Serati's Flame

T.J. Michaels

A SAMHAIN PUBLISHING, LTD. publication.

Samhain Publishing, Ltd.
577 Mulberry Street, Suite 1520
Macon, GA 31201
www.samhainpublishing.com

Serati's Flame
Copyright © 2008 by T.J. Michaels
Print ISBN: 978-1-59998-809-2
Digital ISBN: 1-59998-549-7

Editing by Jennifer Miller
Cover by Anne Cain

First Samhain Publishing, Ltd. electronic publication: August 2007
First Samhain Publishing, Ltd. print publication: June 2008

Praise for T.J. Michaels' *Serati's Flame*

5 Hearts "Serati's Flame is the second book in T.J. Michaels' Vampire Council series. ...great plot filled with action balanced by sizzling sex scenes makes for one great read. What more do you need, humor, hot men, vampires, and a strong alpha female? Nothing! This book fills all those needs."

~ *Fallen Angel Reviews*

5 Hearts, Sensuality Rating: Explicit "This fantastic story is just as good and dangerously exciting as its predecessor. ...hot sexual encounters all while satisfying your hunger for non-stop action. I, for one, am eagerly looking forward to Ms. Michaels' next wildly, thrilling book..."

~ *The Romance Studio*

4/5 Stars, Heat Level: H "It had me rooting for their happy-ever-after as much as cheering their kick-ass assignments. ...Overall Serati's Flame has everything lovers of this genre want. I intend to go back and read the first book in the series and definitely watch for the next installment."

~ *Just Erotic Romance Reviews*

Red Hot! "As with its predecessor...this story is one I'm sure fans will enjoy. In Book 2 of the Vampire Council of Ethics series, we are given a more intimate look at a couple who garnered my interest in the first story. As with its predecessor, T.J. Michaels adds plenty of humor and enough supporting cast to make this story one I'm sure fans will enjoy."

~ *Joyfully Reviewed*

Look for these titles by
TJ Michaels

Now Available:

Carinian's Seeker

Coming Soon:

Hatsept Heat

Dedication

As with every book I've ever written, I dedicate this to my kidlets. You've been steadfast and supportive to no end. There's no way I could have done this without you. The secret to my sanity? Absolutely!

Chapter One

The sun rose over the western mountains. The last of the snow on the distant peaks reflected a deep orange. Bare-chested and oblivious to the cold, Alaan Serati stood on the wrap-around terrace of his apartments watching the dawning of a new day. He gazed up at the clear blue sky and fading moon, but his mind wasn't on the crisp but warming breeze, nor the new life just beginning to push up through the softening earth to herald the coming spring.

No, his mind was on one thing—the time. Seven o'clock a.m. Damn, one more hour before the team gathered together for a briefing on their newest mission. He usually looked forward to these strategy sessions, but he was beginning to dread them more and more of late. And it was all *her* fault.

Pushing away from the wrought-iron railing, Alaan strode inside, closed the door behind him and headed for the shower. The glass stall filled with a billowing mist as the scalding spray of hot water shot out of the massaging shower head and splashed with stinging force against his skin. Hot water wasn't doing a damned thing to get his mind off a certain female. Alaan flipped the control to cold and ducked his whole head underneath the flow.

He exhaled with an annoyed huff. Nope, cold wasn't doing any good either.

Before he knew it, his long, chilled fingers followed the flow of water down his body and passed over the planes and ridges of his stomach until the tips brushed against the head of his painfully erect cock.

A long, low, annoyed-as-hell hiss escaped his throat. Damn it, he had better self control than this. Snatching his hand back, Alaan ignored the discomfort of the weight of his cock as best he could. He grabbed a bottle off the caddy, squirted a healthy handful of ginger-scented shampoo into his palm and slapped it into his wet hair.

"Aw, hell," he grumbled when his fingers worked through the strands only to discover there were no suds—he'd grabbed conditioner, not shampoo. "God, I'm really losing it. My head's so full of that damned woman I can't even wash my hair right."

He needed to go down to the workout room and spar or work out. Or something. Anything to get his mind off the raging hard-on thumping against his navel. If he didn't appreciate the wonderful workings of the male anatomy, he'd consider chopping the unruly thing off. Again, all *her* fault. Lately just the scent of the woman, even from a distance, set his fangs on edge and sent his dick on a rampage. He couldn't get her out of his mind. But why was his lust so hard to control? And why now? He'd known Tameth for years and had always been able to keep his attraction to her under wraps. Even before Sher passed he'd experienced an unexpected need for Tameth. But he'd sworn an oath and damn it, he would do everything in his power to keep it. Even if he'd only made the promise to himself.

Dressed in his favorite uniform of all-black loose-fitting urban camouflage pants, T-shirt and SWAT three-quarter shaft boots, Alaan stalked from his bedroom through the large, open living area, tidying along the way. He'd traveled the world on various assignments and found something to like no matter where he went. But he loved nothing as much as his home here in the mountains of Montana.

Designed in an open round configuration, it was similar to the circular Council Chamber one floor below. The living room was the focal point, a sunken half moon with carpets of royal and dark blues. The walls were all white with gold accents along the baseboards and door moldings. When standing in the middle of it, he could walk off to the right into his oversized bedroom, his office in the adjacent room, or into the dining room and gourmet kitchen off to the left. The fourth option was to walk straight through the living room and out onto the terrace.

After having to wash himself twice to get all the conditioner out of his hair and off his skin, he only had a few minutes for breakfast.

In the kitchen with both doors of the fridge open, Alaan settled for bacon and eggs. Flipping the hickory-smoked meat over in the pan, he huffed with annoyance. The insides of his stomach quivered and tightened as his mind drifted to the clean strong lines of Tameth's body. Again. God, he'd never make it through the meal with his gut turning somersaults like this.

The woman always sparred in a tight stretchy one-piece affair that made him think of lethal ninjas running about with painted-on clothing. When she moved across the floor practicing her forms, blades flashing with deadly accuracy, the sweat from her body mixed with the air. God, he could all but smell her now, and she smelled so...

"Oh shit!" Alaan snatched the damp towel from around his neck and tossed it in the sink. Another few seconds and he'd have been toast. Literally. At least the food hadn't burned, but the damned towel had caught fire while his head conjured the rich, sexy scent of the female who was driving him nuts. The strong, fine tendons in his gums tingled and burned, threatening to let his fangs slip free of their sheaths. Yep, he needed a fight desperately. Keeping his head together in the middle of a battle was a piece of cake, but here in his kitchen he was helpless as his amorous thoughts swirled around his head and spared him no mercy.

The smell of charred cotton filled the space, doing away with what little appetite he had. After an irritating round of hacking and coughing while getting the windows open, Alaan settled for a glass of milk and a bag of AB-positive, along with some snarling and brooding at the table.

A familiar and most unwelcome vibration snaked down his left butt cheek. Snatching the vid phone out of his back pocket, Alaan flipped it open and noted the caller ID with a roll of his eyes. What stupidity would he have to deal with now?

"Serati here," he grumbled into the tiny speaker.

"This is Randall. Sorry to disturb you, sir." The voice on the other end sounded as irritated as Alaan. *Oh here it comes,* Alaan thought to himself, already half-tuning out a very agitated Seeker. Damned vampire politics were a pain in the ass.

"What is it, Randall?"

"We've stocked Stealth Two for the trip overseas. We're all ready to go but the mechanics won't sign off on the pre-flight inspection unless you personally order it. And the Iudex Judges say they haven't received any orders from you for the upcoming mission so they're not ready to assign anyone to..."

Cutting the man off, Alaan said with an implacable tone, one all his teammates were familiar with, "Look, you're flying Stealth Two at my request. Tell those damned mechanics and Iudex Judges that I'll be down there to personally kick their asses if I have to wait a single minute past the scheduled time for take off. Clear?"

"Yes, sir. Perfectly. Thank you, sir."

Alaan snapped the unit closed and stuffed it back in his rear pants pocket with a grimace. Ever since one of their Liaisons went bad a few years ago, everyone seemed stuck on proving who was more loyal, who was most politically correct, and who could impress the V.C.O.E. with their dedication. It was ri-goddamned-diculous. And given his current horny state, he didn't have the patience for this crap.

Pulling the phone back out, Alaan blew out a frustrated breath and hit the speed dial. The voice on the other end was as familiar as his own.

"Bixler here."

"Damn it, Bix, how the hell do you put up with all this bullshit?" Alaan growled into the vid phone. With Bix on vacation, he was stuck as Head Seeker, which meant dealing with all the bickering and petty politics of the Vampire Council of Ethics.

"I rely on my right hand a lot. And I mean a whole lot," Bix said seriously.

Alaan knew exactly what the man meant because Alaan *was* that right hand. Taking care of the details of a hunt and kicking ass was his job as Second in Command. But acting as Head Seeker without a Second meant entirely too much work and too much bull for one man. Dealing with the Council plus selecting and prepping the teams that would go out on every assignment was work enough. He also had to find time to train, or appoint a qualified subordinate to train, the continual rotation of Seekers, Beta Seekers and Iudex Judges in both their physical and administrative roles and responsibilities.

But if Alaan had to choose between being piled with a stack of duties he'd never crawl out from underneath and asking the person who was supposed to act as his Second to do her job, he'd rather bury himself in work.

"Hey, I hear my little sis in the background," Alaan said, not at all subtle about changing the subject. "Tell her I said hi, and I can't wait for you two to get back here." And boy did he mean it with all his heart.

Bix chuckled. "Carin says hi back to you, Alaan."

It was amazing how much being a father had mellowed the vampire out. Actually, it was a combination of Bix's mate threatening to kick his ass if he put his life in danger more than necessary, combined with being a father. Bix, Carin and their adorable hellion three year old, Alaina, had gone on a three month hiatus at their English countryside manor house. The much needed vacation turned into an extended leave of absence when their second child, Russian, decided to put in an early appearance. Mother and baby were doing fine. But they weren't due back to the Western territory headquarters in the Montana mountains for another month.

"God, please help me not kill any of my subordinates before Bix gets back," Alaan mumbled under his breath. But not quietly enough for Bix's keen vamp hearing to miss it.

"Look buddy, seriously, you need Tameth. She's the Second when I'm away. There's no way you can do it all by yourself. I've been Head Seeker for the past forty-two years and with all my experience I still can't do it alone. What makes you think you can?"

"Because I'm more man than you."

Bix laughed heartily. "Yeah, you're more man than just about everyone with your tall, lanky ass."

"Lanky? I'll show you lanky as soon as you get back here, son."

After a few minutes of good-natured ribbing, Bix took it back to business—which was just where Alaan didn't want to go.

"Come on, Alaan, I mean it. In fact, I order you to let Tameth do her damned job as your Second. I will also relay my orders directly to her."

"Damn it, Bix," Alaan snarled, raking his hands through his damp blond curls. "I relieved her of duty as soon as you took off on vacation."

"And she said?"

"Said? Hell, I didn't give her a chance to say anything. Just told her I'd handle it alone until you returned."

"I don't give a shit," Bix snapped. "Tameth is your Second, period. And if you don't reinstate her position, I'll relay my orders to Tameth *and* your mother. As the Matriarch of Clan Serati and Elder on the V.C.O.E., Alaana Serati is still responsible for every vamp in all of the Western territories, including your sorry ass."

"All right, already," Alaan relented, far from happy. The last thing he wanted was his mother getting involved in Seeker business. Not only was she an absolute dragon, she'd be happier than a man with two cocks if there was even the remotest chance that Tameth might become associated with their family.

After all, if he was considered the most eligible bachelor in the territories, Tameth was definitely the most eligible and sought-after female. And a true Serati warrior at that.

"I don't need you to tell Tameth, Bix. I'll take care of it myself."

"When?" Bix pushed.

"Today," Alaan countered.

"Not good enough, Alaan."

"Fine. It'll be settled within the next half hour, just long enough for me to walk up to her apartments. Soon enough for you?"

"Absolutely." Bix snorted. Alaan wished he could reach his large hands through the phone and pull Bix through it. The man was his best friend, but sometimes he wished he was on the V.C.O.E. Most Wanted rogue list just so he could have a good excuse to try to whip his ass.

"And Bix?"

"Yeah, buddy?"

"Have I ever told you how much I hate you?" Alaan asked sweetly.

"Of course." Bix chuckled. "And it's always been at a time like this. Now get yourself up to Tameth's and tell her you need her. If she doesn't cooperate, just lay that deep Barry White voice on her. I guarantee she'll do whatever you need."

"Damn it, Bix, one day I'm gonna..."

The line clicked followed by a clear-as-a-bell dial tone. The son of a bitch had disconnected the call, leaving a frustrated Alaan running his fingers through his already mussed hair.

"Damned woman," Alaan grumbled to himself. "Of all people, why does Tameth Serati-Cole have to be my Second? Nothing but trouble, hanging out with that Clan Hatsept pipsqueak, pale-faced, stringy-haired pimp. Who cares if she outranks almost every Seeker in the Western territories? She's still a royal pain in the ass..."

And strong, reliable, beautiful. Hair so thick and long he wouldn't mind wrapping himself in it. Not to mention a killer body that called to him whenever she walked by, and an ass so perfect... Wait a minute. What the hell was he thinking? The more he thought about the woman, the stronger the longing was that crept up the back of his mind and surrounded his heart with the need for a mate. But he couldn't walk that path again. He couldn't feel this way about Tameth, or anyone else. It wasn't worth the heartache. His position as both a Seeker and son to the Serati Matriarch made life too dangerous for any woman foolish enough to love him.

Pushing away the dull, empty ache centered in his chest along with the raging hard-on that accompanied images of Tameth these days, Alaan painted on his customary scowl and walked the last flight of stairs up to her apartments.

He stopped cold in the middle of the wide, long hallway. *What the hell was that?* It sounded like...moaning. Sensing no danger, he moved towards Tameth's door with slow, measured steps, his boots silent as he padded across the plush carpet. All was quiet except for a murmur so faint Alaan was sure he would have missed it if not for his exceptional hearing. Something about the sound made his heart rate kick up. The sheaths covering his fangs tingled and itched, and the typically smooth skin over his brows furrowed into a deep frown. The barely audible sound caused a fierce physical reaction as his keen eyesight raked the area from one end of the long stretch to the other. There it was again, a feminine gasp and sigh that sounded like...

"Oh, yes, God, that feels so good. Mmm, a little lower."

Tameth?

"Whatever you want, baby, however you want it," whispered a seductive male voice. A very familiar, too-smooth male voice.

Before he'd even made a decision on what to do next, Alaan sprinted the final distance to Tameth's door, and the source of the noises.

Her cries of pleasure wrapped around his cock and

squeezed, while at the same time the very thought of her with another male had his gut twisting in knots. A scorching surge of anger whipped through him so blazing hot, the ends of his hair singed a coal black.

So she was moaning, eh? Well, the person who made her create that sound had better be prepared to have the living shit kicked out of him.

With one huge shoulder braced against the door, Alaan readied himself to force it open, then decided to change his tactic. To hell with the subtle approach. He stepped back, lifted a heavily-booted size thirteen and kicked with all his strength. The door flew several feet into the room followed by a pissed off six-foot-five, two-hundred-and-fifty-pound Seeker.

Fangs bared in fury, Alaan burst into Tameth's living room ready to do some serious damage. His fingers automatically closed over the handle of the customized laser-sighted titanium pistol in the holster at the small of his back. Then his whole body went completely still.

Please, God, let the earth open up and swallow me now.

A fully clothed Kenoe sat on the couch, knees spread, with an equally clothed Tameth sitting cross-legged on the floor in front of him receiving a shoulder massage. The two couldn't have looked more like best girlfriends if they'd tried.

And both of them had the smirk from hell plastered across their smug faces.

"Uh, please tell me you're going to pay for that, Alaan," Tameth said easily, nodding towards the ruined door flat on the carpet. Without waiting for a response, she leaned her head to the side and Kenoe pressed his pale fingers into an obviously sore spot on her shoulder.

"Yeah, right there. How can something feel so good and hurt so much? Ooooh."

The sound emanating from the woman's throat was like a full lick to his balls. Damn she was sexy as all get out.

"I told you to see Dr. Lyons for a muscle relaxant for this shoulder, Tameth. It gets worse and worse every time I work on it," Kenoe crooned in that agitating, come-hither voice of his.

Tameth's black SWAT-issue boots thunked on the rug as she settled her feet out in front of her. Dark, soulful eyes raked over Alaan's body, moving from his feet and up his legs to linger on his groin. Her gaze burned into him, the sensation so acute it was as if she'd used her fingers, stroked the tips up his thighs, and curled them underneath his sac. Damn.

Okay, boy. Rein...it...in, he snarled to himself, his attention plastered on a spot on the carpet four inches in front of his boots. After a few seconds of deep breathing, Alaan looked up and a crash of awareness rocked him back on his heels. Sheer possessiveness crossed Tameth's face the second her dark brown eyes met his iced blue ones. Every muscle in his body tensed as he tried to tamp down the instant heat her gaze ignited as the nerve endings from scalp to toes caught fire. And not the painful kind.

Now both Tameth and Kenoe watched him.

Tameth lowered her head and groaned.

"Ow, that hurts so good," she sighed.

Kenoe's pale eyes took on a mischievous light. What was he up to? Was he trying to seduce Tameth? Damned Clan Hatsept pimp. If the bastard was trying to lure Tameth away from the V.C.O.E. and into one of his slimy relatives' harems, he'd find himself *disappeared* from the face of the earth.

Watching Alaan as if deliberately goading him, the white-haired vamp lowered his head and used his chin to ease Tameth's T-shirt down away from her collarbone, exposing the flesh there. His tongue snaked out and licked a path from the

19

knot he'd been working on clear up to her ear. Tameth lifted her gaze, locked eyes with Alaan once more and gasped with an expression so hot and needy, Alaan took a step back.

What the hell did that pale-eyed punk think he was doing? How dare he stir up Tameth this way? He was nowhere near good enough for a woman like her.

Suddenly all Alaan wanted to do was tear Kenoe, a fellow Seeker, limb from limb, then lay Tameth across the back of the couch, push her pants down around her knees and fuck her brains out.

Barely remembering why he'd originally come up here, his mind filled with the image of a deliciously bare-assed olive-skinned Tameth. On her knees, spread out in front of him, she would look over her shoulder and sweep aside her fall of silky black hair so he could mark her. Bite her. Mate her.

Alaan blinked, forcing the thoughts away.

His cock pulsed with such strength, it threatened to burst through the front of his pants. Okay, time for another deep breath. What the hell was wrong with him?

His body slowly calmed but his teeth, which he'd managed to sheath earlier, now extended fully and without his permission. Good Lord, when was the last time he'd lost control of his fangs? Forcing his incisors to obey his wishes, Alaan pushed his words through gritted teeth.

"Tameth. Kenoe. Report to the Council Chambers. Twenty minutes. Come packed and ready to deploy." His voice sounded harsh even to his own ears. But when the corner of Tameth's lush mouth kicked up into a sultry smile as Kenoe's fingers eased up and down her bare arm, an uncontrollable growl crept up Alaan's throat. Clamping his lips shut, he turned on his heel and stomped from the room. Without even bothering to right the ruined door, he stalked down the hall, down the stairs and headed straight to the sparring room to find something to beat the hell out of before reporting to the Council Chambers.

What caused the irrational need to strip Tameth bare? To keep her from other vampire males? It sort of reminded him of the mating heat he'd felt when he and Sher had been together so long ago. But this was stronger, stranger. Then the bell went off in his brain... *bondmate*. Alaan cringed at the thought. No, it couldn't be. And even if it was, he was strong. He could control it. Better yet, he would forget ever thinking such a thing.

There was no way between here and hell he was going to acknowledge the heat, the need, the only thing that burned beyond the craving for a mate. Bondmate? No way. No how. Not ever.

ॐ

Her vision full of Alaan's broad retreating back, Tameth almost forgot about the searing pain from the hard knot on her shoulder. She loved nothing more than working out with her blades but she'd overdone it during last night's session and now suffered the consequences. And all in an effort to clear her mind of the growing need for the very man who'd just ruined her damned apartment door.

A formidable Seeker serving the V.C.O.E., Alaan Serati was one of the most gorgeous vampires of her clan, and son of the Matriarch herself. Tall, deliciously muscled, and expertly skilled with a variety of weapons, surely he must be good with his hands. And those eyes, such an unusual shade of blue, like the finest cut tanzanite gemstones. His perfect body was topped off with a mass of blond curls so light they were almost platinum. And just listening to him talk was enough to make her cream. The deep bass of his voice never failed to make her think of slow ballads and dirty dancing in the dark.

Kenoe's quiet chuckle brought her out of her musings.

"Well, that was interesting, don't you think?"

"I've never seen Alaan turn that particular shade of red before. Ow," Tameth yelped as Kenoe dug into the same stubborn knot he'd licked in front of Alaan. Strong fingers pressed into her lean trapezius muscles and sent a screaming ache to the base of her skull. After a few seconds of pressure, a dull throb spread through her shoulder blade and settled in her chest. Kenoe's thumbs worked deeper, forcing the tendons to pop over the bone with a snap. Sharp pain was followed by an ease of tension so profound, her stress leached out of every pore and the nerves settled down until they stopped twinging altogether. Maybe he'd adjust the bones in her neck and save a trip to the clan chiropractor.

"Go see Dr. Lyons about this shoulder, woman. And yes, Alaan looked ready to kill. As grumpy as he is all the time, when was the last time you've seen him bare his fangs at anyone, even a Hatsept?"

"In all the years I've known him I've never see him do that when he wasn't hunting. What do you think...?"

"Wasn't it obvious? The man was jealous."

"Are you kidding? He can be such an asshole sometimes, I can't tell when he's upset for some legitimate reason or if he's just being his typical good-natured self." She snorted.

"Well if the way he started growling when I licked your neck is any indication, I'd say the vampire has it bad for you, Tam."

"I'm not so sure. Everyone knows he swore never to mate again after that disaster with Sher. He hasn't been the same since the day they found her all those years ago."

"That was then, this is now. Bottom line, Tam, do you want

him?"

"If you ever tell anyone I'll skin you alive, but yes, I want him. It's the strangest thing, Kenoe. I'm drawn to him somehow, like we complete each other. I swear I can almost feel him sometimes. Now that I think about it, I knew he was outside the door before he kicked it in."

"So that's why you didn't flinch when the splinters started flying, eh?"

Tameth nodded with a choked gasp as Kenoe hit another tight lump of muscle that set every nerve underneath his probing fingers on fire. The flames carried up her neck and settled behind her eyes. Great, just when she'd started feeling better, now she'd have a headache to get rid of before the briefing.

"Okay, Kenoe. Enough. I can't take anymore of your pounding." Thankfully, she'd be all healed up in a day or two.

"Come on, baby," he teased, kissing her earlobe. "You know you like it rough."

A naughty giggle escaped her lips as she leaned her head back to rest in his lap. "I like it, period."

Of course she'd explored relationships with other vamps, but if she were honest, it was only because Alaan had never shown any interest in her. But lately his beautiful blue eyes and platinum curls appeared unbidden in the back of her mind and she found herself unsatisfied. There had always been a certain something about Alaan that drew her, but lately her very skin reacted to the handsome, deadly vamp. Tameth was so aware of his presence, she was beginning to sense his whereabouts even when he wasn't around. It was damned unnerving. But strangely enough, she needed it, needed the smallest contact with him. Wanted it in a way she couldn't explain to anyone, not even to herself. Unsettling.

Easing to her feet, Tameth rubbed the suddenly goose bump-covered skin of her upper arms. Pacing in front of Kenoe, she came to an abrupt halt when she realized she was well and truly agitated, but the feelings weren't hers. They were Alaan's and the man was beyond irritated. No wait, he was working out his frustration on someone or something. But how the hell did she know that?

Kenoe moved up behind her and pulled her back against his chest, nuzzling her ear. "What is it, Tam? What's wrong?"

She sighed as his gentle touch moved from her shoulder, down her arms and around to tease the planes of her firm abs in a gentle caress of a hug.

"I-I'm not sure and I have no idea how to explain it. Damn it, Kenoe, why do I feel this way? Right now he's mad as hell, but unsure and... How do I know the things I do about Alaan?"

Kenoe spun around and riveted her with a blue-white stare.

"How long, Tameth?" he asked, matter-of-factly.

Tameth knew exactly what he meant, but God, she didn't want to.

"I've felt this way about Alaan since I enlisted in the V.C.O.E. law enforcement academy and came here to work under Bix. Close to ten years ago. My mother was thrilled I'd be able to sit under her good friend, his mother, the Matriarch of Clan Serati. I remember the day I arrived. Alaan came to welcome me and to acknowledge my station as a Serati female. The first time I saw him, something wild and weird erupted inside of me. God, my stomach was upset and I actually broke out in hives. My hands went all clammy and I stuttered like some kid fresh out of school." She smiled at the memory.

"Woman, you know he's your mate. So why haven't you pursued him, then?"

"First off, I'm a lady who doesn't chase men. Second, when

we met he was already seeing Sher. There was nothing for it except to get over the fact he was going to mate with her. I just kind of pushed my feelings aside and found my pleasure elsewhere." She flashed a wicked grin that quickly faded to a somber smile. "After Sher died, I respected his decision never to mate again. And that's that."

"But that was years ago, Tam. Perhaps he just needs a little bit of persuasion. Unless, of course, you believe he's much better off without you."

Before she even thought to stop it, a balled-up fist slammed onto her hip as she tapped a booted foot into the carpet in agitation. "Don't be ridiculous, Kenoe. I'm the best thing that's ever happened to that prime male, but..."

"But he needs to realize it. The man was out of his mind with jealousy when he burst in here thinking God knows what. You know you're my best friend, and if you want him I'll help you get him."

"So that's why you licked my neck? I was wondering what you were up to, but figured you'd tell me later. You were pushing, trying to make Alaan lose it. Oooh, you're a bad, bad vampire."

"Yeah, I know. Now kiss me."

With a shared intimacy born of seeing each other through life and death battles, Tameth went willingly into Kenoe's arms. If she'd ever had a best girlfriend and occasional no-strings lover, he was it. A quick peck on her cheek and he eased away from her.

"I'm going to go pack. See you in the Council Chambers. Oh, and just one more thing."

"What's that?" she asked absently, already headed for the duffel bag she always kept half-packed in a corner of the living room.

"The way you feel when Alaan is around, it doesn't sound normal. Have you ever thought that he may be more than your mate? Perhaps he's a bondmate as well? I've heard the heat is much more intense with someone who meets the criteria of both mate and bondmate."

Now that was the last thing she expected him to say. Alaan Serati, bad boy extraordinaire, her bondmate? Oh, please. Surely the man would have said something by now. Then again, he'd sworn off women when, on the heels of Sher's death, an endless string of females had tried to wiggle their way into the life of the most eligible bachelor in the Western territories. It had been a circus, all of them claiming to be his mate, and after such an awful thing as the murder of his fiancée. It had been too much for him.

Even now, after so many years, it was foolish to dwell on such a possibility as mating Alaan. Besides, half the time he acted as if he didn't even like her, let alone want her for anything more than a partner on a hunting expedition.

She snapped her head up and said, "Kenoe, I don't think..."

He was gone. The ruined door was propped precariously on its hinges.

Chapter Two

Lowan sat in his favorite antique chair, a replica of a Pharaoh's gilded throne. Sure, he was as blue-blooded as any good Englishman, but there were none in this day and age as ruthless or as cunning as the old conquerors of the East. Their absence resulted in a breed of vampires who were soft and easily herded. If he had his way, he would pick up where good old Hatshepsut left off. Yes, even his kin would kneel in surrender and call him a God.

Just like the beautiful female kneeling at his feet paying homage right now. Oh, she was so good. Skilled in all the ways of pleasing a vampire in his prime. After all, he'd had the pleasure of schooling her personally. It had taken some breaking on her part—she had put up a good fight after being stolen from her supposed mate. But given enough time and incentive, any woman could be taught to heel. And like it.

She chose that moment to look up. What pretty hazel eyes, such a light brown, rimmed with gold and glazed with passion. So eager in her ministrations. Lowan gasped audibly as her talented tongue snaked out to circle the head of his cock before she took him clear to the back of her throat.

Oh yes, on her knees was where she worked best. And after she sucked him dry, she would go about her duties and service the other males in his specially chosen company. Rogue or not, he was Clan Hatsept and his harem was a place of order. Duties of both the household and amorous kind were undertaken by all of his women to the best of their ability, favored or not.

The first signs of a glorious climax simmered just underneath his full sac. The sweet high-voltage current circled his balls and inched its way up to the base of his cock. She sucked harder, pulled him into her warm mouth.

Fingers buried to the scalp in her dark, curly hair, Lowan couldn't help pumping his hips up to meet her luscious lips.

"Oh yeah, suck it for me, love. Suck me dry."

Her answering murmurs of approval urged him on, faster, harder. She liked it that way, strong and deep no matter which hole he used. The humming around his cock combined with the building pressure was so acute, he slammed his head back against the backrest of his throne as he shot his seed deep on a bellow of approval.

She licked him clean while he gently eased his fingers through the thick curls on her head. Such an obedient and compliant lass. Now that she was trained, Lowan never had to tell her what to do. And she was so passionate in bed, it was almost as if this calm and docile side was some kind of alter ego.

He stood, folded his arms over his massive chest. She rose with him, her fair skin aglow from the small golden flames of the candles he'd asked her to light earlier. Interesting. She used to be uncomfortable completely naked while he was fully clothed. Now she seemed to enjoy prancing around for him.

Lowan nodded towards his semi-hard cock but didn't say a word. She understood. He watched her small but strong fingers gently tuck him back into his loose-fitting pants and tie them closed.

"Myles," he called to the quiet figure seated across the

room. Shrouded in shadows, his best friend and Second rose and walked silently across the hardwood floors until he reached the carpet that marked the edge of sacred territory. Lowan's throne sat in the middle of that hallowed space and no one dared step onto it unless given permission.

"Come." Before Myles could bend to untie his boots, the female was there unlacing them, then helping him toe them off so he could step onto the large carpet.

"Report?" Lowan sat down in his place of honor and waited.

Myles opened his mouth to speak. Instead of a report, a harsh groan slipped out. She'd already undone his belt, unbuttoned and eased the flap aside on the front of his gray and black camouflage pants.

Lowan felt one side of his mouth kick up into a smirk at the look of bliss on Myles' face. The man moved his lips twice more in an attempt to speak while she eased his quickly hardening cock out of the fly of his boxers.

On the third try he said, "The Seekers we bought off in London have...oh God!" Myles' fingers clenched into fists. He resisted the urge to sink his hands through her hair while she sucked him with perfect cherry lips. But no one dared touch Lowan's private stock, recipient of hair-raising blow job or not.

"Sher," Lowan crooned. "You're so good, sweeting. Back up so Myles can form a complete sentence."

Lowan patted his thigh. Her big light brown eyes sought those of her master as she released Myles' now wet cock with a soft popping sound. She left Myles just as he was, turned and climbed into Lowan's lap. He could have sworn he heard a quiet purr as she settled down so he could pet her.

Myles cleared his throat and tried again.

"The Seekers we bribed in London haven't been seen in a few days."

Lowan eased his hands around two perfect breasts and gently played with the puckering nipples. "And this is significant because?"

"Because if they've been reassigned, it's possible that the V.C.O.E. might send *him* here to figure out why you haven't at least been spotted by those assigned to this region."

Him. Lowan knew exactly who Myles meant. Alaan Serati, the meanest fucking Seeker the vampire nations had ever known, outside of Jon Bixler. And for those considered outlaws by the Council, neither of those vampires stalking anywhere within a hundred miles of them was a comforting thought.

"Sher, leave us."

She hopped up and left the room without a word, her beautiful breasts bobbing as she went. When she reached the huge double doors, she turned and waited. With a frown, Lowan nodded his head and she pushed the little button on the wall and walked down the long hallway. Lowan watched her shapely backside until the doors slid closed.

"It may be nothing, sir, but I can't recall London ever lacking Seekers, especially in Knightsbridge."

Lowan rose and bore down on his man. "Find out what the hell is going on, Myles. The last thing I need is Alaan Serati prowling around this city or anywhere in England."

"Not to mention the woman," Myles said quietly, looking down at his deflating cock's sudden burst of life at the mention of her.

"I'm not worried about that. She is, and will remain, mine and mine alone."

"Yes, sir. Good night, sir."

Lowan sat on his throne, stroked the hieroglyphs painted on the gilded, paw-shaped armrest and pondered the words of the man making his way towards the door. V.C.O.E. had managed to thwart all his attempts at planting a mole among their ranks since the last one was uncovered three years before. Alaan played a hand in capturing the rogue, Aleth Sidheon, along with the liaison for the Western territories. Rather, the former liaison for the Western territories.

No hope in that quarter. So, perhaps it was time to call in a favor? After all, rogue or not, he was still a Hatsept.

ℰℴ

The Council Chamber doors stood open to admit fifty of the Full and Beta Seekers assigned to protect the Western territories. Iudex Judges accompanied them into the vast hall, filling less than a quarter of the huge room. The rest of the force, on assignment throughout the U.S. territories and around the world, stood by waiting to be conferenced into this morning's briefing.

All ten clans were represented here among the soldiers and the Council Elders seated around the raised half-moon dais on one side of the room. The Vampire Council of Ethics convened here in the Western U.S. territories during the winter months. The Elders responsible for the U.S. Eastern territories, as well as those in Europe, Asia, the Pacific Rim and Africa, had the duty spread among them during the rest of the year. With spring quickly approaching, the Council Elders and their mates, which included Alaan's parents, would be off to Europe to meet with the constituents there. And now that he and Bix were responsible for all Seeker activity throughout the vampire nation, he still occasionally ventured abroad to meet personally with their subordinates to keep the force running smoothly.

Though most clan members had their own holdings, all

V.C.O.E. properties were unique, tastefully done and oversized to accommodate the number of vampires that might gather at any one time. Given the vast riches of the collective clans, they could afford to build and own vast estates of extreme beauty. But this chalet-style mansion was home, spread over four hundred and fifty acres in the Flathead Valley of Montana. Alaan had been born here, embraced the changing of the seasons on this land. The subtle transformation of thick green tree-covered hills and rolling meadows into an explosion of gold, red and rust-colored leaves called to his soul every fall. Walking across the snow-blanketed lands was just as cleansing to his spirit as hiking through newly sprung grass and wildflowers in the springtime.

Finally, the Council filed into the round, opulent space through a side door. All ten Clan Elders and their mates walked up the carpeted steps to the high dais to the only seats arranged in the room. Nine sat down at the table. Matriarch Alaana Serati and her mate, Ralen, Elders of both Clan Serati and the U.S. Mountain region, were responsible for these proceedings. They remained standing as the Seekers and Judges settled into their ranks in an orderly fashion, their voices at a low hum. Alaan and his elite team stood at the front of the ranks, side by side. All were present...except one.

Alaan glanced to his left the second he sensed Tameth enter. God, he could practically smell her as his eyes took in the lithe movement of her limbs. She strolled across the floor, all confidence and feminine grace. More than enough woman for any vampire, she was a lean, mean fighting machine, yet so soft and compassionate he wondered how she managed to have two such opposing inclinations housed in one lovely body. The long leather trench denoting her rank as Seeker draped over a form-fitting leather shirt and matching leather pants, all done in a shade of turquoise that set off the blue highlights in her long coal-black hair. The exotic beauty was all business, bristling with knives and weapons, some seen, some unseen, he was sure. He caught the dull glint of the hilt of her sword poking up from the hidden sheath between her shoulder blades as she strolled to her place at the head of the pack awaiting her orders. Damn, she was glorious.

And five minutes late.

If she noticed that all of the Seekers on the property were present rather than just their extraction team, she gave no indication of it as she took her position next to him on the front line.

The second she reached his side, his irritation at her effect on him spilled out.

"Glad you could join us, Mizz Serati-Cole," he drawled for her ears alone.

"Thank you for waiting, Barry," she answered sweetly. He bristled, hating the nickname bestowed on him by none other than Tameth herself. After hearing him speak for the first time years ago, she'd claimed his voice was so deep it reminded her of Barry White. The woman had even begged him to sing her a song. And she'd teased him ever since.

Separating himself from the ranks, Alaan walked to the base of the dais and stood on the bottom step. Silence filled the room.

"Elders, we are ready to begin the briefing."

"Go ahead, Seeker." This from the Matriarch of Clan Serati. Alaan repressed a knowing smile as his mother gave him the order with a sneaky little gleam in her eye. He'd shared Bix's orders with her regarding Tameth before entering the Chambers and she was well aware that those present were in for a surprise. But he wondered if his mother had a surprise or two for him as well.

The soft leather of his trench swirled around his booted feet as he turned to address his subordinates.

"For the rest of my time as Head Seeker in Bix's place, Tameth Serati-Cole will act as my Second." He almost laughed out loud at the echo of gasps quickly swallowed up by Seekers immediately regaining their composure. But an expression of shock skipped across Tameth's lovely features. From forehead to chin, the muscles of her face twitched underneath her flawless skin as if they had trouble deciding whether to appear happy, humbled, or flat out amazed.

Continuing quickly, he said, "She holds the highest rank next to Bix and myself. She is also second to none in blade skills and combat experience. Now, for the next couple of weeks, or however long the hunt requires, I and a select team will be away from headquarters. Those on the extraction team for this mission have already been notified and should be prepared to depart on Stealth Two exactly one hour after this briefing."

He glanced over at Tameth's still-changing face and quirked a brow.

"For those on this mission, be advised that if you have any questions about the coming hunt, please see Seeker Serati-Cole before you bother me."

Well, he hadn't intended to be quite so glib, but he was too amused watching Tameth to be serious at the moment.

"Seeker, are you with us?" he queried, wondering if she realized her mouth had fallen open and remained wide enough to catch flies. And such a lovely mouth, too. Lips so lush and full. The thought of pressing his mouth to hers flash-flooded his thoughts. And what about having those lips wrapped around various parts of his body? He hadn't allowed himself to consider such things since Sher's death.

Aw hell, he'd done it again, let his head get away from him, and in the middle of a briefing, of all places. Well, if he wanted to keep the rumored size of his cock from being proven true or false through his pants right this moment, he'd better get it together.

Shut it down, man! Think about something else, like extremely wrinkled grandfather vampires in the shower. Better yet, old people sex! Alaan cringed at the self-inflicted ghastly image. Okay, that did it. He was definitely under control and breathed a sigh of relief as the cock that had threatened to rage only moments ago settled down to sleep against the inside of his thigh.

Addressing the Seekers once more, his voice rang clear throughout the huge chamber.

"Seeker Xian from Clan Li and Seeker Clouds-of-Light from Clan Akicit will be responsible for the Seekers here while Seeker Serati-Cole and I are away. Judge Earlon of Clan Vanett will be responsible for the Iudex Judges. However, Seeker Serati-Cole is still Second even while she is away on the coming mission. If you must, please contact her on her private vid-cell. And last, you will all work together or you'll have to deal with Bix, myself, and Seeker Serati-Cole the moment we return. Any questions?"

At the group response of, "No, sir!" he dismissed them and the small horde of the deadliest and most feared vampire soldiers filed out without a sound, leaving Alaan and his extraction team alone with the Council.

Once the massive double doors clicked shut, Alaan motioned them to stand at the foot of the dais below the Elders. Their pilot, Randall, Slade from Clan Li, and Alex from Clan Akicit had all proven their worth during many a hunt. Kenoe from Clan Hatsept and Tameth from Clan Serati were the senior Seekers. Collins, a seasoned warrior from Clan Sewell stationed out of Scotland, would also be joining them.

"The mission is to locate and apprehend the rogue and fugitive, Lowan Shean," Elder Vannett, Bix's uncle and the leader of his birth clan announced.

"Who? Sounds familiar..." Tameth said, obviously over her surprise at being announced Second. ˙

All eyes were glued on the huge screen mounted behind and just above the Council dais. An image appeared and a collective silence reigned in the room.

"Lowan Shean," Alaan said with a growl as the rogue's photo was displayed on the communications screen. "Lowan Hatsept-Shean."

℘

Tameth was not easily surprised, caught off guard or intimidated, but two shocks in one day? First, Alaan announced she would be his Second, a position she should have had anyway but knew he was too stubborn to allow her to fulfill. And now, the face that flashed up on the screen looked so much like Kenoe, they could have been brothers, only this man was clearly colder, more ruthless. It was evident in the hard glint in his icy bluish-white eyes and in the harsh lines of his mouth. Thick white hair, a distinct and marking trait of every male Hatsept, hung well past his shoulders. Lush but manly lips tipped up into a small smile and gave the only relief to the arctic picture he presented.

Those lips were parted just enough to show sharp fangs. Clan Hatsept males hardly ever sheathed, not caring to conceal their true natures or hide from what most of them considered an inferior subspecies: humans. Amazing they'd never exposed the vampire world in all these many long years. Every Hatsept Tameth had ever met had gleaming white teeth and a respectful and kind countenance, regardless of the fact they tended to horde women. But this particular Hatsept made her veins fill with ice. Something about the bastard screamed cruel.

"Note him well," Alaan said firmly. "We've made several attempts to apprehend this rogue. He is good at flying under the radar, so to speak. It's been almost six years since we've gotten a good lead on Lowan. And if he hadn't been sighted and ID'd in London by one of our informants, we still wouldn't know where he was."

Tameth watched Alaan's fluid movements as he walked the line of Seekers who would assist in the capture. As he approached Kenoe, she didn't miss the fact that her good friend, who sported the Hatsept ultra fair skin, had gone paler than usual. At the same time her insides were alive with the blaze of Alaan's passion in regard to this particular mission. Made perfect sense since Lowan Hatsept-Shean had been responsible for Sher's death. And the outlaw had made it crystal clear he'd taken great pleasure in the malicious act.

Pacing slowly, Alaan said, "This will be one of the most dangerous missions we've taken on in a while. More dangerous than the apprehension of Aleth Sidheon. Why? Because this one comes back alive, if at all possible, at the Council's request."

The hunt for Aleth Sidheon three years ago had been one of the most important busts in V.C.O.E. history. Vampire law enforcement was a family that looked past clan lines. But the Sidheon bust had caused an elite team to rise from within what had already been considered the best. The team working together in pursuit of this Lowan Shean rogue was part of that special force. The most skilled and ruthless of every rank of Seeker and Judge there was. And Kenoe Hatsept was counted among them.

Alaan stopped in front of the slender but athletically built Seeker and quietly asked, "Do you have any problem bringing down a member of your own clan, Kenoe? It's something I've had to ask every Seeker at one time or another. No offense."

And Tameth was surprised to instinctively know he genuinely meant every word.

Kenoe held Alaan's gaze with never-wavering blue-white eyes full of something akin to pure hatred. A hatred that flared at Alaan's mention of Lowan Hatsept being in the same clan as him. Tameth kept her features schooled but made a mental note to ask Kenoe about it later.

Kenoe Hatsept might not be Alaan's favorite person in the world but he'd proven himself in battle. He'd also saved the V.C.O.E.'s collective asses with what had proven to be a clear aptitude for science. He'd used that scientific gift to help reconstruct Carin Bixler's biological ammunition rounds and used them to defeat the very rogue who'd kidnapped her—Aleth Sidheon. Those rounds turned Sidheon into nothing more than a black greasy spot underneath a pile of ash.

"No problem taking down a rogue, no matter the clan, sir." Kenoe's voice was strong, steady. Tameth felt pride well up in her breast as his words rang loud and clear, spoken with such lack of emotion and conviction, it was clear he was completely serious.

Alaan nodded his respect and turned to answer questions from the other team members.

Tameth followed him with her eyes, but her thoughts and emotions were a swirl of amazement and wonder. Alaan was fronting. The tough guy persona he projected all the time didn't feel real just now. And she now understood what Carin meant when she said she used to have a habit of projecting her thoughts when she was emotionally overwhelmed. Alaan might not be projecting to the world, but he was certainly getting through to her.

She felt his stance on Kenoe as clearly as if it were her own. So what else could she learn about Alaan with this newly discovered connection? A wicked smile kicked up at the side of her mouth. Thankfully Alaan wasn't looking at her. Aw damn it! This thing must work both ways. The second she started grinning, he whirled around and pinned her with an accusing glare as if she'd kicked him in the ass or something.

Features schooled once more, Tameth cleared her mind of all thought and returned Alaan's stare. But it didn't erase her newfound knowledge that through all his bluster he didn't really hate Kenoe Hatsept. He just didn't like the gorgeous white-haired hunk hanging around with...*her?* Huh. What a revelation, though an unspoken one.

Tameth's lungs began to burn the longer Alaan held her gaze. Well no wonder—she was holding her breath. She painted on her Seeker's kiss-my-ass expression, inwardly relieved when Collins, a veteran Seeker and Iudex Judge, asked Alaan an important question. One the rest of the team probably wondered about as well.

"Seeker Serati, what about weapons? What have you in store for us this time?" A deep Scottish brogue accompanied a sexy, crooked smile. So, this was the grin that had supposedly stripped off the very clothes of many a vamp female, eh? Not to mention his efficient and clean way of taking down an enemy. The man was almost as feared among vampires as Bix and Alaan. And it was obvious from his question that Collins was eager to stomp a mud hole in some rogue vampire's ass.

Matriarch Alaana quietly cleared her throat and Alaan turned his clear jewel-blue eyes to meet hers.

"Seeker Serati, if you and your team would please turn your attention back to the video conference screen."

Alaan cocked his head in question but didn't say a word. This might be his mother speaking, but she was also leader of every Clan Serati member, no matter where they lived on this earth. And when she stood in her office of authority she brooked no nonsense, especially from a subordinate male.

One of the Council Elders tapped a button on the conference phone sitting in the middle of the large table and a dial tone sounded throughout the room. Seconds later the big screen lit up and flashed as the call connected.

To everyone's surprise, including Tameth's, the beautifully vibrant image of Alaan's adopted sister appeared on the huge video screen—Dr. Carinian Bixler, biogeneticist extraordinaire and mate to the Head Seeker, Jon Bixler.

Alaan's deep bellow made the muscles in Tameth's stomach dance, even as it shook the rafters clear up to the high vaulted ceiling.

"Damn it, Carin, you're supposed to be resting after having a baby, not working!"

"I have been resting, thank you very much. And I had a baby, not heart surgery, big brother."

Alaan glared at the video screen, his stare so hot and angry Tameth was surprised the smooth lacquered floor didn't burst into flame. But Carin wasn't moved, so everything must be normal.

Tameth stifled a giggle when the woman glared right back and said, "Alaan, don't you dare tell Bix I had anything to do with this mission." Amused at Carin's wit and sauciness, Tameth watched the byplay with a smile. Before Alaan could say another word, Carin, as usual, managed to shut him up. She wondered if the woman could teach her how to do that.

"Look, don't you piss me off, Alaan Serati, or I'll fly back to Montana for the sole purpose of kicking your ass. As your adopted sister, I'm a Serati female. Now whatcha got to say about that?"

Alaan's lips may have pressed into a line so thin you could cut frozen meat with it, but he didn't say another word. Who wanted to risk pissing of the top biogeneticist in all of vampiredom? Besides, there was nothing quite like a black woman's wrath, or so Bix claimed. Funny how that statement was always followed by a smart-assed grin and a sated sigh.

"Besides, I have the Matriarch's permission, as well as the rest of the Council," quipped the gorgeous, dark-skinned image on the video conference screen.

Whoa! Tameth rocked back on her heels as Alaan's feelings swept into her head and she *felt* him clear as a bell.

If only Bix would let me spank her, I'd wipe that damned smirk off her gorgeous face. Damned woman.

She bit the inside of her cheek to keep from laughing out loud. So Alaan wanted to spank Carin? This intuitive empathic stuff was a bit unnerving but highly convenient. Alaan's feelings for his sister were tender and brotherly, while his opinion of Kenoe was reluctantly respectful. And his feelings towards her? Hell, did she really want to know? Perhaps she was better off without this weird bond thing between them...

Wait a minute. Bond thing? Oh, goodness. No, she was being ridiculous. It just couldn't be. Could it?

"Now that we've dispensed with the family pleasantries," Elder Ralen Serati chimed in, "let's get on with the details of the mission."

Carin nodded with a pleasant smile, then addressed the room in general. "I've been working long distance with Seeker Kenoe—" nobody called him Seeker Hatsept, "—and Dr. Lyons to prepare some special items for you. I can see everyone just as clearly as you can see me, so we'll do this interactively, all right? Boys, if you're ready, let's do this."

As if on cue, Kenoe and Dr. Lyons stepped over to a long, covered table off to the side, picked it up and carefully carried it over to the team. The doctor pulled back the black cloth to reveal a number of shiny and interesting-looking items while Kenoe gathered up a stack of papers and passed them to each member.

"Okay, here's what we've been working on," Carin began. "The document Kenoe's handing out has a full description of how this stuff works. Let's start with the improved allergy shots for those of you still struggling with a silver allergy. And Alaan, your sun allergy is pretty much under control, but your hayfever is going to kick in with spring right around the corner."

Tameth burst out laughing at Collins' rough grunt. He obviously wanted to get on to the weapons. But Carin, in typical form, wasn't moved at all.

Instead she said, "And for you, Collins, I've been working on an ugly pill."

The entire room tried to stifle their humor but Tameth laughed harder. Collins grimaced.

"I also have a nice new set of long knives for each of you. A nasty and very unfriendly bacterial serum coats the blade. Major skin irritant that'll have you sick as a dog in seconds, so don't cut yourselves. We also have some new rounds for your pistols. Kenoe will explain what he and Dr. Lyons came up with in that regard. After we cover the new modified weapons and ammunition, Dr. Lyons is going to give you a special inoculation to reduce your body's need for hemoglobin. Works for forty-eight hours. During that time, you'll have to increase your protein intake. It's been fully tested and that should be the only side effect. If it's not, be sure to let me know."

As Carin, Kenoe and Dr. Lyons carefully and thoroughly explained all, Tameth felt Alaan's irritation diminish and his admiration skyrocket. But she couldn't sort out for whom. Just Carin? Just Kenoe? Or all of them?

Chapter Three

After the briefing and a quick stop in the kitchen for a snack, the entire team boarded Stealth Two, strapped in and prepared for take-off. They had state-of-the-art military grade aircraft well beyond anything you'd see in the movies, but Alaan still had to wait until they reached twenty thousand feet before he could turn on his MP3 player? It was driving him nuts. He needed something to do. Anything to get Tameth out of his system, even if only for a minute. He wasn't a strong psychic like Bix or Carin, but damn it if the spillover of her excitement about this mission hadn't seeped through his head and into his blood.

Randall's voice cut through his thoughts and a thankful Alaan had to force himself not to shout for joy.

"I've turned off the fasten seatbelt sign. You may now move about the cabin and use your personal electronics."

Oh, thank God! He unfolded his long body out of his seat, stood and stretched. An ice cold drink would do him good right now. Headed to the galley in the back of the huge, sleek plane, he passed by Slade and Alex in one of the six private compartments. They were each sprawled out on oversized bench seats covered with soft suede-like fabric. Their all-black garb blended into the furniture. A low glass table sat on the floor between them where Slade was about to make a very poor move on a black and white sculpted marble chess set.

Alaan stood in the doorway for a second and noted his inability to tell what either of them were feeling the way he could with Tameth. The thought tied his gut in a pulsing knot. Moving on, he spotted no one in the second compartment across from Alex and Slade, but Collins relaxed in the third space alone. Alaan's keen ears picked up the smooth but risqué words oozing from the Scotsman as he spoke quietly into his cell phone. His freaky choice of phrases made it clear he spoke to his mate back home. A mate he was eager to return to after his mission was done.

Once at the galley, Alaan pushed aside the thick drapes at the entrance, stepped across the threshold and almost ran into Kenoe's back. The man had his arms wrapped around a practically purring Tameth. Alaan could feel his cheeks burn as his temper flew out of control. His hands were stretching towards the other vamp's neck when Kenoe turned around and said, "Oh, hey there, Alaan. Excuse me."

And with that, the pale-haired, pasty-faced shrimp of a Seeker released Tameth and headed back towards the front of the plane.

Alaan watched him go, flexing his hands at his sides while trying to keep his feet planted to the spot. If he moved now, he'd be right behind Kenoe trying to rip his Hatsept head off for touching Tameth. Nobody should be touching Tameth, damn it. Nobody but...him?

He spun around and grimaced. The dreamy smile plastered across her pretty mouth rankled his nerves. Damned woman.

"Tameth, what the hell do you see in that pale-faced, skinny-assed, white-haired asshole?" Alaan fumed.

"Skinny-assed?" Now her temper flared in cadence with his.

Not exactly what he was going for. "And why do you always call him skinny?"

She was kidding, right? The sharp angle of her brows didn't say she was.

"The man is six feet tall, Alaan. That makes him as tall as me, you idiot. And while most Hatsepts are slim and athletically built, in case you hadn't noticed, Kenoe is ripped, packed, and damned good-looking. As for the asshole part, may I remind you, my dear Alaan, that so-called asshole helped save both Carin and Bix when we were hunting Aleth Sidheon. He's been invaluable in helping Carin develop new biological weapons to use against outlaws from the day he joined us."

"I know what he's done, damn it." His words didn't make sense to his own ears, but even though he snapped his mouth shut, the thoughts just kept rolling along. Kenoe didn't deserve a woman like Tameth. Didn't deserve to breathe the same air she did, let alone touch her. Hell, the thought of any other male coming within a hair's breadth of this beautiful warrior made the backs of his eyeballs burn and his teeth throb. The realization was way too much to deal with right now. First let him get his fangs under control, then he'd deal with the surging tangle of emotions.

He almost had himself together, but noo-ho-ho-ho. Mizz Tameth had to go and mess it all up with just a few words.

"Not to mention Kenoe is a hell of a fighter, and not too bad a lover."

Sure, Kenoe had been a good Seeker, and could more than handle himself in a fight. But Alaan's brain zeroed in on that last word. The L-word.

"Lover? Did you say lover?" Alaan's voice was much too

quiet and controlled for her taste. She'd known this particular prime male for a whole lot of years. Had worked with him. Fought with him. Even played poker with him. While his deep baritone voice was enough to make her pussy clench, take that same voice, add a growl and a quiet menace, and it became a volatile mix that made her more than a bit nervous. Not afraid, but definitely nervous.

Time slowed and it seemed as if Tameth stood and watched this happening to someone else. Alaan's fingers slipped into her hair just underneath the tightly wound scrunchie holding her ponytail in place. When it became clear what his intentions were, Tameth tried to turn away but found her head plastered to a smooth curved wall. She couldn't move it an inch in either direction. Well, no wonder—Alaan had his big hand wrapped firmly around the thick ponytail, holding her to the spot. Pushing against his wide, heavily muscled chest did no good, not if she wanted to keep her hair in her scalp. Besides, the subtle play of tightening pecs felt good to her fingers.

Well, now what? She wouldn't dare attempt a swift kick to the nuts. After all they weren't actually fighting, not to mention her innate need to preserve the jewels connected to the impressive cock nudging against her groin. In seconds, curiosity and a slow thrum at the base of her womb overrode the desire to get loose.

If it had been anyone else, righteous indignation would have overridden sound judgment as she pounded the poor idiot into the floor. No vampire, no matter the clan, was foolish enough to touch any Clan Serati female uninvited. But this was Alaan.

So what? She was a woman from a matriarchal clan. She might not outrank Alaan in the law enforcement society of the Seekers, but being a female alone elevated her social status above every Serati male, including him, Clan Matriarch's son or not.

Alaan's sea blue eyes glinted dangerously, even in the dim lighting of the little alcove just inside the galley entrance. His platinum blond curls beckoned her hands, the silky stuff cut just short enough to bury her fingers in. They itched, fairly burned with the sudden urge to touch that hair, to touch him. Everywhere. The man towered over her, his body almost twice as wide as hers, packed with firm, solid muscle and the natural abilities born of a vampire. The raw power rolling off him was a spark of enticement. And she was dry tinder ready to be ignited.

Her breathing deepened without her permission and the full globes of her breasts, correction—now swelling breasts— wanted him to caress, stroke and knead them. A pulse of pleasure tickled the base of her spine and eased its way down to her plump lower lips. And he hadn't done anything except grab her by the hair and push her up against the wall.

Oh boy, she was in trouble. Big, nasty, needy trouble.

Time seemed to slow when Alaan bent at the waist, gently pulled her head back to expose the pulse beating at her neck. His tongue left a wet trail from that sacred place up to the shell of her ear. The spark that was Alaan became a fanned flame held to the wick of dynamite threatening to blow her swelling clit out of its little protective cowl.

And then his lips were on hers. Plundering, taking, claiming. Oh, dear Lord, he was simply overwhelming. A deep groan reverberated up out of his chest and straight to where their mouths connected. The spine-tingling sound struck a chord in her belly and she answered with a moan of her own. His scent, the delicious taste of his mouth, the wall of man holding her pinned to the spot assaulted her senses. And all she could think of was *more*.

He released her from the kiss, whispering her name. Her

knees trembled.

"Tameth." The sound was desperate. Broken. Yet still uncertain. Hmmm—it was exactly how she felt. But she wanted those lips back, along with the insistent probing of his warm tongue that took, tasted. Tormented.

His hands had left her hair so one could blaze a teasing trail down her bare arm while the other slid along the ridges of her stomach, making her belly twist and jump. Higher, and higher still, he stopped just below her left breast. The nipple of the damned thing was so tightly puckered, Tameth half expected her breast to jump out of her tank top and into his waiting hand. God, she wanted him to touch her.

And she felt his need to do exactly that. But he fought it. His hands and mouth didn't say so, but Tameth discerned that something deep inside of him wasn't sure if he should run to her or from her. The growing connection between them flared when she grabbed him roughly by the head and pulled his mouth back to hers.

Maybe she could just die now, because Lord knew she didn't have the will to come up for air. There'd never been a sensation like this in her life. Not in all her long years had she wanted a man as urgently and deeply as she wanted Alaan. And now that he'd finally touched her, it wasn't nearly enough.

Thank goodness he had sense enough to push away. Tameth was so far gone she would have preferred to pass out than to stop kissing him, to push away enough to breathe. Besides, why breathe air when she could breathe Alaan?

Feminine satisfaction welled up when the man took a half step back and laid his forehead against hers. She sensed his amazement at the depth of arousal he was experiencing where she was concerned. For a split second Tameth wondered if he had the same awareness of her that she had of him.

Panting like two winded race horses after a quarter-mile sprint, they stood, gentling and easing each other with warm caresses and murmured words. Nonsense mostly, but who cared?

His beautiful blond head rested on her shoulder now as they both fought to catch up to their pulses. Her head spun dizzily and the deep call of his blood reached out, wrapped around her lungs and squeezed. She wanted him. And if his nuzzling the base of her neck whispering her name was any indication, he wanted her just as much.

Her bottom lip throbbed dully where he'd nipped her. Gently Alaan touched the spot with the tip of a long, slightly calloused finger. A drop of blood, her blood, stood out like a bright beacon of life against his fair skin. His tongue snaked out and slowly licked the drop away.

"Damn it, Tameth," he sighed. "I just can't do this. Not since Sher. Not since that day... Shit, I just can't. It was wrong of me to kiss... I—Aw hell."

Her mouth fell open as he turned and stalked away. The man was on the edge, barely leashed. His fight for control was evident in his gait, and in the ripple of rock hard quads flexing with each step.

Damn, he looked good in those jeans.

ജ

"Can I help you, sir?" Randall asked when Alaan stalked into the cockpit and plopped down in the seat next to him.

"No thanks, Randall. I'm all good."

Alaan was grateful when the man didn't press the point. He was still reeling from Kenoe's comment in the aisle. The imp had stepped out of his private cabin, took one look at Alaan and said, as bold as you please, "Mmmm, she smells good on you."

What the hell had he meant by that? Alaan scrubbed his hands over his eyes and sighed. Who was he kidding? He knew exactly what Kenoe'd meant. Besides, he could smell Tameth on his hands, on his shirt. The woman was everywhere and he couldn't tell if it was because he'd held her, or because of this enhanced ability to scent her any-fucking-where.

Even up here in the cockpit cut off from the rest of the crew, her scent tickled his nose and sent a message to his balls to pull tight against his body. Perhaps he should go back to his compartment and change into something more loose-fitting? These jeans were too tight for his unruly cock.

"How long before we land, Randall?" The sooner the better. He couldn't afford to ever touch her again, not if he hoped to stay sane and work side-by-side with her on this mission. The mansion, located outside of the city proper, was big enough to get lost in. Surely he could get a room far enough from Tameth to keep himself halfway under control?

A doubt niggled at the back of his mind and he wondered what it would be like to lose himself in a woman like Tameth. He ignored Randall's questioning looks, put on the copilot headset and closed his eyes. Quieting the roiling thoughts that ran around his mind, Alaan unconsciously reached out to Tameth. Then wished he hadn't. It was so easy. So easy to touch her, to read her. And her emotions were all over the place. The woman, who'd always been the pillar of calm soundness, now flipped back and forth between pissed off and surprised, to finally land on hurt. Alaan felt like a heel. He'd done this to her. Made her feel rejected, less than adequate by kissing her as if he couldn't live without her, then walking away as if she meant nothing.

With a deep sigh, he opened a secure channel and called down to the caretaker of the property they would borrow for this hunt. After informing the man of their arrival time and the sleeping arrangements, he disconnected the call and brooded.

There was no doubt in his mind now. Tameth was the one.

One of few women he could both mate *and* bond with.

Unbidden, the image of a bloody pile of flesh and bones intruded his thoughts. And with it came an ache, a dulling and less jarring ache, but an ache all the same. Sher. There hadn't been much left of her after that damned Lowan finished with her. If it hadn't been for the locket given to her by Alaan himself, it would have been next to impossible to identify her corpse at all. The woman was supposed to have been his mate, and even after all these years, he still remembered what loving her felt like. But this strong bombardment of wild emotions and singing in his blood for Tameth was beyond those feelings of long ago.

He hadn't had the insane need to hoard Sher, to keep her from everyone else. Nor was there the strong need to bond with her psychically, thought-to-thought, mind-to-mind, heart-to-heart. No, this thing with Tameth called to him on practically a cellular level. He'd never been so close to losing himself in a woman from something as simple as a kiss. It was fucking nuts.

He thought about Bix and Carin and shook his head. One thing was sure—from this day forward, Alaan would definitely have more patience with Bix and his overprotective stance in regard to his woman.

When Bix had found Carin and discovered she was his bondmate, Alaan thought he knew what his best friend had been going through. He'd thought it was just a strong attraction. But now he realized that he hadn't had a clue. How in the world had Bix kept himself in check while Carin decided whether she would have him or not? When Carin had lain in a pool of her own blood close to death, how had Bix remained sane? Tameth was hale and whole, yet Alaan was still close to losing his grip on his common sense and wanted nothing more than to send her right back home and away from danger.

Humph. He'd be sure to give Bix an apology and a round of foot kissing now that he really understood the wild range of emotions his friend experienced during that trying time. Hell, if Bix asked, he'd strip naked, jump up on the dais and sing a country song at the next Council meeting just to prove he meant it.

Later that evening, after flying in under cover of darkness, Alaan fought back the need to cry. He hadn't been this miserable since his fangs had grown in during puberty. But it wasn't his tears gathered behind his eyes. They were Tameth's. Her confusion and disappointment swirled around him, penetrated his long leather trench and settled into his skin like a thick mist after a spring rain. Damn, wasn't there some switch he could flip to turn off this awareness of her? The barely controlled lust? The need to shelter and protect her? After all, it wasn't about what he wanted to do. It was about what he had to do. And that was keep away from Tameth. Just the thought of something happening to her because of a relationship with him made him grit his teeth with a consuming combination of fear and blazing anger.

No, he couldn't let it happen. Not to her. Not to anyone ever again.

Off the plane with their gear loaded into four large SUVs, they split up into teams of two, with a spare. Alaan rode alone. As if he had a choice...riiight. He could barely stand to be in the same room with Tameth. There was no way he was riding in an enclosed vehicle with her. Slade and Alex hardly ever parted. Kenoe and Collins both wore his patience to a thin line. Kenoe, because he was...well, Kenoe. And Collins with his stories of ancient battles past and constant yammering of Scotland this and Scotland that grated on his already shredded nerves. Randall seemed the only one capable of shutting the Scot up long enough to get a word in edgewise. That left Tameth to ride with Kenoe, the Hatsept 'ho.

Fine, let her ride with that spindly-armed Hatsept. It was probably what she wanted anyway. Besides, Alaan was no fool. He knew how deeply she cared for Kenoe. They were always together, and it was no secret the two had a strong abiding affection for one another. So let them have at it.

After tuning the radio to a local classical station, Alaan ratcheted up the volume and forced himself to concentrate on the coming rogue hunt. From the intelligence he'd read regarding Lowan Hatsept-Shean and the goings-on in London, they didn't want to be seen approaching their temporary headquarters. Once to the edge of the V.C.O.E. property, at his signal, all headlights were flicked off. Acute eyesight revealed a long drive that led up to a mansion he hadn't had the pleasure of visiting since before the Sidheon takedown. At the end of the quarter-mile driveway, the staff waited in the dark atop the wide stone stairs of an expansive porch.

Alaan pulled up to the edge of the grass across the drive and jumped out of his car. The second his feet touched the ground, he felt her. Tameth. Damn it.

Leaving everyone else behind, he tossed the keys to one of the housemen, grabbed his bags and strode across the pavement. He took the front steps in one bound.

"You made good time, sir. It is rather nice to see you, Master Alaan," said Higgins, an older and very wise-looking vampire who'd been serving in this same building for as long as Alaan could remember. If there was anything he needed to know about this part of town, whether vampire or human-related, Higgins would know.

"Yes, Higgins. It's been a long time."

"We held dinner until you arrived. You may eat whenever you are ready."

Alaan didn't think he could handle sitting at the table knowing Tameth was annoyed with him, upset because of him. For the first time in life, he was out of his element. And he was running. Ashamed, but running all the same.

"Thanks, Higgins. Just send a tray to my room. I'll manage my own gear. Be in the second-floor office at eight tomorrow morning and we'll go from there. Take care of the others, all right?"

"Very good, sir."

"Thanks, Higgins. See you in the morning."

"Good night, sir."

"Good night."

Alaan took one last look around and spotted Kenoe crossing the wide driveway with a pissed off Tameth by his side. They both stared daggers at him as he turned away and gave them his back. He cleared the foyer and flew up the staircase. The last thing he heard was Higgins' efficient voice.

"Please leave your gear at the door and follow me to the dining room. When you have dined, we will show you to your rooms. Your things will be waiting for you and..."

And Tameth's essence followed him all the way up the stairs and down the damned hallway like a specter of the night just waiting for a chance to knee him in the balls.

Chapter Four

Alaan came around the corner and stopped short, taken aback by the couple engaged in a sizzling, passionate embrace. Here were two Seekers in the hallway of the mansion they were using as their headquarters where anyone could walk up on them—not that it would have been strange in a house full of vampires to see them practically making love in the hallway. One of the woman's legs was raised, exposing the firm flesh of her thigh as it wrapped around the man's waist.

If it had been anyone other than Tameth and Kenoe, he wouldn't have batted an eyelash. But that damned Hatsept's hands were all over her perfect body. Stroking the bare skin of that thigh. Fingers buried in the thick hair at her nape as he plundered her lush mouth. It looked like they were on fire for each other.

His eyes involuntarily followed Kenoe's fingers as they made a trail from Tameth's firm round backside up under the itty bitty leather skirt painted onto her body. When the vamp's hand disappeared under the scrap of black leather, Alaan's stomach clenched as tightly as the fists at his sides.

He looked down as if he were watching someone else's body. His large hands unfurled as he imagined Kenoe's neck firmly grasped between them. After choking the life out of the white-haired punk, he'd pull Tameth into her room and lay her across his knee. How dare she share those thighs, those lips with another? Alaan didn't care that he'd never actually claimed Tameth. All he had to do was reach for her...

Emotions fully engaged, his brain kicked into gear as Tameth's odd curiosity slammed into him. Huh?

In spite of what his eyes told him, it didn't *feel* like the two people humpin' in the hall were on fire for each other. While he sensed nothing from Kenoe, Tameth was a jumble of questioning and turmoil, not wound up in passion for the man she was grinding against the door to her room.

Perhaps Kenoe had pressured her into...no, that wasn't it. Tameth would have flattened him if this wasn't what she wanted. Maybe she'd simply given in because she trusted Kenoe? Or because...because what?

What kind of game was being played here? Whatever it was didn't add up and Alaan didn't care for it one bit.

But one thing was certain—the woman was his. Period. And Tameth would surrender to him of her own free will, and not because he snatched Kenoe up into the air by the throat.

Time to be real with himself, and with Tameth. Time to admit that even when Sher was alive, there'd always been a soft spot in his heart for Tameth. As well as the urge, the need, to protect her from any and every threat. Like a sister, right? Yeah, right. Alaan rolled his eyes upward in self-irritation. He had to come clean or he'd go bananas. In truth, he'd never seen Tameth as a sister. Ever. The feelings were simply too raw to decipher, even now, so he'd just buried them, pushed them away and tried his best to ignore her.

But now it was no longer possible to pretend he didn't care for her, didn't want her. If he saw her in Kenoe's arms one more time he'd...hell, he didn't know what he'd do.

It was clear as day. Tameth was his mate, damn it.

It was time to claim his woman. And he wouldn't go another day without doing so.

Alaan pieced together his shredded patience, backed up without a sound and returned to his apartments. Planning his next move, he quickly changed into a comfortable pair of jeans and a light gray sweatshirt.

With his trench coat tossed over his arm, he grabbed the keys to one of the vehicles off the rack near the front door and headed out.

ॐ

"You know Alaan was boiling mad," Kenoe whispered into her ear.

"You knew he was there, didn't you?" Tameth queried, unable to suppress a soft chuckle at her friend's smug nod. "Kenoe, you are such a sneaky dog."

"Glad you think so, kitten."

Practically squealing, Tameth tightened her arms around his neck and squeezed tight while he nuzzled her warmly, laughing quietly along with her.

They untangled their arms and legs from around each other's bodies.

"We still on for the British Museum today?" Kenoe asked, moving towards his own room a few doors down.

"Yep. See you in half an hour?" At Kenoe's nod, Tameth ducked into her own suite to get ready for the day.

After picking up her room, Tameth stepped out into the hallway. She had everything she needed except the gear bag she always carried. She spotted Kenoe locking his door before he strolled down the wide corridor to meet her.

"Ready?"

"Yep, I just need to run out to the truck and get my gear bag."

"I was down in the dining room a few minutes ago and saw Alaan stomp by. He looked like he was headed that way."

The unmistakable tease in his voice reminded her of a little brother who knew you were sneaking out the window in the middle of the night and demanded candy to keep quiet about it. For some reason it grated on her nerves at the same time it sent a tickle down her belly. He was so good at being bad.

"So is there some reason I should be concerned about Alaan being down in the parking area?" she asked with a lazy smile.

Now it was Kenoe's turn to grin. And as always, it was a breathtaking display of pure male sexiness. In spite of the trademark pale skin of the Hatsepts, his features were the perfect mix of tough guy and rock star. Bright, perfect teeth and all that platinum white hair. God, a woman would die for a head of hair like his. She loved it when he wore it down his back. The mass of waves and curls were twisted into neat locs so fine they looked like little silver braids.

She allowed him to back her up against the door and plant his warm hands on either side of her head, caging her between his toned, muscular arms.

"You know, kitten," Kenoe purred, "if I didn't know better I'd think you're having second thoughts about our agreement."

Damn, he smelled so good. Dipping his head a scant half-inch, he eased his lips along hers, gently nipping her with a bit of bared fang.

"Nope, no second thoughts." It took every bit of Tameth's strength not to giggle as she thought about how Alaan had paused, growled and turned on his heel after seeing the two of them in the hallway a little while ago.

Hugging Kenoe again, she planted a quick peck on his cheek and took off towards the stairs with a giddy pep in her step. Once out the front door of the sprawling home, she headed for the row of big black SUVs lining the circle driveway. She made a beeline for the one her spare gear bag was in.

"Damn it," she grumbled, half her body laid across the back seat as she reached for the big black duffel. "I don't remember packing so much crap in this bag. Damned heavy." With a huff, she hefted it up from the floor and set it back down with a clunk. She unzipped it and went completely still. A strange knowing in the back of her mind told her she was no longer alone.

Alaan stood right behind her. In typical Seeker fashion, the man hadn't made a single sound during his approach. But she knew he was there, could sense it clearly. The soft skin at the nape of her neck danced in step with a wild and quickly spreading heat. Her pussy joined in and pulsed in time with the beat.

And just like a prime male, the man had the ability to make all her soft gooey emotions go stone cold with just a few words.

"Come with me," Alaan ordered harshly.

Okaayy? So who the hell did he think he was talking to? It was obviously not a request. And not a drop of tenderness. Not even a damned I'm-sorry-for-being-an-asshole-on-the-flight-over. One kiss on the plane and he thought he could order her around? Puh-lease.

With one dark brow cocked in question, Tameth glanced over her shoulder and took him in slowly from his solid Doc

Martin boots to the top of his gorgeous blond head. Her expression read, *Yeah, right,* and she knew it.

"Look, Alaan, this is my day off. So right now I'm not a Seeker nor your Second, but a Clan Serati female, which puts me a little higher on the food chain than you. So guess what that means—no ordering me around until I'm back on duty. Now go away. I have things to do." With a snort and a roll of her eyes, she turned away. A hint of self-consciousness made her more than a little aware of how high her little black leather skirt rode, baring a good bit of thigh to the man standing behind her. Pushing the thoughts away, she wrapped her fingers around the handle of her grip bag and hauled it from the floor onto the seat.

Annoyed at Alaan's intimidating and scrumptiously sexy presence, Tameth looked back over her shoulder again. If she was going to be bad, may as well go for broke and ruffle his Seeker feathers.

"Besides, I have plans with Kenoe. Important and, uh, definitely delicious plans," she murmured with a deliberately sassy edge, letting her tongue slide over a lengthening incisor, then trail along her top lip. "So, maybe next time, stud." Turning her back on him, she dug in her bag. She had no idea what she was looking for.

Her only warning was a quiet, menacing growl. Unable to hold back a yelp when she was propelled into the back seat of the SUV, Tameth found herself simply along for the ride as Alaan took over. And damn what a ride it was.

The vehicle door slammed behind her and she was suddenly and completely overwhelmed by the presence of the only man she'd ever really wanted. And he was pissed off.

"Kenoe will have to make other plans," Alaan hissed. His voice was as hard and cold as arctic ice. But his eyes? They told an entirely different story. An interesting mix of iced blue and raging hot possessiveness sent a streak of sizzling anticipation down the backs of her legs.

The gear bag went flying into the front seat just before her back slammed hard against Alaan's wide, thickly muscled chest. Nothing about the man was small. His hard, chiseled pecs flexed against her shoulders as she sat with her ass flat against his groin. Large, strong hands settled on each knee, spread them wide and lifted them to settle over his until she was wide open like some offering to a pagan god.

She shivered, but not because her miniskirt bunched up around her waist. The little scrap of material that passed for today's underwear barely covered her labial lips and the cool air evaporated as it came in contact with the suddenly too-warm skin between her legs.

Wait a minute. She was supposed to get her stuff and meet Kenoe in the breakfast room ten minutes ago. She was a Clan Serati female. There was no way a male, prime or otherwise, was supposed to affect her this way. Right?

He held both her hands in one of his and lifted the other to her hair. Unyielding fingers wrapped tightly around her ponytail, angled her head and tilted it backward.

"Damn it, Alaan! I told you I have...mmmmfffff!" And just that quickly, the situation exploded.

He laid a soul-searing kiss on her like a parched man and she was his own personal oasis. And she had no control whatsoever. Oh, Lord, yes!

She tried to hold back the moan bubbling up in her throat but couldn't. Hell, she couldn't even remember why she wanted to resist him in the first place.

smashed against the cool leather of the front seat and bent over at a serious angle. Tameth's hands flew out and instinctively planted themselves as she sought to keep her balance. Slightly bent knees pressed into the firm panel of the seat in front of her. Alaan knelt on the big bench of the back seat between Tameth's spread legs. His chest pressed tight against her back as if he couldn't bear to lose the contact. The huge bulge nestled against her practically bare bottom said what he hadn't spoken aloud. He wanted her. Badly.

A hard grind had her breath puffing out of her lungs in shallow gasps. His fingers burned through the thin, supple leather of her jacket. One hand eased up her back, then crept around underneath her shoulder and wrapped around the swell of her breast with a firm but gentle squeeze. The other eased down the back of her thighs, massaging the sleek muscles as it went. Then inch by inch, talented fingers eased upward to play at the creaming slit of her pussy.

All the while, he pressed decadent open-mouth kisses along her neck and shoulder. Oooh, with an occasional nip of his fangs.

Dear Lord, she was irrevocably and truly lost.

Watching Tameth lean into the SUV showing all that succulent skin had almost been too much for Alaan. He'd stood there shaking his head at himself. Hell, he seemed to be doing that a lot lately.

First he'd been insane enough to kiss her like an old lover while they were on the plane. Then he'd stood there out in front of the house with his eyes plastered on her endless thighs and contemplated walking up behind her, lifting what little bit of clothing covered her nice round ass. In the driveway? In front of the house? God, he was worse off today than he'd been last night. Alaan couldn't remember feeling so strongly about a woman, not even Sher.

His balls had tied up in knots and his cock throbbed as if it were barking orders to a platoon of soldiers. And his little soldiers were suddenly anxious to find a home between Tameth's legs. After round one, he would hold her, stroke her, then drive her back up the wall until she screamed for him.

Still, his brain insisted he turn around, go directly to the sparring room and beat the hell out of something. But his cock wrestled with his common sense. And damn it if his cock hadn't won.

And he knew the moment he'd blown it—about a half a second after he'd opened his mouth and ordered her to come with him. What the hell was he thinking? She was a Clan Serati female. A warrior. And when he was not standing in his office as Head Seeker or Second, he was subordinate to her. Oh well, too late to take the words back. And too late to leave the woman alone.

How he'd managed to stuff himself into the back seat was of no consequence. All he knew was he needed the scent, the taste of her. Right now.

The fine little tendons that controlled his fangs throbbed painfully. Finally he let his incisors slip free of their sheaths just as he positioned her in his lap with her back to his front.

Alaan buried his fingers in her hair and turned her head just enough to make her lips available to his ravenous mouth. The curve of her tight, firm ass fit perfectly into the hollow of his groin. A hollow quickly filled with his aching cock. Tameth squirmed against the cement-filled ridge, driving him towards madness at a dizzying speed. With her legs looped over his, she opened to him freely. The dewy scent of her arousal spilled into the cab of the SUV even as her moist lips softened under his, releasing the sweet taste of apples and spice.

The most desperate, hungry growl he'd ever heard filled his ears. It was wild. It was urgent. It was his own.

The kiss quickly became far less than enough. His very blood was on fire for this woman. He could smell her need. Smell the faint musk of her sweat as it formed in a light sheen over her soft skin. Damn, he could even smell her blood as it thundered through her body, swelling her breasts, her cunt, her clit. He'd never smelled blood *under* skin before. Had never heard thoughts so clearly in his mind. Had never experienced someone else's yearning. *So, this is what Bix meant when he'd tried to explain what it felt like to encounter his bondmate?*

Alaan was a healthy vampire of breeding age. And while vamps were highly sexual people, indulging was something he'd not allowed himself to enjoy in years. It had taken an enormous amount of self-discipline and lots of hours in the sparring room pounding on fellow Seekers or whoever, whatever was available. But with Tameth's enticing scent and soft cries filling the vehicle, the only thing that could have kept him from stripping her bare on the spot was her request that he stop. And she was not asking him to leave her alone. If anything, she was begging him to move faster.

Alaan was so damned glad the woman wasn't human because there was no way he'd be able to hold back with her.

Angled over the front seat as she was, her barely-there underwear didn't stand a chance. One good yank and they were done for, dropping uselessly to the floor of the vehicle. His fingers explored the silky skin of her thighs. But her breasts called to him, too. He could hear them screaming for attention. Easing her jacket off, he pushed up her blouse and gave in to their demands to be kneaded. The stiff nipples plumped further under his fingers and he suddenly knew what she liked. Call it instinct, but the knowledge just jumped right into his brain.

The harder he tugged them, pinched them, the more urgency poured into the grinding swivel of her hips. Soft cries and needy moans wrapped around his cock and pulled. Hard. His hips pumped in tandem with the undulating movement of her body, seeking, wanting.

Sitting on the edge of the bench seat, he lifted her clean off her feet into the air and smashed his face into her bare, sopping pussy. The tangy dew of her cunt hit his tongue. The unique flavor slammed through his system. Imprinted her on him, *in* him for all time. As long as he lived, he would never forget it. It was enticing and addictive, holding him suspended in awe for long moments as he feasted on her quivering flesh. His fangs dragged across her fully erect clit Tameth's entire body went rigid on a desperate gulp of air.

Then he suckled the little bundle of nerves standing so erect for him. Tameth screamed. The sweet honey of her orgasm creamed his face as he wrung a fast and furious climax out of her. But he didn't stop the torment.

Tameth's hands scratched and dug into the leather of the front seat, seeking something, anything on which to anchor herself.

"Oh, baby! Alaan! Just like that," she howled and gasped as he pushed her on and ever upward, not letting her descend from the high. His tongue extended to lash, lick and torment the slick folds of her pussy until she was a quivering mass of flesh and bone. Then she drew in a raspy breath and yelled at him. He couldn't help smiling into her pussy.

"Oh God, fuck me, Alaan. Hard. Now."

"Really?" he asked, lifting his mouth away, drawling with just a hint of sarcasm. "Determined to remain in charge, Tameth? Not going to happen, baby. Not with me."

She lifted her dark head and tried to turn around to face

him. He kept her pressed down over the front seat with one hand instead.

"What? I'm a Clan Serati female! How dare you...oooh!"

He'd unbuttoned his jeans, freed his cock and settled one knee on the seat and a booted foot on the floor. Leveraging his greater height in such a confined space, Alaan leaned over her and slammed home in one smooth, solid stroke.

"Oh, yes!" Tameth cried.

It almost killed him but he stopped moving. Tameth she groaned out her frustration. But he had to begin as he meant to go on. She would yield to him. End of story.

She was so pretty with her golden skin flushed a beautiful caramel. Something inside of her, soft and welcoming reached out to him, embraced and accepted him. But her mouth told a different story.

"Alaan, move your ass, damn it!" she snapped. Dark eyes flashed with a volatile mix of impatience and need.

"Not quite what I was looking for, Tam."

She stiffened with indignation. He slid out of her suctioning heat until only the head of his dick remained inside. God, he was toturing himself—the need to bury himself inside her and stay there rode him hard. But his nature wouldn't let him give in. Couldn't allow his woman to see him as anything less than a real man. Her man.

With short shallow strokes, Alaan teased her with the meaty flared head, gritting his teeth all the while. Damn he was glad she couldn't see the strain on his face.

"Alaan, stop teasing me!" She was panting, writhing, trembling.

"Then tell me what you want in a way that'll make me want to give it to you."

"You want me to what?" she gasped as he slid in deeper then pulled away. Her body shook and quivered, stomach muscles bunched along with the clenching walls of her sex. "Oh, God. Alaan, I-I..."

"Come on, baby, you can do it," he crooned against her ear.

"I want you to fuck me," she growled.

Gripping her hips, he slid home and said, "Again."

"I want you to fuck me!"

Yep, he was definitely going to die. But he'd die happy as hell.

"Again, but sweeter," he said through gritted teeth.

"Please," she whispered. "I need you. Deep and hard."

"Ah, baby, I'm more than happy to give it to you."

His heart melted even as his lust flared wildly. Then he rode her from behind like a madman. Gripped her hips firmly and slammed his girth into her tight hole until the fluttering of her walls told him she was on the edge.

"Is this what you need, Tameth?" he ground out, feeding her juicy slit more of his cock.

"Yes! Yes! That's it!"

Their combined scent filled the cab of the SUV as the sleek walls of her sex caressed him on all sides. The sound of his balls slapping against her bare skin echoed in his ears and he could swear he felt her body temperature rise to just under a boil, right along with his.

"Alaan!" she screamed as she flew apart underneath him. She fell forward over the seat and thrust her ass backward, trying to get more. Nothing could have prepared him for the fist-like grip of her creaming channel when she came. So tight. So strong. And oh so good.

In fact, the woman was good enough to eat. Literally.

Chapter Five

God, the man had a cock poets should write sonnets about—*Ode to Alaan's Wrist-Thick Cock*. Immeasurable pleasure from every delicious slide of the vein-ribbed rod streaked clear down to the little hairs on her toes. Then he seemed to grow impossibly bigger.

"Feel me, Tameth. Feel how you make my dick so hard. God, woman, you make me want to drive into you until we're both cross-eyed and knock-kneed."

"Ummm, yes. I want you driving into me," she panted, wondering how she'd ever formed the words without any air in her lungs.

"Oh yeah, baby." He pushed deeper, riding her with a stamina that nearly took her knees out from under her.

"Oh, Alaan, more. Fuck me. Oh, God."

"I love your pussy, it feels so good, Tameth. But there's something else I need."

"Take it, baby," she panted, yanking the fall of her ponytail away from her neck. "Take what you need, Alaan. Bite me."

The second his incisors pierced her skin, the pleasure-pain streaked through her body, quickly replaced by an exquisite explosion of every cell in her blood. Back arched wildly, Tameth's soul splintered and flew apart as she came exquisitely hard. And yet he moved within her, each stroke sending her on a silver streak towards another wild soul-shattering orgasm.

Withdrawing his fangs, he eagerly suckled the lifeblood from her body. Each pull of his lips in time with the stroke of his cock. In. Out. Deeper. Harder. It was devastatingly beautiful as he fell apart on a muffled cry, soaking her channel with his thick, pungent juices.

Breathing harshly, still draped over the seat, her skirt up around her waist and leather jacket hanging by a sleeve, she reveled in the weight of a sated Alaan spread over her back, panting.

He kissed her softly on her temple and said, "Tameth, love, there's something you forgot."

Instantly, all the languorous heat that had been spread through her body swept into her stomach and transformed into a cold knot of apprehension. Oh, she knew what he meant, all right.

Still buried deep inside, he eased back on the seat and settled her in his lap again. Then he whispered the words that would change their lives forever.

"Tameth, bite me, love."

She didn't answer. Couldn't get the words past the fat lump in her throat. Instead she let him cradle her head, place sweet little kisses against her temple. Needing something to do with her hands as she sat there, Tameth began to ease her blouse down around her body. His expression was soft, so caring, she would have done anything he asked in that moment. Except the one thing she knew he didn't really want.

Gently smoothing the sweat-slick tendrils away from her face, he said, "Bite me back, sweetheart. Bond with me."

She pushed up and off of him, flinched at the sudden loss of him filling her and sat back down on his knee. With her dark gaze fastened on his beautiful London blue eyes, Tameth gave the only answer she knew to give.

"No."

"No?"

While sharing blood with a lover was not uncommon, it was not something to be taken lightly. Tameth had never bitten a lover. Had vowed to keep such a precious gifting just that— precious. The intensity of her connection with Alaan had only grown stronger as the days passed and she was more than sure now that they were bondmates. But she was a bondmate he didn't want. He was just getting off, right? But to her, it meant her heart.

He licked the slightly swollen site of the little wound he'd made on her neck, sending a shiver into her lower back. "Bite me, Tameth."

She looked down at her fingernails and fidgeted. It annoyed her. She never fidgeted.

"No, Alaan. I-I can't."

"Come on, baby," he crooned in that oh-so-deep voice of his that sent the butterflies in her stomach into a frenzy. Scooting down in the seat, he appeared at ease as he gathered her to him and cradled her against his breast.

"I want you, Tameth. I can feel the bond forming between us. Bite me, love. Bite me...right here." She turned to see him motion to the spot on his chest right over his heart.

In a near panic, she sat up and began to straighten out her skewed clothing, more than aware of the growing concern in his mind. Not to mention the rock hard, scrumptiously large, oversized, perfect body.

She blew out a breath and took in a calming one. Then did it again as he waited and watched.

"Tameth?"

"Nope. Not today," she said, fumbling with her bra, blouse and jacket all at the same time. How the hell had he gotten her clothes off? And where were her panties? Oh, now she remembered. He'd destroyed them. The memory sent her pulse racing. Damn it, but she wished she'd brought an extra pair so he could do it again.

"What? What the hell do you mean not today?" She'd never heard him sound so confused and petulant. If the situation hadn't been so serious she would have laughed.

"Just what I said, Alaan. I'm just not ready to exchange blood with you."

He sat up so swiftly she toppled off his lap and landed next to him, half on and half off the seat. Her swollen sex rubbed against the leather as her legs went all akimbo. Why couldn't she manage to get her skirt pulled down, damn it?

"What the hell do you mean, you're not ready? Are you telling me you don't feel, don't recognize what's going on between us, woman?" he fumed. She didn't answer. "But you've bitten that Kenoe asshole, haven't you? Tell me, damn it!"

She started to give him a classic smart-assed retort, then thought better of it. He was obviously pissed *and* hurt. Wouldn't be wise to mess with his prime male sensibilities right now. So she steeled herself for his reaction and told him the truth.

"No, Alaan, I've never bitten Kenoe. I've never bitten anyone in passion. Only to feed."

"What?" Now he really looked baffled, his beautiful blond brows drawn down into a questioning frown. But he didn't stay confused for long. His emotions swung right back around to pissed. And determined. "Well, you will bite me, Tameth. Make no mistake about it."

"Alaan, I..." Wait, where the hell was he going? She

snapped her mouth shut, schooled her features, and suppressed her amazement when quick as lightning, the man yanked his jeans up over his perfect backside and jumped out of the SUV. Well of all the nerve. How dare he leave her in the back seat undressed—well-loved, but still undressed.

Her eyebrows shot up her forehead as the driver's side door was snatched open with such force the whole vehicle shook. A formidable blond-haired god climbed in and peeled out of the driveway with her bare-assed in the back seat.

"What the? Alaan! Where the hell are we going? I told you I have a date with Kenoe."

"Fine," he growled, flipping open his secure video phone. Tameth peered over the seat and felt Alaan force back the urge to howl his frustration when a handsome vamp's face filled the screen.

"White-haired skinny little fop. Damned harem-keeping idiot," Alaan said under his breath.

"Hatsept here."

"Yeah, I know who the hell you are," Alaan snapped.

"How can I help you, Serati?"

"Tameth won't be able to make your date." He spat the last word as if it were some kind of poison.

"Oh? And why is that?" Kenoe challenged. Tameth bit her lip to keep from grinning when the legendary Hatsept smirk appeared on his handsome face. Alaan jerked his head around and snarled at her. "Damn it, woman, put some clothes on."

"Well, you took them off in the first place," she snapped back, not repentant at all that one of her breasts still peeked out of her top.

She could tell he wanted to fuss but snapped his mouth shut instead when a smooth voice floated out of the vid phone speaker.

"Excuse me? What was that about clothes?"

"Nothing," Alaan said, teeth gritted so tight she wondered how his incisors held up under the pressure.

Kenoe pressed the issue and Tameth wished he were there so she could give him a squeeze. "So, why is Tameth indisposed? We had a date to visit the British Museum together. It's not like her to stand me up, Serati. She is an honorable woman."

"Are you questioning her honor, Hatsept?" Alaan sneered.

"Not at all. Just pointing out that it's not like her to leave me hanging."

"Well, she...uh..."

The man was basically breaking her plans with Kenoe. Now he had to cover for her. Tameth wondered what fabulous tale he would weave so he wouldn't make her look bad.

"She just learned that she must accompany me to see Bix. It's about the assignment we're working on. I'll brief the team when we return this evening."

She stifled a gasp. The man lied outright and had no shame. Now what Alaan was this?

"This evening? But it's barely nine o'clock in the morning."

Way to go, Kenoe, she thought. *Keep the pressure on, sweetie.*

"It's going to take all day. You have a problem with that, it's too damned bad. Serati out."

Damned woman, Alaan growled to himself for the fortieth time while speeding up the M1 highway towards the sprawling countryside. His fingers wrapped so tightly around the steering wheel they throbbed.

She felt the bond growing between them, he knew she did. So why wouldn't she just accept him as her bondmate and bite him already? Then again, he felt like a fish out of water, flopping around on the shore. One minute he wanted Tameth with all his heart and soul, the next, all he could think about was protecting her from the dangers of loving him. There was only one person who could possibly understand what he was dealing with.

Why him? Why now? Why the raging hard-on from hell? Well, that one he could answer. The woman's scent filled the cabin of the SUV, swirled around his body and squeezed him like one of those little rubbery anti-stress balls. At least she was dressed now, if the little leather jacket and skirt could be called clothes. And when had he started to care what she wore? He shook his head and focused on the road. Hell if he knew.

"What? What is it?" Tameth snapped. She had every reason to be upset, knew he was sending mixed signals, but he just couldn't help it. His body might be on a one-track road, but his head was all over the map and it pissed him the hell off.

"Nothing's wrong." He snapped the lie right back. Then again, perhaps it wasn't a lie—nothing had ever felt more right than Tameth in his arms. But damn it, he wasn't supposed to yield to it. Not again. But he had to have her, felt his soul shrivel up just a little every time he considered life without her for another single day. She seemed to want him, or had when he was plowing between her luscious thighs, but she chilled up the second he mentioned bonding. So what was the deal? Did she only want some casual sex, a fucking Kenoe replacement? Well he wasn't sharing her, damn it! And to hell with what his catapulting feelings said.

An hour or so later they pulled into the gravel driveway of a modern-looking manor. Tameth immediately recognized the vamp who stood outside the front door. Several more patrolled the grounds in front of the house and, from what she could see, the gardens off to the east.

The second they cleared the car doors, she and Alaan were both embraced by the huge fellow.

"Jaidyn! It's so good to see you. So this is where mother packed you off to, eh?" Alaan clapped the older man on the shoulder with a friendly camaraderie.

"Yes, Master Seeker. She said that if anything happened to Carin or the little ones, she would castrate me herself. Quite a love she has for your adopted sister."

"Isn't that the truth," Alaan said sarcastically.

"So what are you two doing here?"

"Actually, Jaidyn, I'm not quite sure. Ask him." Tameth motioned to Alaan.

Jaidyn cocked his head to one side as his gaze drifted from Alaan to Tameth and back. Alaan felt pride swell up in his breast. Clan Serati might be a ruled by a Matriarch, but Jaidyn, as second bondmate to the Matriarch herself, was one of very few males with serious pull. Yet his woman stood her ground, held his gaze, and practically dared him to askher about what was going on between the two of them.

Suddenly Tameth's expression brightened as she said, "But before you ask him, point me in Carin's direction, will you?"

Alaan allowed himself a small smile. Even though an awkward silence had descended between them, he was glad the decision to drop in on Bix and Carin made her happy.

"Absolutely no problem," Jaidyn replied with a smile of his own. "She's supposed to be up in her apartments feeding the new lad, but I'll give you directions to her labs just in case."

Tameth cocked her head. "Labs? Here?"

The same words teetered on the tip of Alaan's tongue, but should he have been surprised? After all, this was Dr. Carinian Bixler they were talking about.

"Every property she and Bix own has a lab in it. A genius, that woman is," Jaidyn said, admiration clear in every syllable.

"Thanks, Jaidyn," Tameth said quickly, already striding into the house. Alaan's eyes were plastered on her skirt, knowing she wore nothing underneath it. Immediately his head started to swim with a heady combination of desire and frustration. She didn't want him.

"Is something wrong, Master Seeker?"

"No. No, nothing. Where's Bix?"

"In the gardens with little Alaina. You can go through the house if you like."

"No, that's fine. I don't mind the walk. I'm suddenly in need of some good, cool English air."

"Too bloody cold if you ask me." Jaidyn sniffed, turned on his heel and headed back indoors.

Alaan strode around the side of the house. As he made his way to the extensive gardens, he quietly greeted the vampires that made up Carin's personal guard. Every Seeker on the property had been personally chosen by the V.C.O.E. Many he'd trained himself.

And Carin was one of their most important allies in the constant fight for survival. Vampires were in no way weak, but they certainly had enemies. Unfortunately, those enemies were other vampires.

Carin's expertise in biotechnology had royally saved all their butts a few years ago. While she'd been trying to find a way to extend her life by emulating vampire traits in her own body, a rogue scientist was trying to do the opposite. The bastard had actually found a way to destroy vampire DNA without killing the humans he needed to fulfill his sadistic pleasures. And a V.C.O.E. insider helped him. Carin had single-handedly found a way to counteract the rogue's nasty vamp-killing agent, as well as inoculate her mate, Bix, and the others against future attacks.

Their entire race was indebted to one beautiful spitfire of a woman. And as Bix's mate, Carin continued to work tirelessly to ensure that they were all taken care of. Alaan wondered sometimes if Carin had become a vampire, though he knew turning a human was impossible. It just seemed that whenever she was in residence at Council headquarters in Montana, she was forever after one of his veins to draw blood for this sample, or that test. And it was usually after Bix had managed to escape her clutches.

After walking through what felt like an endless canopy of evergreens, Alaan turned a corner and came upon Bix sitting on a stone bench in front of a fountain. He tossed a giggling Alaina into the air. The darling little imp, her long black curls flying around her head, squealed and squirmed with delight.

Alaan stopped short. His lungs seized as his heart overflowed with a longing so complete it was unnerving. And all for something he'd seen a thousand times. It was common to see Bix playing with his little girl, but this time as he watched the two, listened to Alaina scream and yell with glee, "Higher, daddy! Higher!" Alaan's heart squeezed tight with longing for a child of his own. He imagined her with golden skin, a black fall of silken hair like Tameth's. And whether the little munchkin had his blue eyes or not, she would definitely inherit her mother's attitude.

Sigh. Tameth. He was in real trouble where she was concerned.

Finally the invisible bands around his chest released and he opened his mouth to greet his lifelong friend.

"Damn it, Bix, she won't bite me!"

Bix turned a questioning yet amused eye on his bellowing best friend as he held his daughter in mid-air.

ℬ

Tameth found Carin in her bedroom changing an adorable, but very smelly, new baby boy. Little Russian looked just like his daddy, with the exception of his darker hue. He was the sweetest, most handsome little baby Tameth had ever seen. Even at just a month old, his little head was a riot of silky black curls. Fat cheeks with a matching tummy and chubby legs were evidence that he definitely ate well. Tameth had no idea what color his eyes were—he'd slept through the diaper change.

Carin placed the sleeping oversized baby in his crib and shooed Tameth out the bedroom door into the living room.

The second the door snapped quietly shut, Tameth's arms were filled with a squealing Carin who hugged her like they hadn't seen each other in years rather than just a few months. The gesture of sisterly kindness brought tears to Tameth's already misty eyes. She cleared her throat and quickly blinked them back. But not fast enough for Carin to miss her watery smile.

"Okay, chicklet, out with it. And don't even try to play yourself, Tam, 'cause I can see it in your eyes that something's wrong. Not to mention the fact that you're supposed to be on assignment in London. What are you doing way out here in Staffordshire?"

"Well it wasn't my idea," Tameth started, sitting down on

the edge of the loveseat before bouncing back up again. Bare thighs rubbed together underneath her little leather skirt as she moved across the floor. A wince broke through the surface of her calm façade. The tender folds of her still swollen mons brought to mind the cock that had stretched her so perfectly not long before arriving here.

"Tam, you all right? Why are you frowning?"

"Sure. Yeah, I'm fine," she said firmly, easing the frown from her forehead.

"Tam, you know you're welcome here but if Bix finds out I had anything to do with your current mission in London, he'll kill me!"

"It not the mission. It's Alaan. He. Well, we. I mean I..." She turned to stare out the floor-to-ceiling windows. "Oh, God!" A muted yelp erupted from her mouth just before she jumped back as if she'd been scalded. Perhaps because she had indeed been burned. By *him.* Everywhere he'd touched, every spot he'd tasted, the flesh was still deliciously heated. The last thing she needed to see while she sorted out her feelings was that man down in the gardens beneath Carin's balcony windows.

"Damn it, Carin! You could have warned me your apartment overlooked the gardens," Tameth squawked, moving quickly away from the window. Besides, she'd seen enough. A glimpse of Alaan pacing back and forth in front of Bix, slashing his hand through the air. The way his mouth moved a mile a minute, he was obviously cursing a blue streak. The stiff set of his shoulders screamed his anger. He looked furious enough to bite.

And the thought of him biting her again was more than pleasant.

Damn it, she was doing the flip-flop thing. So not like her.

"Tam, sit down. I'll call downstairs for some tea and you

can tell me what's up, 'kay?"

She told the whole story, from the moment Alaan kicked her door in to find her getting a shoulder massage from Kenoe, to the wild sex they'd had in the SUV a little more than an hour ago. Tameth was relieved when Carin took in the tale without interrupting. Or laughing. Or tsk-tsking.

"Well, woman, I won't say he doesn't smell good on you," Carin teased with a big toothy grin plastered across her face.

Tameth blushed so deeply it was a wonder her cheeks didn't sizzle. Carin wasn't a vampire but her mating with Bix combined with the infusion of his blood when she lay dying after a rogue attack years ago had altered her DNA significantly. Other than the need for blood, she exhibited the same natural traits as the nearest four-star vamp, including greatly enhanced strength and a keen sense of smell. Plus the woman was an empath with strong psychic abilities. It wasn't like Tameth could have hidden anything from her even if Carin hadn't been able to scent Alaan all over her.

And regardless of whether Carin thought Alaan smelled good on her or not, Tameth couldn't do anything more than face the truth—he didn't really want a mate.

"But Tameth, if the man said he wants to mate with you— better yet, bond with you—why don't you believe him?" Carin asked directly.

"Because you don't just go from years of a solid I-ain't-gonna-mate attitude to suddenly wanting a mate overnight. He's never shown me any special attention in all the years I've known him, before or after Sher's death. Why now, Carin?"

"Perhaps it's a biological thing?"

"Girl, does everything have to be biological with you?" Tameth chuckled into her tea cup.

"Now Tameth, you know that's a dumb question." Carin

laughed. "Look at who you're talking to—Mrs. Biological, in the flesh. Be right back," she said, setting her tea cup on the table. She rose and went into the bedroom and returned with her and Bix's gorgeous new son. Tameth wanted to hold him, but didn't dare for fear of her heart splintering into a thousand pieces. Suddenly her hand flew to her womb.

It did a funky little erotic flutter just as her mind went blank trying to remember her last menstrual cycle. Oh my God, what if? Neither she nor Alaan had thought about using protection while humping like horny bunnies in the back of the SUV.

Carin laid the baby on his tummy across her lap, picked up her tea cup and took a quick sip. Pinning Tam with a me-big-sister-you-listen glare, she said, "Tam, look, no sex for a human male is uncommon enough, but a full-blood, bad-assed, prime male Seeker not having sex? Girl, it's unheard of yet. Alaan hasn't had any coochie since that Sher person was murdured, what, six years ago? Yet, he gave it up to you. Doesn't that say anything?"

"Sure," she snorted. "It says he was finally too horny to resist the offer."

"Girl, please! Don't be absurd. I've seen women throw themselves at Alaan. He either totally ignores them or blows them off so coldly you can see frostbite on the boot print left on the back of their asses when he kicks them to the curb. But you, woman, you get under that vamp's skin. And from what you told me, you didn't offer, chicklet. He. Took. It."

The finger poking into her chest with every word belonged to a woman who was a mountain of calm reason. Anything coming out of Carin's mouth should be considered, but should she dare hope? Was Alaan really sure about what he wanted? Or was he just having a temporary lapse in his determination to remain single? Sigh. What a quandary.

"What are you saying?" Tameth asked cautiously. Determined to keep her composure, she poured them both another cup of tea. She'd never know how she kept her hands from shaking and sloshing Carin's favorite Earl Gray all over her leather skirt.

"Thanks, Tam. Mmm, that's good. It's chilly today. And I bet Bix has Alaina outside playing without a coat again. Blasted man." Carin rose and headed to the window.

"Carin," Tameth called after her. "You were saying...?"

"Oh yeah, sorry. I get sidetracked, sometimes. Okay, now think about it. Whenever you're around, especially if you're accompanied by a man, he scowls, growls and looks ready to kill, right?"

"He does? I've never noticed..."

Carin's mouth fell open while her head tilted to the side in question.

"Girl, if you tell me you've never noticed how Alaan reacts to you, I may just have to slap you silly. How does everyone notice this stuff but you? Tell me, how do you feel when he's around?"

"It's crazy," Tameth replied, unsure how to piece together what she wanted to say. It was hard to acknowledge in her own mind, let alone explain to someone else. With a huff, she was up on her feet again, and recommenced wearing a hole in the plush royal blue Aubusson carpet. That alone was irritating. She was a Seeker, for chrissake. She wasn't supposed to pace.

"I feel like I know when he's there, but deeper. Almost like I know what he's feeling. I'm not a strong psychic like you, but I could swear I hear the man in my head."

"Tam, I think you're in trouble."

"Why?"

"Because that's how I felt when Bix first came into my life. And you know Bix and I are more than mates. We're bondmates. Do you think Alaan is your bondmate, sweetie?"

What could she say? It was just too much to believe. And since the words were determined to remain stuck in her throat anyway, she just sat down on the edge of the loveseat and shook her head.

"What do you mean, no?" Carin asked, hiking a now wide awake and squirming baby over her shoulder. "You're not saying much, Mizz Outspoken, but personally, I don't see why he couldn't be your bondmate."

Tameth dragged in a sigh. "Then it's a good thing I didn't bite him back. Until I'm sure, there's no way I'd want to be mated or bonded to a man who doesn't really want me. I can't compete with Sher's ghost, Carin. And I shouldn't have to."

"I understand where you're coming from, chicklet." The two ladies chuckled at the man-sized burp that burst out of the little tyke over his mama's shoulder. "But you're being ridiculous, Tam. You know a true bondmating is more than exchanging blood. It can only happen if you both truly want it in your hearts. I'm telling you, when I bonded with Bix it bordered on the spiritual."

Tameth looked down at the floor between her knees, not bothering to school her features or keep the downcast look off her face. Carin left her chair and eased onto the loveseat next to her, putting her arm around her friend in a show of support.

"For Alaan Serati, of all men, to come out and say he wants to mate and bond with you means he feels the bond already forming. He's my brother and I know him. He's not stupid, though he can be an idiot sometimes. I think you're nuts not to believe him. Besides, he didn't ask you to compete with anyone, right?"

"Right," Tameth groaned. After all, Carin really was right. So what was her problem? Her real problem? Maybe she could sort it out sooner rather than later?

"Come on, Tameth, the man is all tied in knots when it comes to you, sweetpea. And speaking of tied in knots...how was the sex? I've heard rumors about a particular blond, deep-voiced, gorgeous vampire that would make my husband lock me away for life if he even suspected I'd heard those stories," Carin whispered conspiratorially.

Tameth smiled, feeling loads lighter, though she couldn't figure exactly why. She hadn't really changed her mind about anything.

"Well, I've heard the same rumor." She laughed. "And the boy has quite a package. Enough to..."

"Tie it in a knot!" the two women crowed in unison.

After a round of good humor, Carin sobered and pinned her friend with a hard, serious stare and asked her flat out, "Tameth, why are you playing games with Alaan?"

"I'm not trying to play games, Carin, I swear. But I have to know that he really wants me, and not still pining away for Sher." She was back to pacing again. "I mean, how do I know he's forgotten her?

She couldn't decide whether to flinch or laugh at the "girl, please" look Carin drilled her way.

"Uh, Tam?"

"Yes," Tameth said through gritted teeth. *Here it comes, Tameth. She's gonna make sense and you're going to feel like a numbskull.*

"Can you tell me why Alaan needs to forget Sher? The woman is dead. She's gone, Tameth. Even if the man thinks about her, he's making love to and going home with you. Spending time with you. Having little fat babies with you." With a flustered wave of her hand, Carin plopped the cooing tot into Tameth's hands. Tameth held him close, buried her nose into the soft folds on his neck and inhaled. He smelled like baby powder and brand new skin.

"Okay, enough about Alaan. Tell me where that gorgeous Kenoe figures into all this? Damn, those Clan Hatsept boys are all so good-looking."

"Well, he's helping me, uh, sort of figure things out." Looking up in time to see understanding flare in Carin's intelligent eyes, Tameth grinned shamelessly.

"Girl, you're using Kenoe to make Alaan jealous, aren't you? Well, from everything you've told me, I think it's working."

"Yeah, but he doesn't have anything to be jealous about."

"Why?"

"Because...Kenoe is gay."

"What! You sure he doesn't swing both ways? I thought you and he..."

"I'd consider him my occasional lover, but all we've shared are a few comforting kisses. Wait, that's not quite true. When I'm bent or stressed he gives a hell of a massage along with the occasional tongue lashing."

"Tongue lashing?" Carin asked with raised eyebrows.

Tameth knew the woman understood exactly what she meant. But there was no harm in painting the picture just a little bit clearer.

"Yes, Carin, tongue lashing. As in female blowjob. Coochie hummer. Clit licking?"

"Okay, damn it. I get it. Hell, after this conversation I may need to go find my husband for a little midday quickie. Sheesh."

Tameth handed Russian back to his mother and laughed at Carin's disgruntled, hornyfied expression.

"We've slept in the same bed, Carin, but that's as far as we've ever gone. We'd get ready to have a hot round of sweaty sex, but before we could do anything we'd look into each others' eyes and burst out laughing. We just don't feel that way about each other. He's like another you to me. A close girlfriend I can share anything with. Only I wouldn't go down on you!"

"Well, I'll be damned. Kenoe Hatsept doesn't like coochie? I've never heard of a gay vampire," Carin crowed, eyes wide with wonder. Bisexuality was common enough, but it was practically unheard of for a prime male vampire to be gay. It had more to do with the genetic compulsion of a slow-breeding race to reproduce than any kind of moral stance.

"I know, but anything is possible, right?"

"Hmmm, I sense a story there."

"So do I," Tameth said thoughtfully. "Unfortunately, Kenoe's not telling. I have a feeling something happened to him when he was younger, but where and with whom, I have no idea."

"Wow, you just made my day. That's the juiciest secret in all of vampiredom. Wait until Alaan finds out. Woohoo!" Carin giggled.

"By the way, the blood suppressant worked like a charm. No side effects so far, so can you give me another inoculation?"

"What for?" Carin asked, already up and headed for a locked cabinet across the living room.

"Just the thought of bagged O-positive, bleecchhkkk!" Tameth's tongue blanched at the thought of the bland stuff sliding over it. It always tasted like it had a touch of cod liver oil in it. Ewww.

Forehead wrinkled with concentration, only seconds passed before the other woman had a suggestion. "Well, just use a voluntary donor. With so many Seekers in London, I doubt they all use the bagged stuff. I'll have to work on some kind of flavor enhancer. In the meantime, I can check with the Matriarch. Maybe for this trip we can set up..."

"No!" Tameth flinched at herself. She hadn't meant to shout. Her feet carried her across the carpet and back to the balcony windows. Damn it, this pacing was becoming a bad habit. Forcing herself to sit calmly, Tameth explained.

"If I can't have a shot, I'll just deal with the bagged stuff. I can't do a donor, Carin." Plowing forward with a deep breath, the words tumbled out. "I-I just can't see myself taking any fresh blood except Alaan's..."

"But you won't bite him? What the hell kind of sense does that make, Tameth?"

The legendary hand-on-hip-foot-tappin' Carin was in full effect.

I knew I'd feel like an idiot before I got out of this room, Tameth thought as her gaze rolled towards the ceiling.

"But you know I love you, Tam."

The injection device from hell was loaded and only inches away from her neck. The cool swab of an alcohol pad was quickly followed by a small prick.

"Yeah, Mizz Bixler, I know." Tameth hissed, grimaced and braced herself at the scalding rush of the suppressant as it entered her bloodstream.

"Damn it! Can't you do anything about the sting?"

"Big baby," Carin teased, stuck out her tongue, then said, "So, how 'bout a shower, lady? 'Cause if you walk into a room with my brother, and he starts growling and unsheathing his fangs because he smells himself on you, I may just have to shoot him."

Chapter Six

Tameth stepped out of a warm, relaxing shower, towel dried her hair and put on one of Carin's too-short sweat suits. Looking down at her wrists peeking out of the sleeves, Tameth shook her head. Carin might be smart as a whip, muscular and athletic, but damn it if the woman wasn't short. And Tameth loved her like a sister.

Well, at least her three-quarter shank boots would keep her ankles from showing. No sooner had she tied up the laces, than out of the corner of her eye she spotted a small bundle of energy hurtling through the front door of the apartment and into the living room.

"Mommy! Daddy said lunch is ready." The little tyke stopped on a dime, squealed at a pitch high enough to break fine crystal, and flew into Tameth's arms.

"Hi, Aunt Tamiff!"

"Hi, baby," Tameth responded happily, catching Alaina at full speed and plucking her up off the floor for a big kiss. "I'm so happy to see you, little miss." She smiled, running her fingers through Alaina's long, windblown curls.

"Me, too, Aunt Tamiff. Uncle Lan said you have to go outside now."

"Outside? Where, sweetie?" Tameth asked. When Carin started laughing behind her back, she almost wished she hadn't asked.

"Out there," Alaina said sweetly, pointing to the sliding glass that led out to the balcony.

"Out there? You mean down in the gardens?"

"Uh-huh," she said with glee, showing a mouth full of sparkling white baby teeth. "Come on, Mommy. Daddy said we have to go to lunch now."

"All right, sweetpea. I'm coming."

"Don't forget my brudder!" Alaina said sternly.

"Yep, that's definitely your daughter," Tameth chuckled at Carin as they were herded out of the apartment by a caramel-skinned, three year old Carin-to-be.

Carin and company walked through the double doors that led out into the extensive English gardens. Tameth held little Alaina's hand and looked on as the other woman called to the brooding giant who had one foot propped up on a fountain bench.

"Hey, big brother."

Even though the clouds overhead obscured the sun, Alaan's expression brightened up the entire courtyard the second he laid eyes on his adopted sister and the new bundle of joy. Tameth frowned. His brilliant heart-stopping smile softened with a tenderness of which she hadn't known he was capable. Would he ever light up like that at the mere sight of her? According to Carin, he already did, but he must've done it when her back was turned or something. After all, imitating the Terminator with a snarled "come wid' me" before screwing her brains sideways and then whisking her away to the one place they weren't supposed to go sure as hell didn't count.

"Hey, sis, how are you?" he called, striding over to the grand double doors to meet them. He laid a gentle hand over the dark tufts of the small head lying on Carin's shoulder. "So this is little Russian Bixler, eh? He's certainly a hefty kid. And cute, too."

"Damned straight. Say hello to your uncle Alaan, Russian," Carin cooed against her son's hair. Gifting Alaan with a sisterly smirk, she said, "We're going in for lunch. Want to join us? You can challenge your nephew here for your meal."

Tousling the little head full of curls, Alaan leaned down and planted a kiss on the baby's brow. "In a minute. I need to talk to Tameth for a sec."

"No problem," Carin told him, hitching Russian higher up on her shoulder. She covered his head with a baby-sized blanket to protect him against the slight chill and headed inside. "Come see me before you head back to London," she called over her shoulder. "I'll be in my lab later."

"Yes, ma'am," Alaan drawled with a mock salute.

God, the man's deep voice made Tameth's toes curl up in her boots. Her attention riveted on his profile as he watched Carin and the children disappear into the house. What an amazing contrast of parts. Hair so fair, a face so handsome and a body so muscularly perfect he could easily pass as one of heaven's protectors. But when he got that prime male gleam in his crystal blue eyes accompanied by a little show of fang, he looked more like one of the Devil's henchmen. Rumor had it any woman would take him in whatever way he chose to present himself. She happened to know those rumors were true.

Her gaze slid down the wide expanse of his chest to the outline of solid pecs visible through his unzipped black-on-black Seeker trench coat. But Tameth didn't care how sinfully attractive Alaan was, nor how loyal he was to the Council and vampire clans. There was no way she'd settle for any man who wasn't willing to conquer hell and high water for her, bondmate or not.

Hmm. The garden seemed strangely silent. Instantly in Seeker mode, Tameth discreetly scanned the area with her eyes. None of the vamps she'd spotted earlier through Carin's window were on security detail anymore. Her senses picked up the subtle scent and faint sound of vamps in the immediate vicinity, none vicious, but none visible. And so quiet, it appeared to be just the two of them accompanied by a light spring breeze, endless blooming flowers, brilliant green grass, hedges and trees.

Being alone with Alaan Serati probably wasn't the smartest thing to do right now. Not while the "want him, he doesn't want me...does he?" perplexity controlled her typically rational mind. Not to mention her body didn't give a rat's rear end where her head was spending its time. All five-foot-eleven and a half inches wanted to lay under him and squirm until she passed out. This was *so* not good.

Thoughts of Sher popped into her head. Well, that snapped her out of her musing. Tameth broke the silence with an irritated clearing of her throat.

"So, you wanted to see me?" Tameth asked, her voice deliberately void of care. Not cold, just...unimpressed. Her conversation with Carin swirled around in the back of her mind. Perhaps she was just being silly. The man she'd always wanted made it crystal clear he had feelings for her. But still...she couldn't help but wonder if she'd have all of his heart or just part of it. And part of it wasn't an option.

"Yes, baby, I wanted to see you," he said slowly, carefully.

His strong fingers extended. He stood as if he had no doubt she would take them.

Tameth's heart camped out just above her esophagus as she took his hand, certain of what she wanted, yet so uncertain. The second his strong grip encompassed her own, she gave up trying to guess what he felt. Instead she stopped thinking altogether and let her mind open to him. Immediately the bottom of her stomach hit the gravel path they stood on as his emotions flooded her head and overflowed her senses. The tidal wave of feeling grew ever higher, then crashed down over her in an overwhelming wave of longing. Oh yes, his need was there, but it wasn't hot or urgent, but deeper, more profound.

Neither spoke as Tameth allowed herself to be led across the expansive gardens, through a wall of tall evergreen hedges that surrounded a thick grove of aspen trees. Suddenly her fingers were cold. She looked down. Alaan had let go and now stood staring down at her heatedly. Amazing. Even at her unusual height, half-an-inch shy of six feet, she felt short looking up at him.

A single digit tilted her head up and she bit the inside of her cheek to keep the gasp from escaping her throat. His expression was raw, dangerous. Delicious. God, the glint in those jewel blue eyes sent a tremor through her whole being—spirit, soul and body. One booted foot stepped towards her. Instinctively, she took an answering step back. Her chin dropped, unable to handle such acute heat and determination. He took another step. Oh, God. The man stalked her like a lion on the hunt in the Serengeti.

Ouch!

The air whooshed from her lungs when the back of her knees slammed against something with such force they buckled out from underneath her. Landing hard, her butt made contact with cold, solid stone. She looked down and could have kicked herself. Just great. So distracted by Alaan's intent, she'd backed herself into a stone bench resting at the base of a huge budding tree underneath a dense canopy of leaves.

And Alaan moved in fast. Bounding to her feet, Tameth had every intention of halting his progress. But instead of pushing him away, her damned mutinous fingers curled into the leather of his long trench coat and held fast.

The baritone of his voice swirled around her as he said, "I will have you, Tameth."

Oh really? Well didn't he have a thing or two to learn? It was her last coherent thought just before he kissed the smart-aleck right out of the remark she'd fixed her mouth to say.

With no memory of rising up on her toes, Tameth stood practically on the tips of her boots doing a terrible imitation of a swivel-hipped Elvis with her arms wrapped around Alaan's thick neck. His answering embrace engulfed and surrounded her until every breath was Alaan and leather. Mmm, demanding lips moved hungrily over hers, extending the kiss until her lungs burned for an intake of air. But who needed to breathe when she could live off of the essence of Alaan?

And what about her resolve to blow him off?

Resolve was overrated.

Mmm, his hard biceps flexed against her back when he eased himself down her body only to pluck her off her feet until they dangled several inches off the grass-covered ground. The ripple of tightly packed abs as they pressed against hers, the expanse and contraction of his wide, solid chest with each breath, could only be described as decadent. Like a dessert so rich, a single bite should satisfy, but so delicious you devoured the whole thing. The tight column of his magnificent cock pulsed against her belly, requesting a response from her fluttering womb. And respond it did, with a spasm so powerful it bordered on pain as every drop of blood in her body sped south to engorge her clit and the lower lips of her sex.

Tameth allowed her tongue to tease the sensitive skin at the base of Alaan's Adam's apple. Exquisite musk mixed with a slight salinity burst onto her tongue. God, he tasted so good.

With one hand buried in the short curls on his head, and the other painting circles across his broad back, she decided to play some more. Pressed kiss after kiss down his neck and around to nibble just below his ear. Nipped at the tendons connecting the base of his skull to the bulging muscles of his neck. Pulled the taut flesh into her mouth and sucked hard enough to make him squirm, but careful not to draw blood. Damn, a beyond-sexy growl rumbled up from his chest. The deep timbre vibrated against her tongue, tempted and teased the little muscles fighting to control her fangs. Whispered for them to release their tight control and let her incisors come out and join the fun.

Come on, woman. Get it together. So damned tempting, but she couldn't bite him. Not yet.

Just when she thought she had herself under control, a wicked flash of erotic sensation streaked from his body, slammed into hers, then back again. It singed the labial lips of her weeping pussy, then sent it up in a white-hot flame that couldn't be doused even by the stream of honeyed dew gathering at her gate.

"Oh dear God." She tried to hold the gasp inside but it was impossible. Rapidly approaching mindlessness, she finally realized what was happening. An infinite loop of lust and madness, both physical and psychic, circled them like a whirlwind until she was dizzy with it.

Oooh, and he was as close to out of control as she'd ever

seen him...well except for the earlier bout of wild animal sex squeezed into the back of the SUV. Her lids snapped open so she could watch him. He made such a beautiful sight.

Eyes closed and head thrown back, Alaan held her crushed against his chest, his nostrils flaring wildly. She could have sworn she heard his teeth groan in protest of him clenching them. And damn if she wasn't in the same sorry shape.

"Tameth, I swear if I don't have you..." he hissed.

"You'll what?" she panted, falling deeper, faster under his spell.

"I don't know what, but it'll be bad, baby. I swear it'll be bad."

She found herself set back on her feet. He spread his legs and ground his thick pole of a cock against her belly. Strong fingers explored the curves of her hips, kneaded the cheeks of her ass, sending a wild zing through her pussy. Her thighs trembled as the fabric of her sweats rasped over the bare cheeks underneath. While his hands were busy exploring from the waist down, his head dipped so he could nibble the tip of a pebbled breast through her sweatshirt. She held onto his shoulders for dear life as her knees buckled.

"God, that feels so good," she whimpered, unsure whether she'd said the words out loud or not.

"Tam, I swear I've never tasted a woman so sweet. I've got to have you again. Mmm, I see my marks are already healing."

Tameth shivered at the mix of menace and desire in his tone as he examined the slightly tender skin just above her collarbone.

"No problem, baby. I'll just make some new ones."

"Wha...?"

Alaan whipped off his black leather trench coat and settled

it over the stone bench. The forest green silk of the lining blended with the dark grass where the edges puddled on the ground.

"Alaan, what are you doing?"

"I thought it was obvious, beautiful." He chuckled. That too-damned-attractive one-sided smirk tipped up one side of his mouth. A mouth she'd like to taste again. A mouth she'd like to...oh God!

He dropped to his knees and took her sweat pants down to the ground with him.

Chapter Seven

To Alaan, she smelled like freshly showered woman with a hint of baby powder. Beautiful inside and out, the woman was both loyal and strong. Like a golden goddess from the Far East, Tameth made him want to bow down and worship her.

His fingers instinctively reached up to take down the mane of her hair pulled back into her customary braid. It was so long, it brushed the curve of her lovely ass. Damn, too damp. The last thing she needed was to catch a cold because he couldn't resist playing in her wet hair. Making a mental note to brush it out for her later, for now Alaan would be content with the soft short curls between her golden thighs.

"Alaan, no!" she squawked, frantically looking from side to side swatting his hands away from her succulent skin. "Damn it, what if someone comes back here?"

Grumbling on a rush of breath, he said, "No one is coming back here. They'd sure as hell better not." His cock pulsed and filled until he knew his zipper would leave an imprint along the shaft.

A slight breeze wafted through the aromatic garden and blew between her thighs. The scent of sweet succulent woman filled the air around them. Alaan's gums itched. Playtime was officially over and he couldn't wait another second to have her.

Capturing her swatting hands, Alaan knelt in front of a reluctant Tameth and settled her bare bottom onto the leather-covered bench. Her soft skin made contact with the silk lining. He wondered if he'd be able to smell her when he put his coat back on.

Reaching up, he slid one hand underneath her sweatshirt to palm a full breast. He weighed one, then the other, gathering a certain amount of male satisfaction at the heat of those luscious points plumping through the lace of her bra.

Burying his nose in her cunt, he inhaled deeply, loving the raw sounds she made. Even after a shower, he still caught the scent of his come lingering faintly between her legs. With his lips just a whisper away from her flesh, he teased her with his words. She was so plump and pretty down here.

"Mmm, look at this. Such a wet pussy." Gentle fingers spread her for his viewing pleasure. "Caramel-coated and so pink inside, Tameth. Does it taste as good and sweet as it looks?" Alaan's mouth watered.

Her unique flavor exploded on his tongue as he slid it along her intimate folds. They blossomed for him as he blew gently over the fevered skin so hot against his mouth. Dipping a single finger into her dewy channel, he stroked into her wet heat. God, she was so tight.

"I like that you keep it groomed, short up top, and bare down on your pussy lips. They're getting all swollen and pouty for me."

"That's from the pounding you gave me earlier," she rasped in a sensual hiss, drawing in a halting breath through gritted teeth.

The sound of her labored breathing, the flutter of her smooth sheath made him hungry, desperate. Alaan lifted her legs over his shoulders and proceeded to devour every dripping inch of her soaked core. A veritable feast.

With the echoes of her building arousal bombarding his mind, Alaan squeezed his eyes shut and tried to process the urgency thundering through the bond forming between them. The woman was on fire, teetered on the edge of insanity. Her need added kindling to his own flames, but he ruthlessly tamped down the wild craving. He had to. Tameth was no prissy female. She was a warrior. A warrior who sometimes forgot her place with him as a man.

Now was as good a time as any to reinforce that whether she was a Clan Serati female or not, he was a prime male. And above all, *her* prime.

Another digit slipped into her scalding sex as he suckled. She arched into him, legs spread wide. Her hips wove a sensuous circle as her warm, fragrant dew dripped onto the silk under her ass. It was a silent plea for more. A deep pull on her clit sent her head backward to meet the bark of the tree.

"Oh, God. Please."

The rising pitch of her voice was like music to his ears, or what little he could hear above the blood pounding through his heads—both the one in his pants and the one on top of his shoulders.

"Please what, Tameth?" he growled, amazed at how much concentration was required to form the words.

"I need more. Something, anything," she wailed, grabbing frantically at his hair, his ears, his shoulders. Anywhere her fingers could reach.

Turning his palm up, Alaan curled the tips of his fingers into the little hollow deep inside her body. At the same time he pressed into that hollow, he turned his head and gently sank his fangs into the supple flesh of her thigh.

She threw her head back and screamed through orgasm

number one. So absorbed and overtaken, the woman didn't even notice when her cries sent a small flock of geese scrambling across the surface of a nearby pond.

"Alaan, baby." She panted between words. "It feels so good. Bite me on the other leg. Now," she half-pleaded, half-ordered. He smiled and deliberately licked the seam of her swollen sex. She snarled at him.

"Unsheath those fangs or fuck me. Damn it, give me both."

"Greedy woman, aren't you? I'll bite you again, but not right now." He exhaled against her skin and toyed with the tiny wounds left behind.

Tameth whined long and loud. Actually whined. Definitely something he'd never seen or heard from her before. Excellent.

Though she'd snapped her mouth shut to keep any further pleas from escaping, her silent cries and accompanying emotions slid along their fragile bond to land hard in the middle of his mind. He *felt* her need beating at his will. Deeper than a desire for sex, it was a craving for him as a mate. A craving she still fought with her heart, yet a battle she'd already lost to her body.

In spite of her verbal refusal to take it further than casual sex, Alaan wondered if Tameth was already half in love with him. One thing was certain—there was more floating through the bond than she wanted to admit. It was the closest thing to an epiphany he'd ever had, and the first time—well, second, since the romp in the SUV—he'd wanted nothing more than to please and pleasure a woman until she lost all reason. If he hadn't been so intent on giving her the tongue lashing of her life, he would have cocked his head sideways in wonder.

The bond brought with it such a threading and weaving of souls Alaan couldn't think of a single word to describe it. And it would only grow stronger until Tameth's well-being was more important to him than anything. But not as important as the lesson he must teach right now.

A hard snatch at the hair on the top of his head refocused his attention. A smile kicked up on one side of his mouth as he teased her inner labial lips with his tongue. Even if their newly forming link hadn't told him how far gone she was, the harsh panting and the fingers creating a bald spot on his crown certainly would have.

Time for part two of her schooling.

He played her like a damned musical instrument. Strummed skillfully until every string pulled taut, every nerve hummed, anxious for release. Her body shuddered, impatient to reach the top, like riding a roller coaster to the top of a peak only to remain suspended in anticipation of the plunge. Just when Tameth thought he would leave her hanging there forever, his lips fastened to her throbbing clit and pulled it into his hot, wet mouth, tongue swirling over the engorged tip.

She fell headlong into orgasm number two as the dam burst inside of her. The waves just rolled on and on, drowning everything in their path. Rather than shivering from being half-naked out in the English springtime air, her wide open thighs trembled against the onslaught of wicked sensation flowing from her cunt, through the nerve endings of her ass, and down her legs.

Sweat rolled like scalding hot beads of moisture between her breasts and along the ridges of her spine, only to be soaked up by the thick cotton of her sweatshirt. Damn, perspiration dampened his shoulders where her knees hung over them.

The deep hum of appreciation rumbled up from his chest, making his lips vibrate against her soaked flesh.

"Come for me again, Tameth."

Was he crazy? She felt like a wet, wrung-out dishrag. There was no way she could come again. It was impossible.

Suddenly her mind filled with images of herself, naked and moaning with an oversized and aroused Alaan behind her. On her knees, chest pressed to the bed... Bed? They'd never been in bed together. So how...?

The answer came to her in a rush of understanding so profound it sent a shiver up each vertebra, wrapped around the bones and sank into the nerves of her spine. These were Alaan's thoughts. Thoughts of what he'd like to do to her. Oh, and what an imagination. Vivid enough to set her insides fluttering all over again. So much for the impossible, she thought wryly as she closed her eyes and let Alaan push her towards another climax.

One particularly kinky scene behind her eyes showed her riding him in a bathtub. He reached up, grabbed her by her ponytail and pulled her down for a wild open-mouthed kiss. It was so real she could have sworn she caught the scent of the vanilla spiced candles illuminating the blue and white tiles of the bathroom walls. Heard the water splash onto the floor as it sloshed over the sides of the tub from their frantic movements.

Another scene saw her bent over his couch, hands tied behind her back with a silk scarf of the same color blue as his eyes. And she was on the receiving end of a spanking.

"Alaan?" Her voice questioned the movie playing in her head, yet begged for more pressure from his smooth, hot tongue. An answering brush of determination smacked into her conscience and filled her mind. What, he wanted to control her? Rule her?

"No, baby, I don't want to control you. But I will be the man in this relationship. Period."

"Yeah, and if you ever spank me," she snarled out loud.

"*...you'll love every minute of it.*"

God, he was so much in her head and felt so right filling that space of consciousness, the surprise she should have felt at the telepathic conversation never surfaced.

But what the hell was she doing, a Clan Serati female practically whimpering under the hands of a male? A male who thought to order her around. She should have been offended, pissed off at the least. But the compulsion to give to Alaan, to allow him to be what he was created to be, flowed through their psychic link. He was a male, through and through, and his clear sincerity simply overruled her pride.

On his feet now, he looked down at her with those vivid sky blues. Thoughts, feelings, desires barreled into her, soul-deep. He took her hand and eased it around his jean-clad cock.

"*Stroke me, Tam. Touch me.*" His need seated itself inside her even as his tempting voice sang to her pussy, setting it pulsing again. The girth of his cock was exquisite against her hand, but caressing him through the fabric of his jeans quickly moved from pleasure to irritation. She needed to feel his hot, velvety shaft sliding over her skin, nudging between her nether lips, sinking deep inside her body. Everywhere all at once.

Glad he wasn't wearing a belt, Tameth yanked at the top snap of his pants and buried her face in his crotch to inhale his masculine scent. Mmm, so clean, so addictive she rubbed her face back and forth across the fabric of his boxers as if to imprint his scent on her skin. Tameth opened her mouth as wide as she could and settled over the cloth-covered column of his cock. Even when her lips strained at the corners, there was still more of him than she could cover. Exhaling, her heat infused his boxers enough to singe off his short hairs. He gasped and she reversed the flow, inhaling greedily until she tasted his scent at the back of her throat.

Mouth watered until it soaked his underwear. Swollen breasts throbbed, stomach cramped with need as her pussy creamed until she felt her own dewy essence glide down the inside of her thighs. Enough playing around. It was time for her treat. And the plan was to eat him up until she couldn't take another drop.

Tameth frantically yanked and pulled on Alaan's shorts until his cock sprang up to meet her in the cool spring air. The deeply flushed tip wept a single clear bead of moisture. Her tongue shot out to capture it. Ginger. He tasted like spicy, sweet ginger.

With her knees spread wide, heels up on the bench, she leaned forward until her chest practically touched the leather-covered bench. The cool breeze playing against her heated flesh did nothing to ease her want. If anything, it made her want him more. Without further ado, his cock disappeared down her throat.

"Damn, Tameth, I always knew you were flexible but I could come just from watching you in that position."

His words made her blush from head to toe. Wanting nothing more than to please him as he had her, she leaned more into her task and hummed around the head of his shaft. In fact, her whole body vibrated like a hummingbird's wings during a courtship flight as she took him as deep as she could. Licked and sucked with one goal in mind—to taste his essence on her tongue until he ran dry. He was close. She could feel, almost hear, his come eager to greet her. Could sense it making its way up his thick shaft.

Bracing herself, eager for the geyser to blow, her goal was snatched from sight. The man jerked out of her mouth. *Noooo! Come back!*

A gasp tore from her throat when her back met the tree trunk and Alaan, dropped to his knees, moved forward and sank balls-deep into her gripping pussy in one plunge.

"Oh shit!" she yelled. The geese on the pond took flight.

He rode her hard. Rode her until she was mindless with each devastating stroke. The walls of her pussy gripped tight, pulling a groan from him. She would have laughed when his eyes crossed with bliss, but she couldn't see straight enough to tell if it was his baby blues crossed hard, or if she was seeing double from the fierce loving he dished out.

A shiver worked its way up her calf. It began in the hollow of her ankle just above her Achilles tendon, then swirled up the blood vessels at lightning speed. Oh, this was going to be bad.

She squeezed her eyes shut and a galaxy of stars exploded behind the lids in a shimmering array of sparkling lights as she fell apart. But he didn't stop moving his thick shaft in and out of her body. Instead, he pushed her towards yet another marrow-melting orgasm. Damn, this had to be some kind of record or something.

"Alaan, I can't take anymore!" she panted, screamed, groaned and pleaded.

"Oh, you can take it, beautiful. Trust me," he crooned as his thumb eased between her legs and found the swollen bundle of nerves.

The slightest touch sent her reeling again. This was it. She was going to die. Then it hit—climax number...number what?

When her breathing returned to something close to normal and she could halfway think clearly again, he withdrew.

A niggle at the back of her brain brought some coherence, enough to realize that as much as he quaked against her body, as much as he voiced his pleasure with deep breathy groans, the man hadn't come. Not once. She'd taken her pleasure too many times to count. But the ultimate pleasure would be for him to experience what she had.

Her mind was caressed with the sweetest, most loving touch she'd ever experienced as his words formed in her head yet again.

"Because, beautiful, this time is for you. Just for your pleasure. I'm willing to wait for mine."

What could she say to such a thing? Nothing came to mind as he held her for long moments after her last climax. Alaan retrieved a handkerchief from his back pocket, gently cleaned her tender folds and arranged her clothes. With a loud smacking kiss on the Clan Serati tattoo around her navel, he pulled up her sweatpants then settled his leather trench around her shoulders. Her boots came next. The man even took the time to lace them properly.

Both fully dressed now, he helped her to her feet, gazed down into her face and pinned her with a no-nonsense stare. No hostility or recriminations, though she'd come and come and come while he'd restrained himself.

"I meant it when I said I want you, Tam. You're mine, and you know it. I never thought you would be the one to run from a challenge."

"Run?" Her head tilted sideways as her fist knotted on her hip. Who the hell did he think he was talking to? "Puh-lease. I've never run from a challenge in my life. And certainly not from a male." She snorted as unexplainable, unrestrained anger lashed out from deep inside her. Suddenly she wanted nothing more than to get back at him for...for what?

"Besides, you don't really want me anyway, Alaan. You've got your fucking memories of Sher."

The rigid snap of his spine and the cold glint reflected in his eyes spoke volumes. He didn't bother schooling his features or masking his emotions. She flinched as they flowed down the new bond like gritty sand through an hourglass, straight into her mind and soul. She'd hurt him. Deeply. Tameth felt like a heel for throwing something in his face he obviously wanted to forget. And she had no idea of why she'd said such a thing. Jealous of a dead woman. Stupid, stupid, stupid.

Before she could open her mouth to form an apology for being such a bitch, she was greeted by the back of Alaan's beautiful blond head as he stalked away from her. Again.

But not before his intentions resonated in her mind—Alaan had made up his mind to pursue her. And she was in trouble.

Chapter Eight

Riding on top of a double-decker bus, Kenoe looked up to the mid-morning sky. He ignored the dusky blue heavens with their occasional wisp of clouds, tuned out the excited chatter of the tourists across the aisle snapping pictures and barely noticed the automated tour guide's voice call out his stop. *British Museum, Great Russell Street.* He hopped off the bus and strode the six-minute walk to the British Museum ticket counter. The closer he got to the front door, the faster his boots moved. His stomach clenched with a funny little flip flop and landed somewhere between pleased as punch and melancholy blue, happy to be there yet acutely aware of the jagged cavern where the missing pieces of his heart should be.

Once through the front doors, a wash of relief poured over his soul like a soothing balm of peace. Whenever Kenoe came to London, he couldn't stay away from this museum. Today he'd hoped to enjoy it with his best friend, but if their plan was working, then Alaan was well on the way to realizing Tameth was his mate. Hopefully they were knee-deep in hot vampire sex right about now.

He lowered his head on a sigh. Tameth needed someone like Alaan—someone who, though a bit gruff and sharp around the edges at times, would be fiercely loyal to her. Alaan would protect her, though she needed very little protection, considering her Class Six rank. But more importantly, Alaan could do something Kenoe would never be able to—love her.

God, he wished he could. It wasn't because he'd lied and told her he was gay, but because the concept involved a certain measure of give and take. And Kenoe had already given more than he ever wanted to, had enough taken from him in his life. So, although it damned near ripped his heart out, he'd resigned himself to holding Tameth when she needed it, lent his ear when she wanted to talk, and even gave the occasional pussy lashing with his talented Hatsept tongue when she needed physical release. And while he gave to Tameth, he couldn't bring himself to receive from her, take from her. Besides, she didn't really want him "like that". The woman's heart belonged to Alaan and Kenoe would do nothing to take away her dream of being with him. Not the way others had taken the dreams he was now prepared to take back.

This was the first time he'd set foot in London in years. Though none of his missions as a Seeker had brought him here, he'd stayed away mostly due to common sense and self-preservation. After all, running into the person he'd feared for most of his life had been the last thing he'd wanted.

He snorted and kicked the thoughts away, refusing to accept his own line of thinking. Damn, he'd moved further along than this, had healed more than this. Yet even now, the bottom of his stomach threatened to boil over, hot with anger at the past that reared its head. The old demons laughed at and haunted him. Kenoe fought against and broke the chains that had held his emotions in bondage as effectively as steel shackles. But no more. Never again. This time, he refused to be bound.

His face a schooled mask of cool confidence, Kenoe kept up his leisurely pace and pushed down the anxious need to run for his destination. His feet automatically took him to the permanent Japanese exhibit in the Asian department. It never ceased to amaze him how deeply moved he was every time he ventured to this part of the museum. His stomach knotted with a different kind of anxiousness just before the bottom fell out. Homesickness, like the longing for a lost lover, assailed his heart.

From Clan Li and its members of Asian descent, to Clan Akicit and their Native American-descended warriors, the vampire clans consisted of just about every race on the planet. The humans of those cultures might not know they had vampire cousins, but they existed all the same. Yet none stirred his soul like the Japanese. Something about the place and its people made him long for the light of that world to stir and diminish the darkness of his lonely soul.

As he stood and took in the detail of an exquisite piece of ancient metalwork, Kenoe felt lonesome, yet more than comfortable in his skin. He'd long since banished the demons that had haunted him every day and night for years after escaping the most loathsome creature ever born—Lowan Hatsept-Shean, his half-brother.

Kenoe knew his clan was ill thought of throughout the vampire nation. After spending time under Lowan's boot heel for what seemed like an eternity, he understood the perception. Actually he owed Lowan some thanks. If it hadn't been for that asshole, Kenoe would have never pursued Seekerhood, would have never had the courage or determination to make it through the grueling training. Only ten of every thirty Seekers ever made it out of the Academy, and fewer still moved past the Beta ranks to full-fledged honors. But he'd made it past Beta, past full honors to elite status. And he'd made it for a reason—revenge.

Pushing the dark thoughts away, he admired a sixteenth-century set of imperial armor. In that moment, in the middle of the British Museum, the pieces snapped into place and settled to form a picture in Kenoe's heart. He knew exactly what he needed to do. As soon as this hunt was over, he would ask for a leave of absence from the Seeker corps and begin a new journey.

No sooner had the realization of the next phase of life imprinted itself in his mind, than Kenoe's enhanced senses picked up a scent. A scent that made his fingers encircle the handle of the samurai katana sheathed in the hidden compartment of the front panel of his long leather trench coat.

He'd seen plenty of vampires in the museum today. A few had even noted the distinct style of his coat, stopped and paid their respects to him as a Seeker, then moved on. But this odor all but burned the fine hairs inside his sensitive nose. There was a Hatsept near. A rogue Hatsept. Kenoe could easily tell the difference in smell and demeanor of his own kind. And there was no mistaking the distinct stench of a Hatsept gone bad. Too bad it wasn't Lowan—a scent he'd never forget. Nor forgive.

With no time to call for backup, Kenoe raised his eyes, tilted his head sideways and appeared intrigued as he studied the movements of every person reflected in the glass. His limber body remained loose and ready to engage.

Interesting. Whoever it was kept his distance, just far enough out of range of the wall of glass housing the exhibit.

"Fine," Kenoe muttered to himself. The small, strong muscles that controlled the release and retraction of his fangs twitched with tension. "Let's get this over with, asshole."

Backing up as if he hadn't a care in the world, a pissed off Seeker moved off to the next display case, then the next. The hairs on the back of his neck kept dancing. If anything they moved with more vigor as his skin tightened and flushed from a rush of battle-anticipated adrenaline.

A throng of tourists moved his way. Not good. He didn't see

anyone familiar but his enemies could easily slide into a crowd, maneuver him into a corner and quietly attack. To everyone else they would appear as a group of friends standing in a tight pack talking and laughing, while he'd be getting jumped in the middle of a pack of rabid disowned vampires.

As the group approached, he changed direction and stopped in the middle of the wide, brightly-lit main hall. Away from any walls, alcoves or niches, Kenoe slid his cell phone out of his pocket and flipped it open.

"So, where are you? Yeah, I'm looking around, but I don't see you." He spoke with enough volume to be heard over almost everyone in the museum, laughing and joking, his voice loud and clear. Not even a group of idiots would attack a Seeker if they believed others were nearby.

"Oh, okay. Uh-huh. Yep, I'm just an exhibit away. I'll see you in a sec." The phone closed with a snap. And during that short conversation with himself, he'd managed to scope out the entire area and everyone in it. But his eyes had to be playing tricks on him. He could have sworn he sighted a female vamp following him. She was a slight little thing, beautiful in a pixie kind of way. Not at all his type. Kenoe liked his women with meat on their bones, feminine with a solid dose of inner and physical strength slipped in for good measure. Kind of like Tameth—all woman, yet she could hold her own in a fair or unfair fight with the best of 'em. And she had the nicest ass this side of creation...well, next to Dr. Carinian Bixler who happened to be a good friend of Tameth's. Those two women in a room together could set the pulses of a dead vampire to racing. Muscular, but with miles of curves and personalities to match.

The female he'd spotted had dark hair and honey light brown. Strange, she lacked the distinct bluish-white eyes of a Clan Hatsept member, but she sure as hell smelled like one. A female resident of one of the local harems, perhaps? But that didn't make any sense, either. She smelled of rogue. Clan Hatsept had very few outlaws on the Council track-em-down-and-kill-em list. Those with the dishonor of being hunted weren't foolish enough to set up house while constantly on the run. Even in their briefing about this current mission, there was no mention of Lowan indulging in the Hatsept tradition of harem-keeping. As far as the Council knew, Lowan was keeping a low profile somewhere in the city, and none of their informants had caught hide or hair of him since Kenoe and his teammates had arrived in London.

Strange. As quickly as he'd spotted the female, she disappeared. Perhaps he'd been so bent and ready for a scuffle, he'd imagined the whole thing? But he'd tell Alaan about it later just to be on the safe side. In the meantime, he would enjoy the rest of his day, firm up his travel plans, and admire the warrior class weapons of the samurai as he palmed his personal replica of one of the ancient works of art hidden underneath his coat.

ɞ

The cell phone perched on the little tray table at Myles' elbow vibrated and hummed. He hated being interrupted in the middle of a snack. He removed his incisors from the donor and licked his lips. Though he no longer savored the rich, sweet blood flowing from the small incisions left on the long, muscular column of the donor's throat, the man didn't move an inch. No surprise there. Every member of Lowan's stable was well-trained, just as Myles' security members were well-trained.

He answered the phone and snapped, "Yeah, make it quick."

"It's Seth, sir," a deep, irritated voice responded. Myles listened to the report of his Second on the other end of the line.

No longer relaxed, he swung his legs over the side of his favorite chaise lounge and sat forward. Tension leached into his shoulders and settled at the base of his skull. Shit, he was going to have a headache. When the other man stopped talking, Myles' teeth clenched tightly as he spoke softly into the mouthpiece.

"Were you seen?" he asked.

"No," the voice crackled across the static-filled line. "I'm sure he sensed us but we kept our distance and were able to remain hidden. But Sher got too close and…"

Sher? What the hell did she have to do with any of this? Myles pressed the phone so close to his tightly drawn mouth, a single sharp incisor pierced his upper lip. "What about Sher?" he snarled. A trickle of blood ran down over his bottom front teeth and onto his tongue.

"She was at the museum, sir."

"What?" Myles bellowed into the phone. His arm shot out and smacked the person closest to him—the handsome, athletically-built young man baring his slender neck for Myles' pleasure. The man scrambled back and away. He rose from the floor, picked up his T-shirt off the carpet and slipped it on over his head. With a toss of his head, he strode from the room with all the dignity of a…of whatever clan he'd been affiliated with before he went rogue and joined Lowan's stable. Myles watched the young man go with little interest. With the news he'd just received, he didn't have time to worry about one vampire's impertinence. Besides, working on the pup's social skills could wait until after he'd delivered this information to Lowan.

"I don't know why she was there but I'm sure the Seeker we were tailing got a good look at her. Even if he didn't recognize her, her presence kept us from carrying out the operation."

Myles gritted his teeth, relieved the team he'd sent out had used good judgment, yet annoyed they weren't able to complete the mission. If they'd gone ahead and things had gotten messy, Sher would have been right in the middle of it. Damn it!

Ear pressed to the phone, Myles listened closely as his Second laid out the details of what he'd seen and heard. And how Sher had screwed it all up. Lowan needed to keep a tighter leash on his spoiled little pet. She was already too full of herself. If it were up to Myles, he'd paddle her ass until it was raw. Fucking woman! What the hell was she thinking, walking into the middle of his carefully laid plans?

And the news only got worse, sending Myles' blood pressure barreling up to the top of his head. Bloody hell! He did *not* need this right now. For once, why couldn't his snitches be wrong? Alaan Serati, complete with a full team of kick-ass-first-ask-questions-later elite Seekers in London was not a good fucking thing. This particular team wouldn't even have to take him or Lowan back to V.C.O.E. headquarters to stand before the Council. Serati was bad enough, but Seeker Collins was with them. Both a Seeker and an Iudex judge, Collins had the authority to impose whatever sentence he felt necessary, even order their heads cut off on the spot. And if Sher was discovered in their company, Alaan Serati would take entirely too much pleasure in such an act.

Then there was Kenoe.

Myles snapped the phone closed, wanting nothing more than to crush the damned thing in his palm and throw it across the room. Rising from his seat with a resigned sigh, he left his suite and headed to the throne room. He didn't look forward to meeting with Lowan. He and his old friend were the only Hatsepts in this harem. All the other vampires were rogues from various clans, the most notorious bunch alive.

With that son of a bitch's unpredictable temper, Myles

would rather face ten rogues right now than one Lowan Hatsept-Shean.

Myles entered the huge double doors of Lowan's room. One wall was full of windows enhanced by black on black window treatments and valances. The drapes were held back with silver cord and allowed bright sunlight to flow in, engulfing the bed with a lounging Lowan in the middle of it.

Thankfully, even rogues who spent little time out in the sunlight could get their hands on bootlegged meds to help keep their allergies under control. The suite was one huge, spotless, white-tiled space with no walls—something about Lowan not liking to feel hemmed in. The first thing visible when one walked in was an ornate throne, the symbol of absolute rule in this place. The bedroom was marked by a plush, light gray carpet. A large glass dining table sat across the room on a creamy white carpet. Except for a small enclosure with a door for the toilet, even the bathroom was visible.

Myles passed the elaborate red carpet with the pharaoh's throne at its center, and strode to the area that served as Lowan's bedroom.

"You. Off," Myles snapped. With those two words, the woman perched on Lowan's backside massaging his shoulders went scrambling. She covered Lowan with a light sheet, then stood next to the bed wearing a garment so sheer she may as well have been naked. And what a lovely body, with endless creamy skin covering lush curves, wide hips and a spankable ass. In spite of his angry, clipped words, her expression held no fear as she stood quietly next to the bed and awaited the next order. The higher ranked males might be able to boss her around, but no one was allowed to touch her without Lowan's permission.

Their clan's harem rules dictated that their women be treated like queens. Even rogues obeyed that rule...after breaking the females in, of course—a nasty but necessary business.

Muffled by an oversized pillow, Lowan grumbled, "This had better be important, Myles."

Myles kept his distance knowing the man didn't like having his daily massage interrupted. Probably because it was almost always followed by some hot, sweaty and fabulously well-trained sex. Clearing his throat, Myles pressed on. May as well get this over with.

"Seth just checked in. The informants were right. There's a team of Seekers in London."

"Don't waste my time, Myles."

"We've been following this particular group with the intent of ascertaining exactly where they came from. Our regulars in Knightsbridge brought them to our attention, then disappeared."

"Big deal. We already knew the Knightsbridge crew was missing and there are Seekers in every city. No surprise there," Lowan mumbled.

"Not elite special weapons and tactics Seekers, Lowan. These are heavy hitters. They could have only been dispatched by the Council."

An involuntary tremor snaked its way through his limbs as he waited for the explosion.

"What else?" Lowan asked impatiently, forcing himself to remain sprawled underneath the covers. Covers that had suddenly lost their warmth.

"Seth's team trailed one of the Seekers to Bloomsbury

district, to the British Museum. The Seeker our men followed today was..."

"I am fast losing patience with you, Myles. What, already?"

"The Seeker we followed today turned out to be your brother, Kenoe. And worse, Sher botched the abduction. They were moving in to try and take him when she popped up. Bitch."

"Watch your mouth, Myles. It is, after all, your fault that so-called bitch is in our service, hm?" The words flowed off his tongue easily enough, but inside, Lowan's blood steamed. Myles probably expected him to jump from the bed and beat everyone in sight to a gory pulp, but in truth, Lowan just didn't feel like it. This little revelation gave him too much to think about to waste his energy pounding flesh.

"Yeah, I remember," Myles grumbled. "Unfortunately."

So, Kenoe Hatsept-Thrace, the proverbial pain in his ass, was in London. Now, *that* was news, and not necessarily bad. He would love to become reacquainted with his little brother. Perhaps pick up where they'd left off all those years ago when Kenoe had fled the harem after their father's death. His mind reeled with the possibilities of getting his hands on Kenoe and persuading him to join the family business. Hmm, his brother was a Seeker, an elite Council assassin and working with Alaan Serati, at that. He couldn't believe it. But there was still one thing he needed to know.

"Is Sher on her way back, Myles?" Before the man could answer, a familiar female scent tickled Lowan's nose. Without bothering to roll over to face his Second or the woman who'd just entered the room, Lowan ended the conversation. His own essence mixed with hers and lingered on every inch of the lovely skin making its way to his bed.

"Never mind, Myles. Just find out where that overgrown

Serati asshole's team is staying and get back to me. And give me a couple of hours," Lowan murmured on an even intake of breath, anticipating the treat of pure feline grace that approached. "I expect to be busy for a while."

Lowan rolled to his back and motioned to the silent long-legged beauty still awaiting instruction. "And take her with you."

Lowan watched him turn on a dime, shoo the female out and depart without a word, back straight and jaw tight with rage. There weren't many who managed to get under his Second's skin, but Sher was an expert at it. Lowan almost smiled at the fury rolling off the man as he made eye contact with no one, not even the men under his command, all dressed in tactical gear guarding the doors that slid silently open at his approach. And he certainly didn't spare a glance for the new arrival now crawling into the big bed, who Myles considered little more than an inconvenient imp.

Lowan lowered his head on a sigh. Sher. Sooner or later, he'd have to do something about her.

Chapter Nine

Sitting up in the grand expanse of the bed, Lowan hissed with a mix of annoyance and pleasure. The sheet slid down and away from his sensitive male nipples and a warm, wet mouth replaced the fabric. Sher was an expert at sucking.

She was also one of the reasons he was hunted as a rogue. Kenoe was the other.

When his brother ran away as a lad, he'd sought refuge in the harem of the Clan Elder himself. Clan Hatsept were the only harem keepers in the vampire nation and held under close scrutiny for adhering to the ancient lifestyle. Needless to say, Lowan's peers didn't much appreciate the extra attention drawn to them by his unorthodox methods in securing and training his harem members. Lowan didn't see what the fuss had been about. He'd taken very few female vampires against their will. Well, fine, he'd taken them all against their will but out of the thirty pleasure slaves in his keeping at the time, only two were female vamps. What the hell did the Vampire Council of Ethics or the Elder of Clan Hatsept care about a bunch of humans? Other than the rule against exposing their world, of course.

Yet in his heart, Lowan knew the abusive treatment of his little brother was what really landed him in a V.C.O.E. cell. He wondered if Kenoe knew they weren't related. Lowan's mother passed away when he was just seven years old. His father remarried a striking dark-haired Egyptian vampire, whom he promptly strangled after Kenoe's birth since the faithless bitch had been knocked up by another male. If not for the fact all Hatsept males were born with the legendary snow white hair and blue-white eyes, their lack of shared blood would have been obvious.

Years later in Vienna, he'd been tried, convicted and sentenced to five years hard time. He'd been waiting to be transported to a prison in Siberia when he'd supposedly caused the death of the woman kneeling between his legs sucking so diligently on his nipples. Her supposed murder put him on the V.C.O.E. Most Wanted list.

One of Sher's small hands squeezed the base of his breast. A pebble-hard nipple and a good mound of flesh stood up for her ravishing. The other hand slid beneath the sheet pooled at his waist and wrapped around his jutting cock. The veins filled and twined around the stretched length, so tight it bordered on pain. But damn, it hurt so good.

With a groan he buried his fingers in her thick curls and pressed her mouth harder against his chest. His left pec leapt underneath her lips when sharp fangs pressed through the skin. He hadn't even buried his cock into her warm inviting cunt, yet he hovered on the verge of orgasm. The little purring sound she made as she sucked his male breast, hungrily slurped his blood, and pulled eagerly on his cock from base to throbbing head, pushed him even closer to blowing his load. But no Hatsept worth his salt would come without his dick buried deep in a lover's body.

"Stop, Sher," Lowan commanded quietly.

Immediately she eased her mouth away, taking one last lick from the trickle of blood just above his nipple. Sher was the perfect partner. Small and feminine, always mistaken for a good little girl. And she knew how to work it to her advantage. Or rather, *his* advantage. Of course she'd missed her old life as a privileged Clan Sewell female for a while, but after her harem training she belonged to Lowan alone, body and soul.

"Call the others," he whispered. She nodded her head in compliance but Lowan was no fool. She hated sharing him with the other harem members. Yet he had to keep her in check or risk being twisted around her little finger. Yes, he must remind her she belonged to him, regardless of the special privileges afforded her.

Not to mention she'd earned a punishment for ruining Myles' plans by being someplace she shouldn't have. And he didn't have to tell her he knew what she'd done. Even with all her expertise at shielding her mind from vamps and humans alike, their bond ensured his quiet rage seeped through.

"Myles is always telling on me," she complained into his mind as she scooted backward off the bed.

"Even if he had not, I would have found out sooner or later, Sher."

Head bowed, she left to do his bidding. Lowan chuckled at the stubborn tilt of her chin, the stiff set of her shoulders. She'd stripped immediately upon entering his bedroom, but now she didn't even bother slipping into her robe, determined to walk out the door and down to the harem chambers without a stitch on. He'd have to punish her for such insolence later. The woman was well aware she was only to be naked in two places—in his bed and at the foot of his throne.

He shook his head thinking how crazy he'd been to steal her six years ago. It wasn't until after her abduction that he'd realized the cause of the strange and much-too-strong attraction between them. Actually Myles had been the one to figure it out—Sher was Lowan's bondmate. It was the reason

Lowan was very careful never to take Sher's blood. Ever. He wanted her, no doubt about it. But he didn't want anything or anyone so much that he'd risk forming such a powerful and irrevocable bond. Their empathic connection was enough. He didn't want to put himself in a position where he'd never be able to walk away from her.

His mind drifted to the first time he'd seen Sher. Six years ago, during the yearly whirlwind tour the Elders took to see their constituents, Lowan had been a guest at the V.C.O.E. headquarters in Vienna, Austria, to await sentencing. He'd already been convicted of crimes against the vampire nation and humanity. Even now, he shook his head in wonder. He never had understood the problem with his methods of securing beautiful young women, and equally beautiful young men, for his stables. They'd all been free to leave anytime they wished. They left in itty bitty pieces, but it was still their choice to go.

Originally from Romania, Sher happened to be in Europe visiting family. She'd stopped in to see the Matriarch Serati before the old hag and the Clan Elders left to visit the other territories. He'd gotten a glimpse of her beautiful face and tempting body standing in a corner of the Council Chambers as they had led him away in silver-coated titanium chains. He still occasionally rubbed his wrists where a nasty rash had erupted and bled as a result of the denial of his allergy meds.

Everyone had known Sher and Alaan were to be mated later that summer, complete with a rare traditional ceremony before the entire Council. At the time he hadn't particularly cared whether the female belonged to someone else. Even if that someone happened to be one of the most feared Seekers in the Seeker corps. The same Seeker who'd captured him and tossed him in vampire jail.

Lowan snorted to himself as the memories slid through his mind. He'd never cared much for authority. Still didn't.

Before the sentence of five years in prison could be carried out, Lowan had escaped, leaving a battered, mangled corpse behind. The face of that corpse was beaten beyond recognition. Among the mass of black curly hair was a necklace with a pendent of the Serati crest Sher had worn around her neck. There was also a blood-soaked note to Alaan claiming that since Lowan couldn't get to him, he'd taken what was dearest to him. The ploy worked...too damned well.

Everyone assumed he'd had inside help from his clan, but all of Clan Hatsept had denounced him. All except Myles, whose genius brought him the last person who'd visited his cell that fateful day. The woman who now entered his bedroom with four harem mates in tow.

Lowan swung his legs over the side of the bed, watching the small group file into the sunlit room. He scratched the red welt on his shoulder and instructed his guards to close the drapes. He needed to get out more, then maybe this damned sun allergy wouldn't act up so much.

He strode across the room, onto the large red carpet and settled naked onto his throne. At times like this he was glad he'd had the foresight to have cushions made for it. With a crook of his finger, he was immediately joined by one of his personal guard. The man removed his boots and, at Lowan's nod, stepped onto the carpet. In his hands was a bronze tray with several lengths of black silk cord laid neatly across it.

Lowan pulled his shoulder-length snow white hair back into a thick ponytail and secured it with one of the cords.

"Bring up the lights," Lowan quietly ordered.

With a slight bow and a mumbled, "Yes, sir," the man stepped off the carpet and back into his boots.

The bright overhead fixtures illuminated the space in front of Lowan's throne like a row of spotlights. In a perfect line, their bare feet exactly twelve inches from the red carpet, stood this afternoon's distraction. Beside a naked Sher stood two females dressed in uniforms of elaborately embroidered, black, loose-fitting harem pants. Created from fine viscose cotton, the pants were paired with matching halters tied around their necks. The sexy tops fell just below their breasts and were loose at the bottom.

Hmm. It appeared Sher had been careful in selecting the participants for the afternoon. She wouldn't have cared about the men she picked, but the women were the newest, least skilled additions to the fold. Something else to punish her for.

Both women, sporting short haircuts as a symbol of the beginning of their new lives, were Sher's total opposites—tall, athletic rather than petite, and neither had dark hair. One woman sported creamy fair skin and red hair, her body toned and slender like a long-distance runner. The other female looked more like a bodybuilder with milk chocolate skin and silky ringlets of honey brown tresses...and she was human, the only one in his entire house.

Lowan turned his attention to the bare-chested males and did a quick study. There weren't many men in the harem, but they were occasionally recruited to fill in the ranks and provide security for the women. Rumor had it that these two were gay. And Lowan hadn't bothered to correct or stop the gossip. It served him well, especially when there was dissension among the women. These two handsome men could get those females to tell them things they wouldn't dare share with the other males.

The men's wraparound kilts brushed the top of their knees. Also all black, the ancient Egyptian-styled skirts were unadorned except for the hem, embroidered with silver thread in the outline of the Egyptian goddess Maat, the sigil of Clan Hatsept. His fellow Clan bastards disowned him years ago, but that didn't change his blood.

Lowan's voice rang out with quiet authority.

"Disrobe."

Immediately the group untied the drawstrings securing their clothing and the garments floated to the floor and pooled at their feet. Lowan fairly bristled with anticipation. None of them approached him or let even the tips of their toes skim the edge of the carpet without permission. His chest swelled with pride at their discipline.

"Sher, come here."

He didn't miss the sly smile that touched the corner of her mouth but quickly disappeared as if it never was. But he had a surprise for the little hellion.

She sidled up to him and started to climb up into his lap.

"Oh no, no, no, my dear," he whispered for her ears alone. "You will sit over there." He pointed to a corner of the carpet at least ten feet from the throne. "And you will not take your eyes off of us." He felt her irritation flare, then snuff out like a candle in a windstorm. Her emotions were put in a stranglehold of control, as expected.

"And you are not allowed to touch yourself, Sher."

This time her anger ignited and continued to burn hot. Not being able to join in the fun was a harsh punishment for someone whose body was trained to crave pleasure. The exclusion would add a level of intensity that would drive her to the brink of madness and leave her hanging there.

"Sit over there facing me. Hands behind your back. Bend your knees and spread you legs as far as they will go so I can watch the juices run from your pretty, soon-to-be unsatisfied pussy." Back ramrod straight, Sher walked slowly to her designated spot for the afternoon. He watched her ease down to the carpet with all the dignity she could muster, her face a mask of bland boredom. Lowan was sure he was the only one who noticed her fingers trembling as she smoothed an errant wisp of curl away from her forehead before grasping her wrists behind her back.

Lowan lay on the thick, soft, perfect-for-fucking carpet, and stretched his body like a big cat.

So Sher thought to choose women he wouldn't find attractive? Once again, she proved she didn't know him as well as she thought. Especially with the darker woman. Lowan's eyes slid back to her.

"What is your name, beautiful?" he asked silkily, his cock beginning to stir just from the sight of such endless luscious skin. His keen hearing picked up her quickening heartbeat as she held his gaze and answered steadily.

"My name is Kimora."

Such lovely light brown eyes, tipped up at the sides, almost feline. The color of old-fashioned root beer ice.

"You are of mixed race?" he inquired.

"My mother is African-American, my father, Japanese. They met as students at the University of San Francisco while he was there on a scholarship long ago."

Lowan had sworn off humans since his run-in with the law, and didn't usually care for large women, but Kimora not only caught his attention, but held it. In all his long years he'd never seen such a perfect body. He found himself wondering if she tasted like the cocoa her skin resembled. Her breasts were large, not overly so, but stood proud and firm with big areolas made for sucking. A small diamond stud winked at him from the bellybutton above her smooth, trim tummy. Hips flared wide and curved around to a perfectly round ass that made his mouth water. He just knew the cropped curls at the vee of her thighs hid a sweet, dewy treasure. The woman had some meat on her bones and Lowan couldn't wait to taste her.

He'd always heard black women didn't take any shit from anyone. How her handler had ever gotten this one to accept their lifestyle, he'd never know. But her passion ran hot, so close to the surface it set a hungry glow in her beautiful whiskey brown eyes.

Folding his arms behind his head, he spread his legs and said, "Kimora, come here and pose for me, luscious." Lowan almost grinned at the shock streaking along the underdeveloped bond with Sher. Oh, she seethed like a cauldron with a top on it, but in record time Lowan's focus shifted away from the woman across the carpet. His mind and thoughts filled to overflowing with nothing but the beauty standing with a foot on either side of his slim hips. Yes, a proportioned vision of sculpted grace. His gaze traveled from the firm thighs she flexed and tightened with ease to the glistening lips of her pouty sex. The toned muscles of her quads and hamstrings were easily visible. Hands on hips, the woman dug a toe into the carpet and tightened a calf muscle. He reached out and trailed a single finger up that lovely rounded bulge covered with so much cinnamon brown skin.

Then she bent over, planted her palms flat on the floor, and used her stomach muscles to pull her legs up off the floor. She remained perfectly balanced on her hands, legs spread wide in a decadent vee. Strong and flexible—nice combination.

"Very nice," Lowan crooned, following her movements as she gained her feet. "Turn around and flex that lovely ass for me."

She did, along with her nicely developed back, shoulders

and biceps. Damn, she was gorgeous.

He almost shook his head in dismay when it was time to proceed with Sher's lesson. After all, he couldn't let her get away with leaving the property unescorted, sneaking after Myles' men, then walking into the middle of a potentially dangerous situation. There was no love lost between Sher and Myles. Lowan knew that. But his Second kept them all one step ahead of the V.C.O.E. and they simply couldn't afford to have the damned woman foiling Myles' operations just because she didn't like him. And he was under no illusion the woman didn't know what she was doing. The question was, why had she really done it?

"Thank you, Kimora."

Her smile lit up the room. Lowan turned his head until his cheek rested on the carpet and his blue-white gaze settled on the others still standing along the edge of the carpet. "The rest of you may serve me now."

His fingers wrapped around Kimora's ankle and held fast when she started to move away.

"You." His voice had kicked up a notch, sounded strained, urgent. He pointed to his lips and said, "Right here." She sank to her knees and her labial lips parted just enough for him to glimpse the candy pink inner folds. He inhaled and groaned with delight. The scent of her fragrant sex filled his lungs, reminding him of tropical coconut mixed with something piquant and savory that he couldn't quite put his finger on.

"Closer," he ordered.

Kimora did as he asked, but not fast enough. With speed born of a vampire he grabbed her about her solid hips, yanked her forward and pulled her down over his face.

His tongue slid up and down the seam of her warm pussy. Lowan hummed with satisfaction as her unique flavor burst

131

over his taste buds. Her hips swiveled and her breathing deepened. Soft little moans escaped from parted lips with each exhale. Such a sensual creature.

"Mmm. Oh," she gasped, grinding her sex hard against his mouth. He stiffened his tongue and slid it just inside her weeping entrance, teasing her without mercy. The lips of her cunt swelled beautifully. Dipping deeper into her hole, he rejoiced in the scalding heat of her channel as he pushed his tongue through the tight ring of clenching muscles. He eased inside, and then retreated with a sensual rhythm until Kimora anticipated the next shallow plunge.

One of the males knelt at his side and wrapped his lips around one of Kimora's puckered, swollen nipples, and pulled it deep into his mouth while one large hand palmed and weighed the other.

Her moans were louder now, hips moving frantically. "Yes, eat me up. Just like that. Oooh!"

A glance at Sher told him her hands were knotted in her lap now. She was completely still, except for the rapid rise and fall of her chest as she called to him.

"Oh, Lowan, I want to fuck you so bad. I was wrong and I'm so sorry I disobeyed the rules of the harem. I want it. I want to be filled with your cock. Please let me come to you. Please!"

Lowan turned away. He doubted she was aware she projected her thoughts so loudly, anyone in the building with a bit of psychic skill could hear them.

Kimora's cries of delight combined with Sher's silent, hot, horny thoughts drove Lowan to such heights of longing and desire he was surprised he didn't exhale smoke with each breath.

He sank a finger, then another, into Kimora's juicy cunt. She creamed and fluttered around them. Her head fell back

132

when his other hand spread her open and suckled on the sensitive knot of her clit, now unhooded and reaching for him. She came on a muted cry. Stomach muscles clenched and rolled wildly in time with the erratic beat of her heart.

The male sucking one of her Hershey's Kiss nipples released it with a loud pop. She didn't hesitate when he stood facing her with the rock hard head of his glistening cock just inches from her full, lush lips. Now it was her turn to suck. Opening immediately, she circled the tip with a wet, talented tongue. It was the sexiest damned thing Lowan had ever seen, and he'd seen a lot.

The male pushed past her lips to seat himself at the gate to her throat. Kimora didn't resist, but relaxed her jaw muscles and took him until her nose was buried in the short curls at his groin. Then her neck began to move. In seconds she dictated the pace. And the male loved it.

In fact, so did Lowan. His cock was a thick-veined pole of throbbing lust, so hard and hungry it was a wonder the skin didn't split. He needed some pussy and he needed it now. He'd just fixed his mouth to instruct Kimora to slide her juicy channel over him when a warm tight sheath slid down over his cock—the redhead.

He didn't have to look up to know her mouth was wrapped around the cock of the second male. The loud slurping and humming sounds made it clear enough.

Lowan buried his face back between Kimora's thighs while the other woman bucked his hips, riding his cock as if he were a wild, unbroken stallion. Her knees gripped his hips and she ground her body down hard, seated to the hilt. Then rose up until only the head of Lowan's cock remained inside, and slammed back down. Over and over. Lowan wondered if the woman was a country girl.

Hell, for a pair of novices, these women worked his body so thoroughly, he felt like both the pimp and the 'ho, demanding and giving it up to them all at the same time.

Holding nothing back, he let the pleasure of eating sweet Kimora and the delight of being milked by the redhead—he'd have to remember to get her name—flood his thoughts. The second Sher picked them up, along with his reeling emotions, her desire for him transformed to anger, then remorse, and finally resolve.

Lowan heard all of this flash through Sher's mind while he, Kimora, the redhead and the two males exploded together, then collapsed into a pile of sweaty, sated flesh.

The second they'd managed to catch their breath, as if on cue, all four rose to their feet, left the carpet and stood in a perfect line once more, their skin glistening with the light sheen of their pleasure.

Sometime during the interlude, a towel had been placed on the armrest of his throne. Lowan didn't bother using it. Instead, he rose from the plush rug, sat on the gilded symbol of his status and critiqued the harem members on their technique one at a time. In short, they'd all been very good.

"Your trainers are doing an excellent job with you." Motioning to the two women, he said, "You two have been here all of three months. I am impressed with your ability to time your movements for maximum pleasure of your partners. Also, neither of you faked orgasm. If you did, you fooled me. And believe me, I am not an easy man to fool."

Focusing on the two men, he said evenly, "You anticipated the females' needs well. You've been good additions to our family for several years now and have lost none of your touch. I would like the two of you to continue to assist Lars and Seth in training these two lovely ladies. And make sure the redhead receives an extra portion of chilled blood confection with her dinner."

All four bowed slightly. None of them so much as smiled—it would have been inappropriate. But their bright expressions showed they were pleased with their evaluations.

Sher was pissed. Resentment rolled off her like hot lava bubbling up in the crater of a volcano just before it blew. But he refused to acknowledge her in any way. Not yet.

"You may dress now." With a negligent wave over his shoulder, Lowan said, "Sher, you may dress as well. Then escort them back to the harem."

She rose with urgency, anticipation. Lowan knew what she expected—to be ordered to take her harem mates back to the common rooms, then return to him alone.

He could no longer afford to give her what she expected.

Dressed quickly, all of them filed towards the entrance with Sher at the head of the orderly column. Lowan's personal guard opened the door to let them out. Sher had taken a single step across the threshold when Lowan's voice rang out once again.

"One moment."

Five heads swiveled around to face him as they continued to move towards the quiet hallways.

"Kimora, please get a change of clothes and come back here. Alone."

Shock registered on Kimora's face. The two males smirked. The redhead showed no care whatsoever.

Sher stumbled.

Chapter Ten

Alaan rose from his spot on the loveseat to stand in front of the blazing fireplace. The door eased open.

Higgins' dignified voice rang quietly through the expanse of the library. "Sir, do you need anything before I retire for the evening?"

Yeah, Alaan needed something all right, but he certainly didn't want it from Higgins.

"No thanks, Higgins. I'm fine." What a bald-faced lie. The older vampire's soft footfalls approached the door when Alaan yanked his mind away from what had him all tied up in knots. Remembering why he was in the library in the first place, Alaan turned to the longtime servant.

"Higgins?"

"Yes, sir?"

"We'll be heading out shortly to hunt. Be sure to secure the doors after we leave. No one gets in. No one leaves. Understand?"

"Of course, sir. I may be getting along in years even by vampire standards, but I do remember protocol. The few humans who work in the mansion have long gone home, sir. Don't worry. Anyone who wants in while you and the others are gone had better possess a key or..." A wrinkled finger pushed aside the lapel of his long formal waistcoat. Black metal glinted against the flames dancing in the grate. "They had better be able to, as you say, dodge bullets. I've a full clip of the special biological rounds, compliments of Dr. Carin."

Alaan chuckled. He should have known. Carin would have sent anything she thought they needed well ahead of time. He turned and took in the packed crates of supplies piled against one wall. He'd been so caught up with Tameth and her ridiculous notions of what she believed he wanted and didn't want, he hadn't even finished going through them all. Sigh. Sorting out vitamins and blood enhancers from deadly poisons was probably best left to Kenoe anyway. He was a natural scientist and worked with Carin whenever they were both at Western headquarters in Montana.

"Goodnight, Master Seeker, sir." A wink crinkled the corners of Higgins' still-bright gray-green eyes as his gnarled fingers gently patted the holster hidden under his coat.

Alaan smiled at the old vamp's back as the library door snapped quietly closed behind him. Once more he stared into the crackling fire. His chest expanded with a deep sigh and contracted on an irritated huff while the events of the past several days sifted through his thoughts.

Well, one good thing about declaring Tameth his Second—he'd been able to avoid just about everyone while she handled the details of the mission. And even when she assigned partners and routes to scout together, he'd simply pulled rank and took the routes that allowed him to do his surveillance alone. When he returned from scouting, he'd spent his nights in his room practicing his telepathic blocking and shielding, reading, pacing and ripping his hands through his hair. Other than their daily team briefings, he hadn't spoken to Tameth since her little dig about Sher after he'd just given her the fuck of a lifetime. Why didn't the woman get it?

After what seemed like forever, Alaan was ready to leave his past behind to be with the woman he believed was the perfect mate for him. And just like a female, she'd dug up the hurt he'd finally buried and rubbed it in his face like a fresh mound of dog shit.

After her smart aleck remark, Alaan had left her standing in Bix's garden and run up to Carin's labs. It was obvious he was pissed but thankfully Carin hadn't asked any questions. Instead, the good doctor pushed him down in a chair, swabbed his neck with an alcohol pad and gave him his overdue allergy shot. Once he finished complaining about the sting, she shoved a meat and veggie pasty left over from lunch into his hand. He'd been so shaken by all the over-the-top psychic business he hadn't realized he'd been projecting his thoughts like some untried baby vampire. Carin had tactfully suggested he "work on that". Unfortunately, no matter what he tried or what level of telepathic skill he possessed, all he could do was turn it down a little. None of his psychic blocking would ever work against Tameth. And thankfully, only Tameth.

Now, Alaan was fast losing his resolve to just stay the hell away from the woman. And *that* pissed him off.

Sigh. Beautiful, honorable, all-woman, Tameth.

The very same woman whose fingers wrapped around the knob on the other side of the door. She hadn't made a sound but he knew she'd come into the room. Even if her scent hadn't stolen to him and filled his head. Even if she hadn't called his name out loud, or brushed lovingly against his mind, he knew she was there. Would always know. This bond business sucked.

"Alaan?"

He stood, soaking the heat of the flames into the front of his body until his clothing burned so hot against his skin, it almost surpassed his need for Tameth. Was that the quiet click of the lock? No. Not only would the team be down soon, but she'd all but called him a liar after making love with him. What would be the point of getting cozy now?

He almost wished she'd just go away. If she couldn't accept him, believe him, what more was there to say...other than "ouch" from the tight bands of steel squeezing his heart until it threatened to burst like an overfilled water balloon. God, he wanted her. Sheesh, his brain must have shriveled a bit from standing so close to the fireplace.

He looked up to the ceiling and mocked himself. Amazing. Mr. Bad-Assed Prime Male Seeker was having his heart ripped to shreds just being in the same room with a female. A female who didn't trust him. Didn't believe he wanted her.

"Alaan?" she queried again.

He didn't bother to turn and face her. Not until her strong fingers wrapped around his large biceps and squeezed. Hands braced against the mantle, he turned and looked down into her face. Like all Seekers, the woman was trained to school her features and keep her emotions under tight rein. But right now she didn't bother with either. Miserable was the only word he could think of to describe the sorrow rolling through her.

"Alaan, I'm so sorry. I shouldn't have said what I did about Sher. Forgive me?"

"Why, Tameth?" His tone serious, he managed to push the question past the choke of tears in his throat that almost kept the words stuck there.

"Because, Alaan, I..." She paused, lowering her lashes as if she couldn't go on. He faced her fully now, comforted by the subtle caress of her fingers on his arms. Her chest rose and fell on a deep flustered breath.

She backed up a step and let it all fly out on a rush. "It's killing me to lay down my pride and say this, but I was wrong, okay? It's just that I've been attracted to you for so long I just couldn't accept that we might finally be together. But it's beyond attraction, and I..."

"You what?" He hadn't meant to sound so gruff, but he had to know if he was reading more into what she was saying than what she meant.

"I-I need you." Stammering, Tameth blushed hotly but raised her eyes to boldly meet his gaze.

She really needed him? Alaan calmed his mind, cocked his head, and listened while the tightness restricting his lungs tried to decide whether to release or squeeze harder.

"I haven't been able to think of anything else the last few days. I've felt this way about you for so long, it seems like forever."

She'd wanted him forever? How could that be true and he not know it? Or had he known but not accepted it because of fear?

She paused. He pushed.

"Go on."

"Alaan, I need to hear your voice when I wake in the morning. Need to feel you pressed against me when I fall asleep at night. Now with a bond forming between us, I can't ignore it any longer. Please, I...mmppffhh!"

He yanked her into his arms and slammed his lips down over hers. He'd heard all that was necessary. Right now, he needed to touch, to taste, to savor. A hunter by nature, Alaan had never felt so much the predator. It was impossible to hold back the cyclone of emotion, the blur of longing mixed with affection and pent-up anxiety. And he didn't want to. Instead, he let it burst forth and engulf him until it soaked him through. He'd never been so free as he moved in tandem with the rush of raging passion.

There was nothing tender in the kiss. Alaan threw himself into the touching and pulled her into the deep with him. Stroked and caressed, lip to lip, tongue to tongue, and chest to chest until the two of them burned together in a conflagration of sizzling heat.

More than a melding of the mouths, but a joining of the hearts. Everything she'd said, everything she'd confessed was all there on the surface of her mind for him to experience as if they were one being. Along with a strong yearning, the sorrow and guilt of hurting him with her little Sher remark were like deep pits of remorse in her head. The longer he held her and whispered endearments between kisses, the more those potholes filled with happiness and love until, finally, the slate of her mind was as smooth and clean as hand-blown glass.

Arms wrapped around Tameth's tall frame, Alaan bent his knees, gathered her against his chest and lifted her clean off the floor. Four steps had him at the nearest couch, but he couldn't bring himself to release her soft, supple lips. Not yet.

Instead he set her booted feet on top of the cushions— Higgins would kill him for that—nudged them apart and settled between them, all without leaving her mouth for a second.

She tasted of vanilla and mint, like his favorite holiday candy melt-aways. So pliant and giving, she offered up everything, let him take anything, holding back nothing in mind or body. On a gasp, she broke the kiss and looked deeply into his eyes.

"So does that pole in your pants mean you forgive me?"

The thought and all the passion behind her words whispered through his brain. Forgive her? Hell, yes.

"Now I have some making up to do," said Tameth.

A bone-deep shiver passed through his body when her fingers wrapped around his very-there erection.

"Tameth," he said aloud. "We don't have to have sex in order for me to forgive you." Okay, her fingers were still moving across the front of his body, and his hips were beginning to chase them around. "It's not necessary, baby, really..."

"Shut up and stand there."

Yep, she was a Serati female all right. Through and through.

"I may be a Clan Serati female, Alaan, but I will never." A strong finger landed in the middle of his chest with a hard poke. "Make the mistake." His belt hit the floor. "Of forgetting you are." All five buttons on the crotch of his pants gave way. "All prime male."

She squatted down until her nose was level with the waist of a pair of quickly retreating jet black camouflage trousers. His cock sprang free and fell into her hot little hands. "Mmmm, commando style?" She tilted her head, licked her lips, and stared. His cock jerked.

"Damn, woman."

Pulling him gently by the throbbing plump head, she sat on the ledge of the couch and bent forward. No fooling around. No preliminaries. Just took him to the back of her throat in one stroke.

His head fell back on a muffled shout. His bottom lip stung where he bit into it to keep from yelling. Her strong teeth nipped the pulsing column of his rod. His eyes squeezed shut—were those stars? She nipped him again. Damn it, but not enough to blood him. Just enough to send a sliver of pleasure-pain streaking through his balls. He would never last like this. Her mouth just felt too good.

He almost started to pray for strength when a deep moan eased along her vocal cords and sank into his dick. The unfathomable, seductive hum wrapped around the base of his spine, caressed every nerve ending up and down his vertebral column. Even his ribs vibrated when she expressed her pleasure.

The wet hot channel of her mouth surrounded him from root to tip, pulled away just long enough for him to get a breath, then slammed back over his hard flesh. The woman sucked his cock like it was her favorite pastime. He'd never felt so wanted, needed by a female as he did right now. Her honesty about her feelings for him reflected in every suck, every moan, every pull of her mouth. And he fell more under her spell with each lick.

Not long ago, he would have fought tooth and nail against such feelings. Now, all he wanted to do was drown in them. The woman was like a potent drug, sweeter than the finest wine, and more restorative and fortifying than the freshest blood. She was his sustenance.

Easing her lips away from his cock, Alaan took over.

"Stand up for me, beautiful."

He had no idea where his patience came from but "grateful" was the understatement of the century. Slowly, he eased her leather Seeker's trench coat down her shoulders and off. It became a puddle of black leather at her feet. Her scent whooshed up to meet him as the folds of her coat settled onto the cushions of the couch.

His long fingers curled into the collar of her shirt. The Kevlar buttons on the front of her tactical fatigues flew around the room as the shirt fell down around her elbows.

Funny. She was the toughest woman he'd ever met. Hard as nails, reliable and skilled enough to kick ass with or without a weapon. He'd always expected sturdy, boring cotton underwear beneath her serviceable combat gear. Instead she favored richly colored bras with matching panties—if you could call the little skimpy pieces of cloth panties.

Today's treat was a ruby-colored confection done in a cut where most of the tops of her lovely round breasts were exposed almost to the nipple, but the sides and undersides were fully supported. Lovely.

The swelling peaks of those perfect mounds whispered his name. Or was that her desire winding through the bond to twine with his? Either way, he would give her what she needed.

A swift dive saw his mouth wrapped around the budding areola of her right breast, suckling through the vibrant red silk. His fangs came out to join the fun.

She squeaked. He grinned.

"Damn it, Alaan, you bit through my...aaahhh."

"Don't worry. I'll buy you another one." A mix of triumph and "cheeky bastard" laced his words. Grinning, Alaan pressed his mouth more firmly around her flesh and suckled until her fingers wound through his curly hair and threaded down to the scalp.

"God, that feels so good. Suck it harder, baby."

As he tormented one breast with his tongue, a strong thumb rasped over the bud of the other until her whole body got in on the act. Her breathing hitched and her head traveled back and forth across her shoulder as he nipped her soft skin. Curvy hips, lean tummy and succulent, round ass engaged in their own silent dance as her body entreated him to give her more. Even the fat braid hanging across one shoulder swayed and moved for him.

"Oh yessss," she hissed. He glanced up. Her face was contorted with need. Alaan let his elation at her pleasure fly through the bond. She answered with thoughts of her own.

"Arrogant asshole." But she was smiling and that's all that mattered.

The tie around the end of her braid came loose with a gentle tug. The strands flowed like living silk through his hands. He'd always wanted to play in the thick, black fall. The orange glow from the fireplace reflected off the glossy waves until they resembled writhing fire as he fanned her hair between his fingers.

He traced the curve of her ass with his fingernails, delighting in her uncontrollable shiver. Then his tongue came into play and licked a path from her breast up to her jawbone. With a handful of hair clenched in his fist, he pulled her head back and tasted every inch of caramel skin from her dainty little earlobes, into the hollow of supple flesh at the column of her throat, all the way down to the little scrap of red fabric across her pelvis. Her stomach fluttered and clenched. But not nearly enough.

And how the hell did he manage to appear this calm? He was so hot, his body should have gone up in smoke under his trench coat. His teeth ached, and his cock was so hard he could probably punch a hole in a stone wall with it. Hell, even his toes wanted to come. But not yet. Not until Tameth screamed his name for the whole mansion to hear. Including her Hatsept lover. Correction, ex-lover.

In a move that even impressed himself, he whirled her around by the shoulder and applied the perfect bit of pressure behind her knee. The woman went down with a "humph" and found herself in the same position as the first time they'd made love—on her knees draped over the back of a seat. But this time was a fantasy come true. Tameth, ass in the air, hands behind her back. And soon to be on the receiving end of a lovely spanking.

ଚଠ

First the man had ripped her favorite bra with his fangs and now here she was, ass up in the air, with a pretty good idea of what was to come.

Riiiippp!

"Alaan, damn it." There went her thong. It was soaked through and useless anyway but that wasn't the point. The man was making a habit of shredding her underwear.

With a thigh in each of his hands, Alaan hefted Tameth into the air. By no means a small woman, his ability to lift her with little effort was a testament to his brute strength, vampire or not. Legs spread to the max, a shriek-moan bubbled up from her chest and filled the room as Alaan buried his face between them. Damn, the man sure knew how to eat a pussy.

Warm, wet tongue stiffened and stabbed into her quivering flesh, followed by the nibble of sharp but gentle teeth at her labial lips. Every nerve from her waist down to her toes was alive with pleasure. And just when she thought he would encircle her clit and suckle her to ecstasy, he found a new spot to torment just to the left and below the swollen knot.

There was no way she'd be able to take anymore. It was too good, too sensual, too...deep.

"Oh thank God," she panted, silently grateful he'd let her down to her knees as her arms hung limply over the backrest. Alaan's wide, perfectly proportioned cheek pressed into her back, the Kevlar of his specially designed shirt lightly scratched her bare skin. He could be so tender, it blew her mind.

Biceps jumped underneath his knowing touch as he caressed her arms, then slipped his fingers up to sweep her hair to one side. He buried his nose in it, then let it drape over one shoulder and hang over the back of the couch almost to the floor.

Alaan took one of her wrists, eased it behind her back and kissed a path to her forearm. It was soon joined by the other wrist...and tied?

What the hell?

She tried to rise, but found her chest plastered against the backrest of the couch.

"Shhh, just enjoy this," he whispered against the nape of her neck.

A soft strip of material whispered against her skin. An image of the blue silk handkerchief always tucked in Alaan's inner coat pocket flashed into her head. But hell, she was a warrior. She'd never been tied up in her life, and certainly not on purpose.

"If you don't like it, I'll stop, Tameth. I promise."

The coaxing tone and deep bass of his voice soothed her ruffled feathers. Relaxing, she nodded and let her body sink into the thick pillows.

The second her breathing calmed, it kicked up again. Alaan's fingers were on a marathon to touch every inch of her body. One hand stroked up and down her back, around to her belly, up and down her thighs. The other dipped into the cleft of her butt cheeks and slid down past her puckered hole so he could cup her soaked sex. A blunt fingertip eased back and forth, then swirled around her clit in torturously slow circles.

Her hips writhed side to side, then circled 'round trying to follow his fingers. Back arched on a gasp as that same teasing finger sank deep to massage her honey-dipped inner muscles. Dew-slick walls clenched around him when his hand eased upward to weigh a swollen, sensitized breast before tweaking its aching nipple.

A rasping lick of his hot tongue ducked into her lower spine and tickled up the ridges of her back, while Alaan's fevered cock eased between her thighs. Her skin careened from hot to cold, and every temperature in between. The tight opening of her cunt flexed and spasmed, reaching for the rock hard length teasing her entrance, pushing her towards overload. He was sculpted rock candy—smelled of musk, ginger and sex. Sounded like a male lion in heat, growling against her ear as he took pleasure in every moan and writhe. And he looked like a blond god, with skin like cream, eyes like sapphires and a body that reached to the skies, stacked and padded with endless honed muscle.

And his cock...was currently a big tease.

The flap of fabric on either side of his dick rubbed against the hollow of her sex. Huh. Again, he'd managed to get her bare-assed naked while he was fully clothed.

Knees spread wide, she pushed her ass out, inviting him inside. Wanted him to sink into her pulsing channel. Desperate to be full of him, to feel connected to him—physically, emotionally and psychically.

Yelp! A jolt shot from her cheeks straight to her pussy as a loud flesh-on-flesh smack bounced off the walls of the vast library.

Smack!

Alaan's big hand made contact with bare flesh again.

Wait, this had to be soooo wrong. Clan Serati males, or any male for that matter, didn't hit their women. And Clan Serati females ruled the roost. They gave spankings, damn it. They didn't receive them.

But it felt so good!

A warm flush spread over her backside and sent a heat like she'd never experienced dive-bombing for her clit. It was so agonizingly swollen, her whole pussy ached and throbbed. Oooh, such intense pleasure, she stood on the verge of begging.

148

Smack!

Her sopping wet folds made way for his thick white-hot rod to slide in between them. Inch-by-delicious inch eased inside until he was seated to the hilt. The flesh of his sac lay against her thickened labial lips, so soft, so full. Spreading her knees just a bit more, she reached back to weight them carefully with trembling fingers.

His cock jerked inside of her. Every muscle from her eyeballs down to her toes pulled taut with anticipation. But he didn't move.

"God, it feels so good, Alaan," she moaned pitifully. He eased out a hair and slid back inside. "Oh yes."

"Do you like that, beautiful?" he whispered harshly, pulling out another little bit, then sliding back inside.

"Aaah, yes. More."

Another delicious smack on the reddened cheeks of her ass. But no more cock. What was he trying to do, drive her insane? Then the man lightly scraped his neatly trimmed fingernails over the same path his palm had taken over her ass. She felt the shiver clear down to the red cells of her blood.

"Damn it, Alaan, move your ass!" she screeched, wiggling her hips trying to get closer. Tameth didn't think she'd ever screeched in her life, except in Alaan's company.

Easing out just enough to cause friction, he teased her with just that little bit of movement. God, just wait. She was going to kill him.

"Alaan, I swear if you don't move, I'm gonna kick your...oh shit!"

Well, the man moved all right, but certainly not in quite the way she'd meant. His entire length disappeared from her clutching sex. Damn it!

Then, just as she'd opened her mouth to bite his head off, his wonderously addicting shaft reappeared in all its thick, perfect glory, accompanied by another delicious smack.

Ragged moans became wild and needy gasps, and finally urgent, desperate pleading.

"Oh, yes. Oh, Lord. Fuck me!"

She couldn't believe it—reduced to begging for a male.

"Hell, I'll get over it," was her final coherent thought as Alaan rode her into an orgasm so earth-shattering she swore her molecules flew apart, then reformed into a new creature. One that would never be satisfied with another male. Ever.

Tameth sat cradled in Alaan's lap on the couch in front of the fire. Strong but gentle fingers absently stroked the little wound he'd left above her nipple. A slight, lazy smile graced her lips.

Alaan huffed and groaned. "My skin is jealous."

"What are you talking about?" she purred, unable to keep the contented sigh from slipping out.

"Your skin's got all these nice little bite marks on it. Mine's all smooth and unmarked. Not fair."

Her belly hatched a whole flock of dino-sized butterflies who decided to go for a test flight. God, she really wanted to bite him, badly. Soon, but not yet. Besides, she'd taken the blood depressant. Talk about backfiring. She didn't want any other man's blood, but the stuff also kept her from taking the blood she *did* want—Alaan's.

Worse, Tameth didn't think she could ingest even the tiniest amount of sustenance without getting sick. The craving suppressant worked like a charm but certainly didn't replace the need for some good old-fashioned hemoglobin. Not a long term solution, for sure. And the nausea that accompanied the third dose she'd taken just last night had been unexpected. The very scent of blood, other than her own, had her damned near heaving.

Note to self—let Carin know about this gross side effect. As much as her heart wanted to bite Alaan, all she could do was wait out the next twenty-four hours and try not to blow chunks whenever one of her teammates ingested a dose of the bagged stuff.

"Don't worry, handsome. I'll sink my fangs into you soon." Reaching up, she eased her fingers into his mussed mop of curls and pulled him to her for a sweet kiss. A deep breath filled her lungs with Alaan's manly scent and took the edge off the nausea. The man was delicious. A rasping lick to the side of his neck had him shivering so violently, Tameth felt it as keenly as if it were her own.

A quiet scuffle sounded in the hallway.

Someone said, "Hey, why's this door locked?"

Tameth's head snapped up and bumped against Alaan's chin. With their wild bout of lovemaking, she'd forgotten about the briefing she was supposed to give before the this evening's hunt. God, the man addled her brains. She'd never shirked her duties in all the years she'd served the Council.

"Then perhaps it's time you started. A little shirking never hurt anybody."

She glanced up and wanted to smack him. A smirk accompanied the male satisfaction that filled and overflowed the words easing through her head.

"Damn it, get out of my head, Alaan," she snapped. "And let me up."

With a sigh, he reluctantly released her and Tameth

151

jumped into her clothes while Alaan just sat there and watched with a gorgeous smile spread from ear to ear.

Yep, he definitely deserved a good backhand to the forehead. The door rattled.

"Hey, anybody in there?" Collins called from the other side, trying the knob.

"Just a minute," Alaan replied. But he said nothing more and didn't move any faster, either.

Why didn't he make up something, anything?

"What for? Once they walk in and smell sex all over the place it's not going to make any difference."

And he was still grinning, damn it.

Tameth had never gotten dressed so fast in her life. With her pants halfway up her thighs, she stomped into her boots and promptly fell over onto the carpet.

Alaan burst out laughing. Bastard.

"Can I help you, baby?"

"Oh, now you ask." Sputtering and hissing with a feline-like snarl, she bared her fangs at him, then hustled to the huge mirror over the fireplace and gasped. It did look like she'd been thoroughly sexed up. And she couldn't fault Alaan for her current tousled appearance. After all, she'd started it.

"Here, let me," he crooned at her back, untangling the snarls from the pile of spaghetti on her head that was supposed to be hair. She wasn't surprised she hadn't heard him move. He and Bix were the fastest, most stealthy Seekers in the whole corps. But she doubted any of their fellow vamp law enforcement officers knew Alaan could braid hair like a champ.

In no time he'd wrapped a rubber band around the end of a perfect braid and flipped it over one shoulder. With a loud wet smack on the side of her neck, he walked away and opened the door.

Back straight, eyes front, she took her place at the conference table across the room. Alaan sat clear on the other side. The place reeked of sex, but they both ignored the half smiles and knowing looks of their fellow Seekers. Without another word, Tameth began the briefing.

"This afternoon, we'll be dropped off at various Underground stations." Pointing to one of several huge maps attached along one wall, she continued. "Alex and Slade, you'll take the Underground to Paddington Station, come up to street level and walk the Bakerloo route south. Kenoe, you start at Tower Hill station and walk the District route west."

Thankfully, the buzz about what she and Alaan had been doing in the library with the door locked died down quickly. In between words, her thoughts drifted to the gorgeous prime at the other end of the table. He happened to be doing a much better job of schooling his features than she was, but it was entirely his fault, considering the mental pictures he sent streaking into her head. So, he was inventive with a handkerchief, eh? Nasty bastard. She almost laughed out loud when his stone facade cracked just a hair at her last thought.

A deep breath was followed by, "Alaan gets Piccadilly East, and I'll start at St. Paul's Cathedral and walk the National Railway route. We should all be fairly close to each other about three quarters of the way through the surveillance. We'll scout on foot for about five hours, then meet up near Victoria Station around nine o'clock tonight. We leave in ten minutes. Check in every hour. Any questions?"

Relief didn't begin to describe how grateful she was when nobody had anything to ask. Her soaked pussy was stuck to the crotch of her pants and her bra hung in tatters underneath her shirt. Uncomfortable was an understatement.

A bland expression planted firmly on her face, she concluded the briefing and stalked from the room.

No one but Alaan knew that only minutes before she'd wanted nothing more than to block out the chattering in the hallway and beg him to continue sliding his magnificent cock into her cunt while she purred like a well-mated female.

Chapter Eleven

With all of her senses engaged, Tameth's sharp eyes scanned every nook and cranny of the dimly-lit street as she walked. Not a single sound was missed, the scrape of a boot over cold concrete, the soft screech of tires two streets over, the buzz of the neon open sign in the window of a pub. Very few people walked the street tonight. Every now and then a car or two blazed by, illuminating the shadows. The overcast sky filtered out much of the moon's light, but at least the earlier chill had given way to a warmer evening.

With the top of Tameth's trench unzipped to the waist, a light comfortable breeze tickled the exposed skin at the vee of her stretchy black T-shirt. A pair of her favorite black stretch jeans fit her curves just right. The damned pants would have been perfect if not for the slight irritation of the crotch seam against her still swollen labia—something that was not typically a problem.

Not wanting to carry Alaan's scent on both her clothes and her skin while she hunted, she'd run upstairs, shucked off her typical Seeker's garb and yanked on the first all-black outfit she could find. Not exactly tactical, but with scant minutes to change clothes after the romp in the library with Alaan, a woman had to work with what she had.

Tameth moved quickly past a row of shops and pubs, palming her blade through the flap of the fake left pocket of her trench coat. After the last rogue hunt, Carin suggested the alteration. This way, her blade remained hidden beneath the folds of her leather coat while still firmly in her hand. After all, it just wasn't smart to walk around London with a three-foot katana blade flashing for all to see. For good measure, a loaded laser-sighted Taurus SP-99 semi-automatic handgun sat ready in a holster belted low on her hip.

Rogue hunting was dangerous business, not only for the Seeker involved, but any humans who might happen along. To protect them, Tameth had to be on her toes. She stalked the streets, senses alert and weapons at the ready...and couldn't get her mind off Alaan Serati.

The boy had skills as a lover, no doubt. And the tornadic orgasms he wrung from her before they'd split up to hunt remained fresh in her mind. And probably would for the next twenty years. A half-block ahead, a couple turned out of a restaurant. A soft sigh reached Tameth's ears and she could just guess what the man was doing when he put his arm around the woman's waist, then slipped his hand underneath her short jacket.

Absently, Tameth fingered the spot just above her right nipple where Alaan had bitten her. The skin tingled beneath her bra as a new supply of blood flowed into her swelling breasts. Fingers dipped a bit lower and rasped over a plumping bud. Alaan's manly scent lingered on her skin and wafted up through the opening of her coat. Skin that longed for a repeat of his lips wrapped around the pebbled tips.

Damn, she'd better cut it out. Anyone looking would think she was hard up and horny, touching her own breasts while walking down the dark street alone. The last thing she needed was a fist fight with some drunken idiot who convinced himself that he was the solution to scratching her itch.

Her vid phone vibrated silently in her back pocket. Raising her hand, she pushed a tendril of hair away from her face and connected the call with a discreet tap of the tiny wireless earpiece.

"Serati-Cole, here," she whispered.

"Hey."

Alaan's sexy voice slid across the airwaves and caressed her entire body, like melted butterscotch poured over a rich warm brownie. Delicious.

Pushing away the immediate arousal, Tameth clamped down on an instant hunger for Alaan à la mode and slid back into Seeker mode instead.

After a deep breath, then two, she replied, "Hey, back." But there was no suppressing the grin in her voice no matter how hard she tried. "Shift's almost over and nothing to report."

"What about the others?" Alaan asked over the rumble of what sounded like a train in the background.

"Alex and Slade checked in an hour ago. They're looking into one more lead, then calling it quits."

She bristled with jealousy when the couple in front of her turned into a small Irish pub. The woman's face was flushed with a big grin spread from ear to ear. The man wore a one-sided, self-satisfied smirk. That damned smirk must be universal man language for "I know how to make my woman squirm."

Tameth sighed, both bored and aroused. A quick look over her shoulder as she crossed the street revealed nothing and no one, as had been the case on her whole route. Talk about ready to call it a night.

"Look, Alaan," she whispered, barely moving her lips.

"Between the five of us, we've covered, what, twenty square miles in all directions? No sign of anyone or anything out of the ordinary. Other than very few Seekers in the places where vampires are known to congregate, none of us heard, saw, or sensed anything at all. That worries me, big guy."

"My thoughts exactly." He paused a moment, then said, "Kenoe just met up with me. What are Alex and Slade's current locations?"

With a quick glance at the small GPS unit on her wrist, she replied with a huff, "They're less than five miles west of you."

He chuckled. She grumbled. As Bix's Second, it was Alaan's job to monitor the team's movements. And he'd made it very clear that he took great pleasure in letting the job fall to her as his Second. Damned man knew it was a pain in the ass to babysit Seekers who didn't want or need watching over. He'd practically crowed when shoving the GPS into her hands just before they began to hunt this afternoon.

"Call them back and have them meet us at The Stag for dinner. Afterward Randall and Higgins will meet us at Piccadilly Station and drive us home from there. By the way, Collins is joining us for dinner, too."

"Collins? Why? I don't have him scheduled to go on duty until midnight."

The bottom fell out of her gut. Tameth turned her head to look out into the street. It was much too quiet.

"Believe it or not," Alaan continued, "he happened to be taking in a play at the Apollo Victoria Theater."

"A play? Collins? Gruff, belching, coarse, Scottish-brogue Collins?" With a fake gasp of shock, she breathed, "Say it ain't so."

Alaan's answering laugh warmed her insides.

"Yes, that's the one. When we get back to the house, he and Randall are going out on patrol as scheduled. See you soon?"

"Yep. Serati-Cole, out." Tameth was all business once more as an almost imperceptible and unfamiliar presence brushed against her mind. Her gut twisted as a disconcerting chill made its way across her lower back. Somebody was tailing her, and that somebody radiated an indescribable menace. It was definitely a vamp but she couldn't tell whether it was a rogue or not, or more importantly, one of Lowan's stooges.

Without stopping or changing her body language, she quieted her mind and carefully eased a psychic shield into place. Whoever had the nerve to try to press into her thoughts didn't need to know they'd been busted.

Some vampires just couldn't seem to remember that their world was nothing like the fucking movies. Thanks to Carin's insistence, hence Bix's orders, every Seeker in the Western territories had honed their psychic abilities with some pretty rigorous telepathic exercises. It took excellent psychic skill or a bond to delve into someone else's head.

And this bastard obviously didn't have either one.

With a deep breath, Tameth tried to scent who might be tailing her but only picked up the strong diesel fumes from the double-decker tour buses headed back to their yards for the evening.

Her footsteps slowed as she approached the opening to an alley. "Psss, how stupid," she hissed under her breath. Considering her unique leather trench coat identified her as a Seeker, her unwanted company must be deranged to try to ambush her. If the idiot hid in the alley, she certainly wouldn't just walk into his arms. Instead, she fingered her ear, deftly removed the sparkling diamond stud and let it fall into the top of her T-shirt to rest just inside her bra cup.

A pouty squeak accompanied by a very loud, "Oh, no!" erupted from her throat. Barely ten feet from the alleyway Tameth fell to her knees with a huff in true drama queen fashion.

"My earring! My diamond earring! Just when I thought I was off duty, too! Damn it, this can't be happening!"

Patting the ground frantically, she waited. And waited. The hairs at the nape of her neck throttled back from wild samba to old-lady waltz as whoever she'd sensed backed off, then disappeared altogether. What the hell was going on?

After a minute or two of dirtying up the knees of her jeans playing super-ditz on the ground, she stood, brushed off her clothes and continued on to her destination. Her gut churned with every step. She might not have enjoyed a fight tonight, but her senses remained in overdrive. Something monumentally devastating was about to happen. She could feel it.

ⅎ

Alaan sat on the outside of a huge booth, forcing his jaw to move. The plate in front of him overflowed with an overdone filet of beef, a pile of roasted potatoes and a small round of Yorkshire pudding. A small saucer held a hunk of bread with so much butter on it he almost looked forward to the cold bag of A-positive Higgins would have waiting for him back at the house. With a curled lip, he pushed another lump of chewed bland fare down his throat. God, he missed Montana food.

The Stag was a clean, well-run establishment with friendly wait staff. A pub atmosphere with a full service dining menu that looked better on the classy plastic-covered menus than it tasted. The place attracted a thirty-something crowd instead of the young, loud college students in some of the other pubs they'd visited during this trip.

"Dang, look at that face," Tameth chuckled, more amused than she should have been. "I don't think I've ever seen you look so sour."

"Except when a horde of Clan Hatsept males showed up at the U.S. Western V.C.O.E. headquarters to party," Kenoe chimed in, joining the fun at Alaan's expense.

Alaan growled. That was the last thing he wanted to remember. Aleth Sidheon, an accomplished scientist and a rogue—the worst combination imaginable—had been on the loose. The threat to their existence was so dire, the Council summoned all the Clan Elders and their constituents to his parents' estates at the V.C.O.E. Western territory headquarters to discuss the situation.

A huge ball was thrown to celebrate the collaboration of the clans. Unfortunately Carin and Tameth were on the menu of every unattached male on the property. Then, with the help of a mole, Sidheon arranged Carin's kidnapping. Bix, along with the entire Council, went ape shit.

That had been the first time in at least fifty years a Clan Hatsept prime had served the Council as part of an elite team. And that male had been on Bix's team ever since—Kenoe.

Tameth's husky laugh drew the eye of several men across the dining room. One of the dumbasses raised his glass with a wink. Tameth returned his gaze with a siren's smile and blushed. Alaan couldn't read the man's thoughts but with the wolf's smile spread across his face, who the hell needed to? Tameth was another story—he could feel her up one side and down the other. The leer on the dolt's face across the room clearly said he wanted nothing more than to get underneath her painted-on jeans. And she had the nerve to be flattered? Oh, hell no! His woman had better understand that any wooing and flattering would come from him.

Alaan schooled his features into a bored mask and looked her dead in her beautiful almond-shaped eyes.

"If you want that idiot across the way to receive the ass-kicking of his life, encourage him just a little, Tameth."

She laughed at him. Laughed out loud like she was at a baseball game or something. Damned woman.

"Don't bite the visitors, dear." She grinned and pushed away her pint of cider. He didn't miss the devilish sparkle in her root beer brown eyes. Her tongue peeked out of the corner of her mouth just as the gentle massage of her sock-covered toes slid up and down his cock under the table. Oh, she was so bad.

He'd have to ask her how she'd gotten her boot off without anyone noticing. Mmm, but he sure as hell noticed now. Her toes dipped into the space just below his balls and eased their way up and over. He got so hard so fast it was as if she'd flipped an erection switch and all the blood in his body dumped into his pants at once. It was almost impossible to resist the urge to let his head fall back and enjoy the gentle strokes up and down his dick.

"Damn it, woman, we're in a restaurant. What are you trying to do to me?"

"I thought it was obvious, handsome," she purred.

The bond made it clear she enjoyed torturing him way too much. Lifting her glass to her mouth for a deep swallow, she looked out the window while her toes worked their magic on him. Fine, he'd get her back later.

The man across the room rose with an extra glass in hand. After two steps Alaan's stoic expression fell away with a twisted snarl. Just before a display of fang, a psychic nudge from Tameth and the removal of her lovely toes from the erection straining against his zipper reminded him that he was
162

supposed to remain discreet. But he couldn't suppress a scowl as he glared back at the walking meat sack. The idiot turned out to be smarter than he looked. He sat his pasty ass down and didn't look at Tameth again.

But his whole team stared at him as if he'd grown three heads and two cocks.

Alaan pushed his plate away, folded his hands around a cold glass of ale and leaned towards his teammates. Hissing so only those at his table could hear, "Any of you blockheads look at my woman like you want to eat her and I'll kick your ass from here all the way back to the States."

All eyes turned to a stone-faced Tameth.

Wow. The speed at which her emotions streaked back and forth amazed him. The woman swept from haughty Clan Serati female don't-dare-assert-a-claim-on-me to soft and feminine God-I-love-it-when-you-go-prime. Hell, the pressure of all those feelings should have popped her head clean off. Finally, settled on well-loved mate, she dropped the rock-hard expression and flashed a blinding smile to her teammates.

"You heard him, boys. I'm now taken."

"Good answer, beautiful. Otherwise I'd have to spank you when we get back to headquarters."

"Oh, damn. If I'd known, I would have defied you on purpose," she silently whispered back.

"Told you you'd like it." A good dose of deliberate prime male smugness accompanied the words. *"Back to business, hm?"*

She winked at him and his insides danced a jig. He was so far gone. With a self-deprecating snort and a fortifying sip of his brew, he sat back in his seat and tried to relax.

"So," Alaan said seriously. "Anybody wanna tell me why

there wasn't a single Seeker in all of Knightsbridge tonight?"

Kenoe spoke up. "Perhaps it's related to what I shared with you the other day?"

"What are you talking about?" Tameth asked, clearly surprised Kenoe shared something with him that hadn't been shared with her. A funky silence blanketed the table like a wet cloth draped over his head on a humid day. Alaan shook it off. This was Seeker business. Nothing personal.

"I asked Kenoe to keep this quiet until we could determine which direction to take. I spoke to Bix about it and we agreed there was no need to alert the whole team without reason. Well, now there appears to be a reason."

Collins took a large swallow of the brown syrupy soft drink in his hand and quickly followed it up with a gurgling burp. Tapping his chest as if there was more burp stuck inside, he said between hiccups, "Is this the proper place to divulge whatever is going on? Sounds serious."

Alaan pinned Kenoe with a stare, leaving it up to him.

In his typical straightforward manner, Kenoe quietly gave all the details of his trip to the British Museum a few days past. No one was surprised he'd sensed one of his Clan following him. After all, they were sure word had gotten out about their presence in London on the trail of Lowan Hatsept. But the shocked silence at the revelation of Kenoe's family tie to Lowan was thick enough to choke a horse.

∞

The adrenaline rush Tameth had suppressed while hunting came slamming back into her chest. Only this time it rode the waves of anger rather than pursuit and competed with the raw emotions bombarding her heart. Her head claimed there was no reason to be upset. Even as his Second it was his choice to share information with her or not, especially if Bix had been contacted. But her heart wanted him to confide in her. Share everything. Have a real relationship. His brow was furrowed with genuine confusion, the bond hummed with it. But damn it, she needed to make him understand.

"Uh, guys, would you leave Alaan and me alone for a moment?"

The team rose as a unit, then spread out to strategic spots in the restaurant. If she hadn't been so pissed, she would have chuckled at Kenoe's grumbled, "About damned time. I'm overdue for something stronger than this piss water beer." The white-haired, handsome-as-sin Hatsept Seeker made a beeline for the bar lounge while a burly, surly Collins headed outside to cover the front door.

Even with her intense Seeker's training and experience, it took considerable effort to rein in her reeling emotions. The cider, once sweet and refreshing, was now bitter on her tongue. Downing it in one gulp, she set the glass carefully and quietly on the tabletop and discreetly let it all hang out. For his ears only, of course. She may have been pissed, but she'd had plenty of practice quietly snapping Serati male heads off.

"Alaan Serati, what the hell were you thinking to keep such important information from me?"

The man had the nerve to raise one of those thick blond eyebrows at her as if she'd gone surfing in the middle of a tsunami.

"Er, share it for what?"

"I can't believe you asked me that," she hissed. He couldn't possibly be that dense. No, no way would any man of hers be such a blockhead. She was his Second and he was supposed to trust her, damn it.

"You're very good at that," he said with a smirk.

"Good at what?"

"Keeping your expression calm. You're pissed as hell, but you look like we're talking about having Sunday tea."

"Oh shut up, you...you idiot! I'm your Second, and I can't believe you didn't..."

"Key word, Tameth, is Second. For now, *I*," he emphasized the word, "am Head Seeker, woman. Not you."

"I'm sure I'm supposed to care but..."

"And I spoke to Bix about this. So why the hell would I run a totally unsubstantiated lead, with no facts to back it up, by you? And don't pull the Clan Serati woman crap on me. When on duty, you're subordinate to me, not the other way around."

His argument made sense, but who the hell cared? Fuck him and Bix, too. She wanted to be treated as an equal. Not shut out of his and Bix's little Head Seeker club.

Then he grumbled something about why on earth did he have to be born into the only matriarchic clan on the planet. Now *that* did it.

"Because!" Okay, now she felt stupid, but pushed it away quickly. Besides, no woman in her right mind would want a relationship with a man who refused to understand how much she *needed* to be included.

"Look, Tam, when I stand in my office as Head Seeker or Second to Bix, I'm not your mate and I'm not your friend."

"You've got that straight, asshole. As a matter of fact why don't we just say you're neither mate nor friend, period."

"Speaking of periods, are you coming on yours?" he questioned. For a second he looked as if the big light bulb had gone on in that giant blond head of his, and suddenly he had the answer to life. Idiot.

"And I am *not* PMS'ing. If I were a male Seeker you wouldn't leave me out. I don't want you to treat me differently just because I'm a woman or because we had sex."

"Sex doesn't have anything to do with it. Look, woman, get it through your head. It's not personal. It's. Fucking. Work! And since you're going to be all 'female' about it, tell me which of our team members I shared this information with instead of you."

Her mouth dropped so wide open she was amazed it didn't make contact with the table. Damn, he had her there. As far as she knew he'd only shared it with Bix. And that sure as hell didn't count, considering he had authority over the entire Seeker corps all over the planet.

"All right, Tam, what is this really about?"

Leaning forward, he took her hands and held tight while gently stroking the pulse point just above the center of her palm. Suddenly Tameth felt beyond inadequate. She'd never gotten upset before when Alaan sought council about a mission from Bix instead of her. Hell, nothing out of the ordinary about that. It was normal and had been going on for as long as she'd been a Seeker. But rumor had it that Alaan used to include Sher in everything, including Seeker business he had no permission to share. Yet he'd left her out, and while she was Second on a mission at that. Her gut clenched as the seething fog of anger lifted leaving behind a dull ache in its wake along with a realization she'd never admit to in a million years—a dead woman had her tripping.

Bottom line: She couldn't compete with a ghost.

The second the thoughts cleared her brain, he dropped her hand as if scalded by her touch. Looking up from where she'd watched him softly stroke her fingers, her gaze traveled past the soft supple black leather stretched over his bulging forearms, past the center of his chest, and up to his handsome face. His expression was no longer carefully controlled. Lips drawn tight, brows pulled down into a tense frown, the man looked more ferocious than she'd ever seen him in any battle. Tameth sat up straighter. He'd been annoyed before, but now he was flat out angry, off the charts and struggling to keep his temper in check.

"I heard that, Tameth," he said, referring to the thoughts she hadn't meant to project. "First of all, I never shared anything with Sher that I was honor-bound by Seeker law not to. Second, I never asked you to complete with her ghost. Ever."

He rose without another word and walked right out the restaurant door.

Alaan's presence had been her constant companion, planted firmly in a corner of her mind. Now, the bond was strangely quiet, as if he'd turned himself down to a dull hum. He didn't say a word the entire way home. Not on their walk to the underground station. Not when Higgins and Randall picked them up to drive them the rest of the way. Talk about the cold shoulder. This felt like a piece of her soul was spread thin over a crumbling iceberg. And she didn't like it at all. Partly because she knew she'd been wrong. And partly because she simply didn't like the idea of anyone having this much power over her emotional wellbeing. It was like being on a teeter-totter but not realizing when your partner unexpectedly switched sides. One minute she felt like she was flying, the next, her ass was on the ground with the wind knocked out of her lungs.

But her insecurities were not Alaan's responsibility, and it wasn't fair to hold him accountable for her emotions.

However, he was responsible for ignoring her. And if there was one thing Tameth hated, it was being ignored.

She jumped out of the SUV, boots crunching on the gravel as she strolled across the courtyard, through the rear foyer and straight to the back staircase. The wall of silence in her head dropped just before Alaan streaked along the bond as he called her.

"Tameth?"

Her pace didn't slow, and her mouth didn't move.

"Tameth, do you hear me talking to you?"

Yeah, she heard him all right. Obviously the man was under the illusion he could blow her off all the way home, then expect her to be oh-so-happy he was speaking to her again. Well, as of fifteen minutes ago she was off the clock, so whatever he wanted to talk to her about could just wait until she came back on duty.

Passing the lift, her feet carried her up to her suite as regal as she pleased. Not once did she look back.

Alaan Serati could just kiss her happy ass.

Alaan clicked the vid phone closed for the third time tonight and blew out a frustrated breath. Tameth *would* choose tonight to get all weird on him. The woman was maddening and her timing sucked. According to the call he'd just disconnected, the Knightbridge district's Seekers they'd discussed over dinner weren't missing after all—they were in hiding. Smart group of guys, those vamps. Considering they'd double crossed Lowan Hatsept and were now passing information to the Council through their contacts in Ireland, the Elders immediately granted them sanctuary and arranged transportation for them to V.C.O.E. headquarters in Montana.

While the news was a relief, there was some disturbing information as well. The word on the street was an attack was planned on their temporary headquarters. Tonight.

He'd wanted to tell Tameth about it, but she'd pissed him off with her misconceptions about his feelings for Sher. And to be honest, he was getting sick and tired of trying to convince her she was the one he wanted. Let her stew awhile, realize she was being silly, and hopefully come to her damned senses again like she had in the library earlier. The loving had been beyond spectacular.

He doubted it would happen again anytime soon. The frost she gave off as she stalked away from him would have frozen the balls off of the meanest vamp alive. But there was no time to deal with that now.

The mansion was placed on lockdown the second Collins and Randall left to scout. Inside, Slade played Second while Tameth was off duty, checking and double-checking the monitors in the military-style makeshift communications center set up on the fourth floor. Outside, Kenoe coordinated the reinforcements who'd arrived from various districts around London. The teams, two Beta Seekers each, were discreetly placed around the property in a three block radius.

With security firmly in place, Alaan took the first shift and made the rounds. He made quick work of covering all five floors of the eerily quiet brick mansion.

Tapping his earpiece, he whispered, "Dial Alex P." The phone rang once before Alex's clear voice filled the line.

"Yes, sir?"

"You up? It's almost time for your shift."

"I'm already out the door and headed to the first floor, sir."

"Excellent," Alaan said on a yawn. "I'm knocking off for the night. Serati, out."

Checking his watch with a sigh, Alaan stopped in his suite, shucked out of his coat and sat down for all of ten seconds. He'd said he was going to look in on Tameth, but now that it was time, his pride kept his feet firmly planted on the carpet. After all, the woman was officially off duty and there was no need to disturb her with news of something he was more than capable of taking care of. But keeping information from her set her off in the first place. His desire to protect and keep her safe tugged at his conscience. Then again...aw hell, now *he* was being weird.

This was different from running a possible dead-end lead past her. This was a possible attack on them, life and death. Alaan would never forgive himself if she walked into a deadly situation simply because he'd failed to tell her of potential danger. His heart ached with Tameth's hurt, tightening in his chest, urging him to go comfort his woman. God, he was really turning into a total wuss. Bix would certainly get a kick out of it.

Leaving his coat draped across the loveseat in his sitting room, Alaan made his way up to her floor. Knocking lightly at her door, his gut tightened when no one answered. He knocked again. Perhaps she was asleep? He lowered his defensive shields and reached out along the forming bond. Her emotions immediately swirled around him—fear, confusion, pain. His woman was in distress. Had the bad guys gotten in while he'd been on his rounds? No time to figure it out now. He had to get to her.

"Tameth, open this damned door before I break it in." He waited for the tensest ten seconds of his life. No answer.

Here we go again. He snatched a gun from its shoulder holster at the same time his powerful leg lifted his boot. The door flew inward and smacked against the wall with a bang.

Tameth ran through a door across the living room and stopped short, all beauty and rage, in full Seeker mode. In complete control of her breathing and movements, her eyes

171

flashed dark fire while taking in the situation in mere seconds.

An expertly schooled expression read, "Hello, my name is Tameth. What's yours?" But her unsheathed fangs and perfectly positioned samurai katana said she was ready to cut his head off.

"Aw, hell." Alaan looked up to the ceiling and grumbled under his breath. *God, just kill me now.* His ears grew so hot, surely he'd flushed at least seven shades of red.

The woman was buck naked. Rivulets of water slid down and caressed every curve, nook and cranny of her beautiful caramel brown body. A trail of frothy bubbles dipped into her navel and ran down off to the right into the crease just above the dark, close-cropped curls of her cunt. Her wet mane hung plastered against her back while long black tendrils clung to her temples, neck and collarbone.

Tameth's razor-sharp blade hissed through the air as she lowered her sword swiftly. She stalked up to him and poked her finger in the middle of his chest. Hard. He looked down at the spreading wet spot on his favorite black silk shirt.

"Alaan, damn it. If you don't stop using your big-assed feet to kick my doors in, I'm gonna chop off your balls."

Had she said balls? As in, how great it felt when his balls slapped against her ass when he took her from behind?

"Do you hear me?" she bit out, fangs still bared.

"Uh, yeah, I'm sorry. I'll call. Uh, Higgins. To, yeah..."

"And stop looking at my breasts, you oversized, blond headed..."

What? He wasn't looking at her breasts! Well, actually he was, unsure of when his gaze had slid away from the glare she'd pinned him with. Sigh. Yep, definitely eyeballing the luscious globes of her beautiful, deliciously wet breasts. Breasts that happened to be puckered from the slight chill sneaking into her warm apartment through her ruined door.

"Alaan, did you hear me?" she snapped.

Hell, he'd only heard half of what she'd said, missing pretty much everything after balls and breasts. The wild motioning of her sword towards the door gave him a clue of what she was trying to get him to do.

He backed up and propped the door shut as best he could. When he turned to face her he was rewarded with a perfect view of her firm, bare backside as it moved away from him. Whoa, she was walking away? Where the hell was she going? Wait, had he asked that out loud?

"I'm going to finish my bath, you idiot," she seethed.

Yep, he'd said it out loud all right. If he could only get the quickly growing erection in his pants to release enough blood to keep his brain working, surely he would have realized she was going back to the bathroom. And he was going with her, whether she was mad at him or not.

Oh sure, her anger boiled up out of her pores—naked, dripping wet pores. By the time he finished with her, she'd be purring. He'd make sure of it.

Chapter Twelve

Alaan would never view bathing in the same light again. With a silly grin plastered on his face his mind flashed back to relive the view of Tameth's glistening skin glowing under the golden candlelight as she rode him wildly. And yes, she'd definitely purred, several times in fact.

After cleaning up all the water they'd sloshed over the side of the tub, he'd walked into her bedroom to find her sprawled on the bed, her wet hair hanging over the side as she fingered her still creaming slit. Instantly hard again, he'd all but dived into her pussy, fucked her into a blistering orgasm, and shouted to the rafters as he joined her.

Now they lay snuggling contentedly in Tameth's big bed, legs entangled, her lovely lush breasts pressed into his side as he held her close. Good thing he'd kicked in her apartment door earlier and not the bathroom or bedroom doors. A few more minutes of her strong fingers playing with his balls, sliding up and down his body, and tweaking his somewhat sore nipples, and they would definitely need their privacy. Again.

The scent of her blood was like a siren's song. Dragged him under the tidal wave of longing, drowned him in her very essence. His tongue flicked out and touched the tip of the incisors. After all, he'd only have to unsheathe them when he bit her again. And he would, indeed, bite her again.

And tonight he hoped she'd return the favor.

God, would he ever get enough of her? Stupid question. Of course not. He'd come so hard in the tub he'd expected to at least blow smoke out of his ears. Yet here he lay, wanting her again, yet filled with a peace he'd never experienced before.

"What the hell is that noise?" Alaan drawled lazily, his body a huge heap of boneless, satisfied male. Tameth, just as sated, lay sprawled across his chest gently plucking at the sprinkling of hair there.

His vid cell buzzed and hummed as it vibrated on top of the nightstand next to Tameth's bed.

"This better be good or the person on the other end of this phone is going to wish my foot was considerably smaller when I plant a size thirteen up their ass."

Tameth's relaxed chuckle warmed his heart. She didn't budge an inch, forcing him to drag her along for the ride as he scooted across the bed, reached for the phone and flipped it open.

Tucking his earpiece around the shell of his ear, he disabled the video capability on the small wireless hand unit and yawned into the mouthpiece.

"Serati here." He missed the caller's introduction, too busy laughing. "Hold on a minute," he ground out, then hissed at Tameth between suppressed chuckles, "Damn it woman, will you stop it already?"

She'd climbed on top of him, scooted down his body and blew raspberries against the twitching planes of his flat belly. Damn, that tickled.

In the end he closed his fingers around the mouthpiece with one hand, while the other firmly grabbed a handful of her hair and eased her face away from his stomach. After a few seconds of deep breathing, he was able to continue the call.

Minx.

"I'm sorry to bother you, sir, but we have a bit of an emergency."

It was Higgins. Just the knowledge of who was on the other end of the line sent a streak of alarm through Alaan's gut. Higgins wouldn't dare call him at this time of night, or rather morning, unless the man was sure the world was coming to an end. Then Randall's curt tone cut through the background noise as he and Collins shouted directions to someone else.

Alaan sat up. Tameth tumbled onto her back on the bed. She recovered quickly, her brow drawn down just as hard and tight as Alaan's.

"*What's going on?*" Her voice was laced with concern.

He covered the phone and mouthed, "Don't know yet," before remembering no one could hear their private conversations.

"Higgins, what the hell is going on down there? It's one o'clock in the morning."

"I think you should come downstairs, sir. And I've taken the liberty of calling your sister and Seeker Bixler. They're on their way."

Alaan was out of bed now, the erection that had begun to stir with Tameth's raspberries now slapped limply against his thigh.

"What? What's going on?" Tameth asked, headed to her closet, pulling her long fall of hair over one shoulder into a quick braid as she went.

Raising his hand, Alaan pressed the earpiece closer while whispering, "Hold on a second. I'm trying to hear what's up." Screw it, there was no way he would be able to sort anything out with all the yelling and shouting going on.

"Higgins? Higgins?"

"I'm here, sir."

"Tameth and I will be down in two minutes. Front or rear?"

"Rear courtyard, sir. And you may want to come alone."

"What? Why?"

"Trust me, sir."

Alaan didn't know what the hell was going on, but he certainly wasn't going to leave Tameth behind. Yes, he trusted Higgins' judgment, but he had to show faith in Tameth regardless of the obsession to protect and shield her.

By the time he flipped the vid phone closed, she was two steps ahead of him, fully dressed, gun holstered low on her hip, and her sword unsheathed and at the ready.

He smiled.

"That's my girl."

"Damned straight."

Alaan walked out the backdoor and stopped so quickly Tameth ran into the wall of his back. She tried to look around him but he was simply too tall. She couldn't see a damned thing. Nudging him in the middle of his back and poking him in the ribs had no effect. Finally she stepped close, planted her foot in the back of his knee and pushed.

Alaan stumbled a few inches, just enough for Tameth to push her way around him and get through the doorway. Her katana cleared its sheath and whistled to a stop in midair. Her thoughts pushed against his and echoed his disbelief.

In unison, they silently gasped. *"Oh God, this is not happening."*

Pale as a sheet, as if someone had drained every ounce of blood out of his body, her man stood and looked out towards what appeared to be contained chaos.

Two SUVs were parked on the gravel, engines still running. A score of people ran around the courtyard, all with some weapon or another drawn and at the ready. Randall was yelling into a hand-held radio.

Collins stepped up to Alaan, anxiety rolling off of him in waves.

"Where should we put her, sir?" Collins asked, cradling a small limp form in his beefy arms. Whoever it was looked to have been knifed. A mop of black curls hung as limply as the rest of the body and partially obscured the face. But the fine bruised cheekbones, full lips and small round breasts were enough to give a clue of the victim's sex. Blood covered the simple T-shirt plastered to her body and ran thick down Collins' forearms. Red droplets splashed onto the white and gray graveled walkway.

Alex was right behind Collins now. Slade and Kenoe flew around the corner of the house. Kenoe's katana stood ready to do damage. Slade had a black titanium pistol in one hand and a nasty looking dagger in the other.

Higgins ran forward and eased the mass of blood-soaked hair away from a battered face.

Alaan went still as stone. His mouth hung open but nothing came out. The man didn't even blink. Just stood and stared at what turned out to be a familiar vampire female. Shit.

Tameth swallowed the bile rising in her throat, stepped up and took charge. Pushing away the horror before her, she schooled her features, sheathed her sword and took charge. She could be a shaken, admittedly shell-shocked woman later. Right now, she needed to be a Seeker, and Alaan's Second.

Clear as the night sky over their heads, she yelled over every voice present.

"Everyone shut up!"

The chaos continued. With her index fingers in her mouth, she whistled like a New York taxi driver. Silence immediately reigned.

"Collins, take her to one of the extra rooms on the first floor. Put her as close to the kitchen as possible. Higgins, call one of the staff and have them meet up with Collins. I want you both in a briefing."

Higgins moved to enter the house.

"No," she said, handing him her video phone. "Call the staff on my phone on your way to the library. I want to know what the hell is going on."

Pointing to Slade and Alex, she continued.

"Lock down the mansion, then join the team in the library. Kenoe, circle the property and collect reports from the reinforcements. Then contact the captains of the Mayfair and Kensington Station teams and find out if they saw anything strange since that's where Collins and Randall were scouting tonight."

And perhaps where they'd come across...her.

The second the words left her mouth, Kenoe's vid phone flipped open, fingers dialing, obviously ready to get on with the task.

"Do you have any orders to relay to them?" he asked urgently,

"Use your judgment. Handle it. Randall, call Bix. He's on his way, but if you can catch him before he leaves the house, it may be faster to take the small chopper and go get him rather than have him drive all the way here."

Not a single person moved. What, were they deaf? No, probably just as shell-shocked as she was. "I said move it. Right. Damn. Now. You all have five minutes. Period."

Alaan and Kenoe both turned to face her. Before she moved away Tameth caught fleeting, but odd, expressions as they crossed both handsome faces—surprise, admiration, concern. Unfortunately she didn't have time to explore their feelings right now.

She was having a hard enough time pinning down her own. The churning in her stomach threatened to back up into reverse. She bit the inside of her jaw and commanded the vomit bubbling at the base of her throat to stay down. A fathomless pit of loss opened up in the middle of her soul. God, there was no way she and Alaan could overcome something this monumental.

Collins carried the wounded, bleeding female into the house.

Seekers and staff scattered in all directions.

Tameth squared her shoulders, planted her focus on placing one foot in front of the other, and strode purposefully back inside.

Her head swam with the enormity of the situation.

Sher had risen from the dead.

⨯ↄ

Tameth's thoughts tumbled end over end. Sher was alive and in London. This just couldn't be happening, not when she and Alaan had finally reconciled. Or she thought they had. Perhaps sex in the bathtub hadn't meant as much to him as it had to her.

Wrapping herself in a cloak of calm that almost slipped off and away more than once, Tameth stepped into the role she'd been trained for. Leadership.

Once the team was seated, she stood at the head of the large table in the center of the library. Her gut churned with acid. Honestly, she really didn't want to know what was going on. It would make this all too real.

Damn it. Sometimes she hated doing her job.

With a discreet but deep breath, she made eye contact with each Seeker in the room. They all looked like a bunch of carved statues, still as stone with perfectly schooled faces. They had to be as shaken as she was. Many of them knew Sher, and those who didn't had been told the story of her death at one time or another.

But something was off about this whole situation. More than the woman being alive after six years of absence, her appearance while they happened to be hunting in London seemed suspicious at best. But right now, there were more important things to tackle—like finding out how the hell Sher had fallen into V.C.O.E. hands after such a long time being "dead".

"Was that Sher Sewell that Collins carried to the spare room, or am I out of my damned mind?" Tameth asked.

"It was Sher, all right," Alaan mumbled. His state of shock was as palpable as everyone else's. It was the first time he'd spoken since they'd stumbled into the courtyard to witness the woman's return from the grave.

"But how?" Slade asked. "I thought she was killed years ago."

"So did we all," Alaan said. "Obviously we were wrong."

Thankfully some of the color had leached back into his appalled features. He stood and walked across the room. Eyes closed, he let his head fall back on his shoulders and roll slowly around. Tameth felt him forcing the tension from his body.

Kenoe rocked the room. "She smells like a Hatsept."

Alaan swung around with a snarl. "No way! You're wrong. How would you know, anyway?"

Tameth gaped. He took one look at her and dropped into his chair with a sheepish snort. After all, it was a stupid question. Kenoe's clan shared the same blood and had a connection of sorts, just like every other clan.

"Alaan, you've been out of Vampire 101 for a long time now," Tameth countered sarcastically. Her anger rose with each word. "Snap out of dense mode. Of course clan members can sense and scent each other at close distances. Kenoe caught a whiff of one of his own clan members just the other day, remember?"

"She's not a fucking Hatsept." Alaan was back on his feet, fangs bared on a snarl. Fear and pain snaked down the bond and bit into her like a viper that had just been prodded with a stick.

"Look, Alaan," Kenoe said, "I don't know how she got here, or where she's been all this time, but I know what I scented on her. The real question is, if Sher smells like a Hatsept, how the hell did she get that way?"

"Stop pushing, asshole."

Tameth's heart sank another notch. *Sigh.* Apparently she'd been right all along. Alaan was still all wrapped up in that woman.

"This is getting us nowhere," Tameth interrupted. "Collins, tell us what the hell happened. Where did you find her?"

"Randall and I were scouting Mayfair, near Hyde Park. We sighted a couple of suspicious-looking vamps. The second they saw us, they took off running. We followed them into an alley. That's where we found her."

"The vamps you two were chasing, did they do this?" Kenoe asked quietly.

"No way. We ducked into the alley just seconds behind them. Someone else had to have injured Sher. They simply didn't have time."

"Interesting," Kenoe mumbled to himself. An intent expression remained etched across his forehead as he worked something out in his head.

At the end of Collins' recounting, they were no closer to figuring out this mystery than they had been when the briefing began. But one thing was sure. Nobody was getting into this house and nobody was getting out.

Tameth gave everyone their orders and ended the meeting.

Just then, Carin and Bix bustled into the library.

Carin was all business. "I've brought a ton of medical equipment. Where's the patient?"

"I'll take you to her." Alaan jumped from his seat and practically dragged Carin out of the room.

Tameth watched him go. All of her accusations about Alaan still being hooked on Sher came back to haunt her. Her mother always told her to think positive, because whatever she expected would be exactly what she'd get. Boy, had her mom's words turned out to be true.

Miserable, she followed Kenoe to the staircase and paused, her eyes plastered on her mate's back as he bustled Carin down the hallway towards the room where Sher lay unconscious.

With a sigh, she allowed Kenoe to lead her up the stairs while Higgins offered to take Bix, with a sleeping Alaina bundled in his arms, up to one of the empty rooms.

Choking back a wash of tears, Tameth's heart broke into tiny, sharp pieces, like glass broken out of a once-shiny mirror. Kenoe led her into his suite and promptly locked the door. And she didn't even care why.

ȣ

While listening to Randall and Collins' recount of how they'd come upon Sher's body, the pieces of the puzzle had clicked together in Kenoe's head. Suddenly he knew exactly what was going on. And if he was right, they were all in grave danger.

In classic English style, his en suite room was done in lacquered browns and rich beiges. The large living room sported a hardwood floor centered by a stiff, uncomfortable couch that sat on top of a thick room-sized rug. He'd scooted the only body-friendly piece of furniture, an overstuffed chair, into a corner to make room to exercise with his blades.

His heart constricted with love and concern when Tameth sank into that chair and her big brown doe eyes pinned him with a miserable stare.

"Hey, woman, you doing all right?"

"Do I look all right, Kenoe? The very thing I kept telling Alaan was most important to him has come back from the grave to haunt me."

Leaning next to the front door, one booted foot propped up against the wall, he crossed his arms over his chest and spoke calmly.

"Don't be so sure, Tam."

Her head tilted to the side as her expression cleared. Kenoe knew the exact moment her common sense wrestled free of her bruised emotions.

"Kenoe, you think it's a setup, don't you?"

"Hell, yes, it's a setup. Think about it. A few days ago, without a doubt, I scented a Hatsept rogue in the British Museum, but the only person I saw was a dark-haired pixie chick..."

"...who happens to resemble the one lying unconscious downstairs?"

"Exactly. Looks like. Smells like."

Kenoe's gaze followed Tameth as she popped up off the chair, stalked to the center of the room and paced the length of it. Hands on hips, her long braid whipped around her head and almost hit him in the face as she rounded on him.

"Does Alaan know any of this?"

"I told him what I'd sensed and described the woman I saw. But who in their right mind would think I'd seen a six-year-dead woman?"

Three strides had him over at the wet bar yanking a thick plastic bag out of the mini-fridge.

"Want some?" he asked quietly, pulling a couple of glasses out of the cupboard above the bar. Hmm, what was wrong with Tameth? He hadn't seen her take her usual dose of blood, or supplement her diet by feeding from a donor since they'd been in London.

"You look a bit peaked. You need some blood, Tameth," he insisted.

She scrunched up her face and waved him away, looking like she'd rather throw up. After her throat worked through a few fierce swallows, she glanced towards him.

"It's Carin's blood suppressant. I think I took too many doses. Just the sight of blood makes me sick. Unexpected side-effect, I guess. Should wear off in another twenty-four hours, I hope."

Sounded plausible. Tameth didn't seem to be worried about it, so he relaxed. "Maybe she can give you something for the nausea since she's here."

Tameth nodded, dropped her head between her knees and panted like a dog on a late summer day in the humid south. She seemed so miserable, he didn't have the heart to feed in front of her. After setting the extra glass back in the cupboard, Kenoe returned the bag of O-positive to the fridge and joined Tameth across the room. The last thing he wanted was to make his best friend more ill than she already was. And the greenish tint to her dark olive skin said she was pretty close to blowing chunks.

Easing his arms around her body, he started. She was clammy and shaking, working her throat convulsively. Taking her hand, he turned it palm up and pressed down on the muscle an inch and a half up from the crease where wrist and hand met. Massaging steadily, he worked the P6 acupoint to help control the nausea.

"Come on, Tam, take shallow breaths. That's it, baby, just breathe. Nice and slow." Her shoulders stiffened with his little slip of the tongue, but she didn't pull away. What the hell was he thinking, calling her baby, all sweet and tender like that? Shit, he'd have to really watch it. Better yet, when this Lowan mess was resolved, he'd put his plans into motion immediately rather than six months from now like he'd planned.

As much as he wanted her, Tameth simply wasn't his to love.

"So, anyway," he rushed on to cover the awkward silence. "While I'd already told Alaan about the museum, tonight, I obviously didn't have a chance to get him alone long enough to confirm that it was definitely Sher I'd scented that day. I just think it's more than a coincidence, especially with us being targeted for an attack tonight."

"What?" she screeched, yanking away from the shelter of his body.

"Didn't Alaan tell you?" Kenoe could have kicked himself in the head the moment the words left his mouth. Tameth obviously hadn't known about any planned attack. Must be Seekers-and-stupid-questions night. Damn. He was supposed to be playing matchmaker between her and Alaan, not getting her pissed off at the vamp.

"I'm sorry, Tam. I was sure Alaan was going to talk to you about it when he followed you upstairs after we got in."

"Well, we'd just finished making...uh, well, no. He didn't really have a chance to talk to me about it."

"You're so cute when you blush, Tam."

"Oh shut up, already. I'm embarrassed as hell."

"Why? You've wanted that vamp in your bed forever. Now you've got him. What's there to be embarrassed about?"

"What I had earlier and what I have now may differ. The appearance of Sher might put a bit of a wrinkle in things."

"I don't think so, Tam. Just trust him, trust yourself. You deserve to be happy, so enjoy it."

"Back to the subject, please."

"I rather like talking about your sex life. You look so cute when you get all flustered and..."

"Keep it up, asshole, and we'll spend some time talking about *your* sex life." She groaned pitifully. He reached out and pressed her wrist again.

Snapping his mouth shut, he bit his tongue to keep from laughing. He'd love to talk about sex. Hell, he'd love to *have* sex...but that wasn't an option with Tameth. A few more rubs and he released her.

"Better?"

With a quick nod she was back to pacing. Kenoe watched her wear a hole in the carpet, back and forth. God, she had such a nice ass.

"Kenoe?"

He looked up and was, as always, shaken by the beauty and intensity of the woman. Kenoe grabbed hold of his wishful thinking and pulled it into the present. Lack of participation in the current conversation because he was thinking about Tameth's ass simply was not acceptable. They had a case to solve.

"Why would Sher let you see her if she planned to come here and cause trouble?"

"I know I sensed more than one Hatsept rogue in the museum that day. Perhaps she was with them and I saw her by accident?" Sounded good, but it didn't seem plausible. Suddenly, another idea popped into Kenoe's head. "Then again, maybe it's a diversion? Sher's appearance wreaked havoc on our security layout, and on the same night of a planned strike against us. The whole team is talking about it, as well as the reinforcements who came in to help us. With our attention divided and the house in an uproar, it would have been easy for someone to slip in."

"Son of a bitch," Tameth snarled, already moving towards the door. Kenoe was right on her heels.

"Tameth, where are you going? The house is already in order and security is tight. If someone did get in while we were wigging out over Sher, they sure as hell won't get out easily. Why don't you try and get some sleep? I'll walk you back to your suite."

When it looked like she would resist, he reminded her they'd already spoken to and accounted for every Seeker within five miles of the mansion. Thankfully the forest fire buzz created by Sher's sudden appearance had died down to a smoldering heap.

Since they were already in the hallway, Kenoe stayed in step until they reached her room just a few doors down from his.

"What the hell happened to your door?" The thing hung partially opened and looked well beyond sad. The metal fittings around the hinges seemed fine, but the wood frame surrounding the deadbolt had been shattered to pieces.

"I was in the tub when Alaan came by earlier. I didn't hear him knocking. Give you three guesses about what happened next."

No guesses required. The big boot print on the outside of the door spelled it out clear enough for the dimmest dimwit. Alaan had obviously kicked the thing in. Again.

"Well, you can't stay in here tonight. Not with a door that doesn't close or lock."

After getting her things quickly moved into the room next door, Kenoe went back to his place and took a shower. All the while his mind flashed between the Hatsept-scented Sher, Tameth and Alaan's interrupted mating, and his need to find a love of his own. But it wasn't going to happen tonight. Wanting to be nowhere other than with Tameth tonight, he threw on some pajama bottoms and a robe, wrapped a towel around his head and headed back to Tameth's rooms.

She answered the door with a thick towel twisted around her waist-length hair and the cutest pair of royal blue flannel PJ's. Settled down on another hard monstrosity of a living room couch, he didn't hesitate when she motioned for him to sit on the floor between her knees.

Patting dry his freshly washed hair, Tameth set to work carefully separating each and every one of his shoulder-length, snow white locs. She'd gotten a quarter of the way through, making sure none of the perfect squares of hair intertwined with its neighbor. A smile spread across his lips when she grumbled and fussed about proper hair care.

Reaching up to still her busy fingers, it was time for a little more truth between him and his best friend.

"Tameth, there's something I need to tell you."

"Sure, sweetie, anything."

She squeezed his shoulder reassuringly, the way she always did when trying to comfort him, then went back to work on his hair. The woman was amazing. She'd conducted the earlier briefing, organized all the personnel, and flawlessly executed her duties as a Second. But it didn't change the fact that her man was downstairs with his unconscious ex instead of up here with her. Yet she tried to reassure him. Yes, she was a one-in-a-million find. And he'd let Alaan know that if he ever hurt her, he'd have a Hatsept ass kicking coming.

"Listen closely because I have no intention of repeating any of this. I've never shared this with a single soul other than my Clan Elder." Tipping his head up, he watched four parallel lines trek across her forehead on a furrowed brow. Still he waited. Waited for her to acknowledge the importance of what he needed to say. With a nod of her head, Kenoe jumped in with both feet.

"Lowan took over our harem when I was just a young pup. I was abused. For years."

"Is that why you're gay?"

His first inclination was to blow off her question. But what if something happened to him and he never had another chance to lay himself bare? He loved her and it was time to come clean before he took off.

"Tameth, I'm not gay." Holding her gaze with his blue-white eyes, the wait for her to lose her temper at such a revelation seemed endless. She tightened her grip in his hair.

"Ouch."

"Sorry," she mumbled. "You're not gay? Well, what...er, how?"

"I'll tell you about it, but not right now, okay?" There was no way he had the bandwidth to deal with both Lowan and his gay lie tonight.

"I ran away from the harem and sought refuge with the Clan Hatsept Elder. He had Lowan brought up on charges because of what was done to me. The charges piled up higher when I told the Elder what I'd seen done to others, though he never seemed to abuse anyone the way he did me. He kidnapped humans, which is against our laws. After being subjected to the most bizarre psychological and sexual tactics, they may as well have been brainwashed. His harem came to him by force, but very few humans actually left while I was there."

"But I thought Clan Hatsept rules require all harems be filled voluntarily?"

"They are voluntarily filled, and only with vampires, if the prime male is typical. But Lowan is not normal. He's crazy, Tameth, so consumed with his need for sex and control, it drives him. As for me, he seemed more intent on punishing me for just being alive. His Second, a man named Myles, carried out most of the brutality, but Lowan called the shots. And sure, he gave his people opportunities to leave if they wanted to. But those who took him up on the offer didn't survive long."

Tameth's top lip curled into a snarl. "Bastard."

"You have no idea," Kenoe agreed flatly. Then he revealed everything. All the hurt, pain and treachery he'd experienced simply because he'd been born into the wrong family. It spilled out like the bursting of a dam after an overflow of rain. Cleansing was the only way to describe the result of simply sharing the burden he'd carried for so much of his life. Hell, and it had only taken three years of friendship with Tameth to finally tell her. It amazed him, considering he'd expected to take every ounce of the shame and anger to the grave.

He felt wonderful. Purified. Free.

On the other hand, Tameth sat stone-still, her golden olive skin paled to a ghastly jaundiced yellow. Her whole body shivered.

"I. Am. Going. To. Kill. Him," she swore with cold menace.

"Get in line, darlin', get in line."

Chapter Thirteen

"Hmm. Blood pressure and temperature are both normal. I wonder how she got these cuts and bruises on her neck and shoulders. Looks like she's been in a fight. Strange these marks aren't healing at the rate they should for a healthy female vampire," Carin wondered aloud. All she received was an oh-so-articulate "uhn".

Turning slowly, she shot a black look at the massive lump of vampire sitting on a stool next to her. "Geez, Alaan, that grunt was so helpful. How 'bout helping me get some answers rather than sitting there staring at this woman?"

The needle of a loaded injection gun disappeared into Sher's neck. Alaan didn't even blink, just continued to stare intently with his mouth tightly drawn and the muscle at the base of his jaw ticking madly. Even his eyeballs seemed tense.

"I'm giving her a modified cell reconstruction serum. It'll accelerate her body's natural healing abilities. Wounds like this on a normal vampire would heal in a day. If my calculations are correct, she'll be fine in a matter of hours. I've mixed a sedative in with the serum for the pain, otherwise these bruises around her neck will hurt like hell when she wakes up. But even with the meds, she'll be lucid so we'll be able to get some answers."

Another grunt. The man was seriously getting on her nerves.

Carin sighed tiredly. The flight to London had been hairy at best. Bustling a grumpy, sleepy toddler and the equipment needed into the helicopter to create a lab-like atmosphere had been no easy task. Even if Bix had done most of the work, she *so* didn't need this grunting crap from the man sitting there like some kind of nitwit.

"So why are you here, Alaan?"

He looked up with dark puffy circles under his eyes. Evidently he was as tired as she was. His usual topaz blue irises were more of a weary blue-gray. The lines around a tightly drawn mouth turned down into a fierce frown, covering his handsome features beneath a blanket of worry. Turning his attention back to the woman on the gurney, Alaan shook his head and finally spoke.

"I'm not sure why I'm here. I guess that's what's bothering me, Carin. Part of me wants to be sure Sher is okay, but..."

"But the other part would rather be knocking boots with Tameth."

"Damn it, Carin, do you have to be so...so...?"

She just loved to make him blush, even when he was pissing her off.

"Be so what? So real? Yes, I do. I don't know how to be anything other than straight up. Maybe you should try it sometime."

"Meaning what, exactly?"

Why did the man bother playing this game with her? They were family. More importantly, they were friends. And she was his empathic friend. If anyone could dig into his emotions, she could, and he knew it. Damned man.

"Alaan, why don't we do this a little differently? How 'bout you tell me what's really bothering you, baby-love?" She put a little bit of old grandma impersonation into her voice, knowing it made him wince every time she acted like the older sister.

Still grumbling, he cooperated.

"Fine. I want to be here for Sher but only because I feel obligated to make sure she's okay. No other reason. She doesn't move me anymore."

They both gazed at the still, pale body of the woman who used to cause the sun to rise and set in Alaan's world.

"She doesn't move you at all, Alaan?" Carin asked, as she stepped closer and leaned into his side, careful not to touch him with her sterile gloved hands. "Not even a little bit?"

"No, not even a little. Bottom line is I'm in love with Tam." Cheeks bellowed on a huge exhale of frustrated breath. "God, I've wasted so much time chasing Tameth with my dick, I didn't pursue her with my heart. It's more than just the bond allowing me to feel her emotions, to hear her thoughts. Much more. I really care for her, Carin."

"So what the hell are you doing down here then? Talk about mixed signals. Poor Tameth must be reeling."

She shook her head, fully aware that if Alaan's connection to Tameth began like her and her husband's had, Tameth hadn't missed Alaan screaming "I love you" into her soul while his actions proclaimed Sher as number one.

And why the hell was he looking at her as if he expected her to answer her own damned question? Geesh, the man deserved a smack in the back of the neck. If there'd been even the slightest chance she could get away with planting her fist in the middle of his face to knock some sense into him, she would have gone for it.

"God, you can be so dense sometimes, Alaan. But..." she sighed. "You're my brother and I love you dearly. Idiot." Then another thought popped into her head—maybe she'd call the

195

Matriarch, fill her in on what was happening and let her chew a new hole in his ass. Nah, Tameth would never forgive her if even the smallest piece of Alaan's perfectly muscled butt went missing. Oh well...

Besides, she could feel her brother's pain, feel it spike to heartbreaking proportions. *To hell with the sterile gloves.*

Carin wrapped her arms around Alaan's waist, hugged him close, and promised it would all work out all right. Funny, he was so much taller it was like hugging a big blond tree.

"Well at least you've told her, right? I mean, I'm sure Tameth is glad to know you love her, especially since you're sitting down here at almost four o'clock in the morning with your unconscious ex."

"I, uh, I haven't told her yet. And stop giving me that dear-God-my-brother-is-an-idiot look. I'm going already."

Carin smiled when one of the most handsome and deadly men she'd ever known leaned down and planted a tender kiss in the center of her forehead. Alaan had never made her so proud as that moment when he walked out of the makeshift hospital room, leaving his past behind. His pace quickened the closer he got to the door. He didn't look back. Not once.

Carin stood there a second after the door snapped quietly shut. A slow smile spread across her lips. She knew exactly where he was going. Snatching off the blue examination gloves, they landed in the trash as she chuckled and grabbed a clean pair.

"Tameth, girl, I hope you're ready for the determined prime male coming your way."

As for Sher, this whole situation felt wrong.

"Bix?" she called across the link to her husband.

"I'm here, baby. Need me?"

"No, I'm fine. I've given Sher a sedative and planned to start analyzing the blood samples I took from her."

"I still can't believe she's alive and here in London after all this time."

"Yeah, me either. Key words are 'can't believe'. This is fishy, Bix. Of all the times for her to appear out of the blue, it happens to be while Alaan is in town hunting the rogue that supposedly took her out?"

"I agree. Alaan told me that Kenoe scented a Hatsept on a trip to the museum. Interesting that it was a dark-haired, small-boned female vamp."

"Yeah, kinda like the one lying here in this bed."

"My thoughts exactly, baby. Hey, when are you coming up to bed?"

"Up to bed? The question is, when are you coming in from outside?"

"I never could get much past you."

"And don't you forget it, handsome."

"Listen, Jaidyn understands the situation here and knows we don't have an estimate of when we'll make it back to the vacation house, so no worries on getting back to the baby. Also, Higgins put us on the second floor, third door on the right. There's a key for you hidden on top of the doorframe."

"Alaina…?"

"Higgins just vid phoned me to let me know he checked on her. The little imp is snoring like a Marine who's been on duty for thirty-six hours straight. Thankfully the man put us in a two-room suite so she can rattle the walls without keeping us up."

"My baby does not snore." The ice-cold snap in her voice was followed by a chuckle. "Sher will be knocked out for hours."

"You sure you wanna stay up and mess with blood

samples? I haven't had my dose of chocolate today."

She loved when he called her his chocolate. A shiver worked its way from the top of Carin's head, across every square inch of her milk-'n-cocoa colored skin, and down to her painted toenails. The link with her bondmate hummed with Bix's freaky anticipation. She never had figured out how he made her physically experience the caress of his thoughts.

"The Seekers here have everything under control. I'll race you to the bedroom, baby. Last one in bed gets a spanking." Bix's thoughts caressed the tips of her nipples. In seconds they went hard as pebbles under her lab coat.

"Dayum! In that case I'm moving like a little old lady in a too-tight pair of four-inch high heels!"

"So what about the blood samples, beautiful?"

Blood samples? What blood samples? Morning was soon enough to begin analysis. After some good loving and a few hours of sound sleep.

In spite of the serious implications of Sher's unexpected arrival, Bix's laughter poured over and through Carin. Her eyes went wide as his telepathic question was followed by a mental image of his big, strong hands making delicious contact with her bare ass at the same time his impressive cock sank into her weeping pussy. Oh, he was such a naughty vampire.

"Cut it out. You're making me sweat, damn it," she half-heartedly complained. Carin placed the vials of blood into a medical grade portable cooler, then bustled over to her patient. After tucking the blankets a bit more snugly around the woman, she turned off the lights and eased out the door.

Hopefully Tameth and Alaan were deep into the same kind of blazing memory-making lovin' that she was headed to with Bix.

"You've got one minute, beautiful."

"Get out of my head, Bix!"

"I will, after I've stripped you naked and gotten into someplace else."

God, she loved her man.

℘

Tameth lay perfectly still, with the exception of the hand slowly easing towards the blade underneath her pillow. There'd been no sound but someone had entered her room. Relaxing her fingers from around the hilt of the specially treated long knife, she relaxed as the scent of spiced ginger floated to her nostrils. Alaan.

She cracked an eye open and looked up at the shadow looming over her bed.

"Alaan, what are you doing here? Better yet, how did you get in?" For a moment she wondered if he was going to say anything.

He answered with a sighed question. "Do you want me to leave?"

"Don't answer my question with a question, Alaan."

Forcing herself to ignore the slither of his uncertainty pressing down through the bond, she arched a brow in the darkness. Huh. The man wasn't bothering to shield his thoughts, quiet his mind or control his emotions. No, he just let it all hang out, laid bare for her to see. And his heart was filled with remorse and soul-deep longing...for her.

When she'd climbed into bed alone tonight, he'd still been downstairs with Sher, clearly where he wanted to be. So Tameth had taken her desire for him, along with the knowledge that he was one of few men she could bond with, wrapped them up together and stuffed them in a box in the depths of her heart. But now his raw emotions dug down into her secret place and plucked at the ropes and chains tied around that box.

Her determination to forget about him wavered.

"I was downstairs with Carin while she examined Sher."

"And you're here now because?"

The dark outline of his body knelt down on the floor, reached forward and clicked on the lamp. Her mouth fell open at the blond mountain of a wreck on one knee next to her bed. His hair stood on end like he'd spent the last couple of hours yanking on it. His typically vivid, lively blue eyes were dull and tired. The second she tilted her head to the side in wonder, his spine snapped tight into a rigid column, effectively stilling the questions now stuck in her vocal cords.

"I'm here because I'd rather be with you, Tameth."

Had she heard correctly? "But what about Sher?"

"Tameth, get this through your head for the last time." He flashed up off his knees and sat down next to her. The blankets pulled tight around her body. His large hands clenched into fists, but he didn't touch her.

"Sher is my past. I felt responsible for her death, but here we are six years later and she's alive. I don't know what happened to her, or where she's been, but it doesn't matter. I want you. Only you."

Raising a hand to her cheek, she pulled it away with a bit of surprise at the moisture there.

"Aw, damn," he rasped. "Don't cry, Tam. I can't stand it when you cry."

But the tears escaped before she could stop them, welling up and spilling over in a torrent of pent-up emotion—happiness at Alaan's unexpected presence and declaration of love. Then her thoughts strayed to Kenoe. Immediately, pain and rage welled up inside of her on his behalf. Alaan picked up on it right away.

"Let me wipe it from your mind, baby. Whatever it is that's bothering you, let me love it away, Tameth. Please."

Alaan Serati had never said "please" to her in all the years she'd known him. Any words between them had always been either a command or...hell, that was all. Commands and orders. But tonight his patient plea—along with the fact he could have simply plucked her concerns right out of her thoughts without asking—shattered the rest of her resolve.

How could she resist this man? The bond vibrated and hummed between them and overflowed with his sincerity, genuine care and downright craving for her.

Throat clogged with a barrel of tears, all she could do was nod her head.

Alaan leaned down and kissed the woman he surely didn't deserve on the tip of her nose.

"Be right back. Running to the bathroom."

A quick shower was definitely in order. After being down in the hospital room with Sher, there was no way he would go to his woman with even the slightest essence of his past clinging to his skin.

He turned off the bathroom light and stepped out into a room of shadows. Tameth had turned down the lamp until only the faintest glow reached from the nightstand out into the darkness. Keen hearing picked up the soft rustle of fabric as she scooted across the bed to make room for him.

But he'd had some interesting revelations as he sat next to

Sher's prone body as Carin examined and treated her. He'd spent so many years keeping every woman, including Tameth, at arm's length because of Sher. Tameth could have had anyone she wanted, yet she'd committed herself to the Seeker corps and, whether he'd wanted to acknowledge it or not, to waiting for him to pull his head out of his ass long enough to realize how much his soul called to hers.

Even tonight, he'd let his shock get in the way of rational thinking. How many times had Tameth insisted he still pined after Sher? After all his denials, the woman showed up and he'd gone running after her...just like Tameth said he would. Worse, he didn't care for Sher anymore. Yet, off he'd gone. And Tameth was still willing to forgive him.

And if they never shared blood as mates, never completed the lifebond to tie their lives together, the link would always be there. Even if she gave her heart to another man, when in her presence, he would always have a glimpse of her heart. He had no right to ask for anything more than she was willing to give.

The second his naked backside hit the cool sheets, his arms were full of a warm, equally naked, fragrant woman. Easing her onto her back, Alaan whispered against her lips.

"I do believe I'm in love with you Tameth Serati-Cole. I know you love Kenoe..."

"But..."

"It's okay, baby. I don't care if you still love him. I won't even ask you to mate with me if you don't want it. All I want is for you to love me just as much, just as hard, as you love him. Can you do that?"

And if she couldn't, he would just have to deal with it.

"Yes," the whispered words were laced with tears. "Yes, I can do that, Alaan."

An abundance of care soaked through the uncompleted

bond and wrapped around the depths of his soul.

"Alaan, listen to me. Kenoe and I have never been lovers in the way you're thinking. And while I love him, it's as a close friend. But that's all, I promise. Okay?"

Awed by the depth of his own feelings, and more than a little relieved, he vowed right then that one day the bond they shared would be completed. Whatever it took to convince her that he belonged to her alone, he would do. She had to believe in him, believe in their love. If this thing wasn't heartfelt and genuine, she could bite him all day long and the bond wouldn't close.

Easing his mouth down to hers, he was gifted with a kiss so sweet it almost brought tears to his own eyes. Though he didn't deserve it, the woman was so responsive, so giving, so *his*. Strong, steadfast, yet so feminine and beautiful in her passion. God, how he loved her.

He made love to her slowly, gently easing inside her body with a reverence that took his own breath away. He even refrained from taking her blood, and resisted the mind-blowing sexual rush of pure energy that came with the act. And with every loving caress of her mind, every gentle touch of her fingers along his skin, each welcoming arch of her back, Alaan fell more in love with her.

Hmm. Love. As much as he'd resisted, now he couldn't imagine a single day without it.

Chapter Fourteen

Rubbing sleepy eyes, Carin walked out of the supply closet into the makeshift hospital room with a new vacu-tainer and several clean glass tubes to hold fresh blood samples. She'd left the room dim so her patient could rest when she returned to consciousness. There was only one problem—her patient was gone.

"Strange," Carin mumbled aloud, setting the vials down on the small metal tray next to the bed with a quiet clink. "She was just here when I checked twenty minutes ago. Maybe she took a potty break." But her intuition didn't think so.

Backing away from the empty bed, she carefully watched her back while making her way to the light panel on the wall across the room. Her fingers worked one of the little switches. Nothing happened. With growing frustration, Carin tried another, and another until all six had been flipped up and down several times. But the room remained shrouded.

Heavy drapes blocked out the dawning sun. Damned good thing she could see in the dark almost as well as a vampire. If not, she would have missed the shadow near the window. And that damned shadow had just yanked the phone off the wall and was now rushing her way.

Well, this can't be good, she thought as her back hit the floor and the air whooshed from her lungs. A pair of, maniacal eyes stared down at her as a cute little button nose pressed against hers. Sher. A completely healed Sher.

Wow, guess the medicine worked better than I expected, Carin thought, followed by an annoyed, "Hey! Get the hell off me."

"Sorry, can't do that," the petite pixie replied, baring a bit of fang with each slowly spoken word. Head cocked to the side, Carin took in the female sitting on top of her stomach. So this was Sher? Cute, except for the madness lurking just beneath the surface.

Letting her empathic abilities ease from the tight rein she always kept on them, Carin reached out and almost recoiled at what she sensed. Dear darling Sher was certifiable. Thoughts and emotions from one end of the chaos spectrum to the other swirled in, around and through her, growing more frenzied the longer she held Carin on the floor. *Okay, girlfriend, scientist to the forefront. You've been in this tough spot before. Get some damned answers.*

"You're Sher, right?" Carin asked quietly, hoping her tone and a noninvasive caress of calm psychic energy would ease the nutball sitting on top of her. Instead, the nutball snarled.

"Wanna tell me what the hell you're doing out of bed?" Carin asked, nonplussed. Hell, she'd survived a rogue vampire attack and kidnapping by one of the most notoriously brilliant criminals on the planet. No way in hell was she going to cower before some vampire chick having a bad hair day, crazy or not.

"And who are you, exactly?" the female asked cautiously. Easing back to sit on Carin's thighs, Sher grabbed her by the lapels and raised her back up off the floor. Carin kept her hands at her sides. Oooh, but Lord knew she'd rather stomp a mudhole in the female's backside. Instead she remained perfectly still while she was sniffed about her neck and hair.

What the hell? Was this a female vampire or a damned dog? Oh, that's right—nutcase. Okay, back to business.

"I'm your doctor," Carin replied calmly.

"That's obvious. But I meant, who are you? Your scent seems familiar."

"That's because I was wearing this lab coat while my brother was in here. It's probably his scent you're catching."

"Your brother? Who?"

"Alaan Serati..."

"How?" Crazy Lady cut her off, buried her nose in Carin's lab coat and inhaled again.

"Long story," Carin replied with a slight smile. "I assume we don't really have time for it. So, uh, whatcha up to? And how are you alive after all these years?"

The woman flashed a diabolical smile. The typical *"you're going to die so I may as well tell you"* thought brushed across her mind. Carin almost smiled.

"Years ago Lowan's Second, a man named Myles, used me as a bargaining chip with the guards who were responsible for Lowan Hatsept. I was...taken."

Uh-huh, and from the lust-laden expression that overtook the woman's features, she meant she'd been literally *taken.*

"Why didn't you contact anyone, let someone know you were alive? I'm sure that sometime in your six years in a Hatsept harem you got near a phone a time or two?"

"Why would I do that?"

"Because Lowan..."

"...should be here any minute. But I'll be done with you by then."

"What the hell have I ever done to you? I don't even know

you."

"Just because you're related to that Serati bastard. Everyone always acted as if he were larger than life, when he was really just a big mama's boy."

"Mama's boy?" Certainly they weren't talking about the same Alaan Serati? This couldn't be the woman Alaan would have moved heaven and earth for? And who'd supposedly loved him in return. Damn. Lowan must have really messed her head up good.

"Alaan never really loved me. It was always about what his mother wanted, or what the Council wanted, while all he ever did was treat me like a damned china doll. Hell, he wouldn't even have sex with me, claiming it was to honor me until we were officially joined. But he was a liar," she snarled into Carin's face. "Alaan wouldn't touch me because he didn't really want me. Clan Serati only wanted to tie our families together for the Matriarch's political gain, the old crone!"

What? Now Carin was pissed. Because of this one female Alaan had kept his heart hidden, had remained alone for so many miserable years. Even when everyone thought she was dead, this woman had caused so much trouble between Alaan and Tameth. Now here Sher was, aiding a rogue just to hurt Alaan all over again? And all because he'd been nice to her? Respected her? Oh, hell no! Nobody, crazy or not, fucked with her family and got away with it.

"So just lie still and it'll be over soon. And when I'm done, we'll take care of Alaan," Sher whispered.

Carin's nostrils flared angrily. *Not bloody likely! Consider yourself upgraded from nutball to sadistic nutball.*

"Why is it you vamp bitches think you can always pick on me just because I'm human? Tell you what, endanger my family and your ass is toast. Burnt. No butter. Now get up off me or

I'm gonna have to beat you down," Carin said menacingly, meaning every word to the depths of her soul.

"Mama? Mama, are you in here?"

Aw, hell. The little munchkin's timing really sucked. Carin got Sher by the ankle just as the woman lunged towards the door and the small but confident voice calling for Carin.

"Run, baby! Run!"

"But Mama..."

"Don't you dare 'but Mama' me, girl," Carin said with quiet finality, holding onto a squirming, hissing Sher. Damn. One of the woman's bare feet got loose and connected solidly with Carin's lower jaw. Ouch, that hurt.

Sher bounded to her feet and took a single step. Carin tackled her from behind and they came to a skidding halt a mere few feet from Alaina's little tennis shoes.

"Get your behind out of here, right now," Carin hollered, fingers wrapped firmly around the throat of a struggling Sher. "I can't have my baby see me beat the hell out of someone. It would be traumatic for you. Now go find your daddy."

Immediately the sound of little feet echoed down the hall, then disappeared altogether. Carin released Sher's neck, got a couple of handfuls of hair and swung the woman away from the door and deeper into the room.

The bond with Bix flared. Oh, now what?

"Carin! What's going on? Alaina just ran out into the courtyard babbling something about the short dark-haired lady and Mommy not being friends."

"It's Sher." She hurriedly sent her husband a mental picture of the situation and said, *"Bix, I can't concentrate on kicking this bitch into the next century with you distracting me. Just get your butt in here."*

With a flick of her wrist, Carin locked the door, knowing Bix would still be able to get in. After all, the men in her life were notorious for breaking down doors.

Carin turned back to a growling Sher. God, she wished she had incisors right about now. But no worries. She'd settle for beating the snot out of Sher the old-fashioned way.

"Now, little Miss Traitor. It's just you and me."

ॐ

A woman clothed in what looked like an open-backed hospital gown flew by just as Alaan stepped out of the library. A familiar dark skinned woman ran right behind her. Sher? Carin? What the hell?

Suddenly everyone was screaming.

Sher called frantically. "Help, she's trying to kill me!"

Carin yelled after her, "Damned right! Stop her Alaan!"

Shaking himself out of the surprise of seeing a formerly unconscious Sher running down the hall and away from Carin, Alaan moved into action. The gowned figure was no more than an arm's length away. He reached out and the fabric of the light blue garment rasped against the tips of his fingers.

Out of nowhere, a raging Bix flew down the front staircase, jumped the last eight steps in hot pursuit. And landed on top of Alaan.

Sher was out the front door and disappeared into the surrounding brush as the Head Seeker and his Second sprawled in a tangle of arms and legs in the middle of the front foyer.

"Damn it," three voices fumed together.

It was a rare thing for either of them to screw up while in pursuit of an enemy. But at this moment, neither man wanted to look up, knowing they'd find Carin glaring daggers at them in her classic pose—hands on hips with her serviceable leather shoes tapping a cadence on the tiled floor.

Chapter Fifteen

A human boy walked up the road, into the circular drive and right to the front door. A score of semi-automatic weapons were trained on him as he skipped and whistled along. The Seekers on the roof and on the sides of the house remained so well hidden the boy was completely oblivious of the danger surrounding him. And that's just what Alaan wanted.

Alaan watched the kid through the door's viewpiece. He was a handsome kid, no more than seven years old, with a mop of tousled strawberry-blond waves and a mass of freckles across the bridge of his nose. Smacking on a big wad of pink bubblegum, he happily chewed away. A small gap was visible between perfectly straight, white teeth.

A little finger reached out and pushed the bell.

Alaan backed off. He and Bix stood hidden on either side of the door as Higgins cracked it open and greeted their guest with years of perfected butler grace. The conversation concluded quickly, with Higgins passing the boy a five-pound note for his trouble before closing and locking the door.

The second the tumblers clicked into place, Alaan's hand stretched out to receive the note that had just been delivered. He read it, then read it again. Son of a bitch. The note contained exactly what he'd expected, what they'd counted on. But that didn't mean he had to like it. Hands folded into fists so tight, the echo of cracking knuckles sounded around the tiled foyer. Tapping his earpiece, Alaan turned on his heel and connected a private call on his way to the library.

"The operation is now underway. You two move into position."

Kenoe's smooth timbre, which no longer grated so heavily on his nerves, flowed through the earpiece with confidence and iced, deadly intent.

"Is it what we expected, sir?"

"Yep, it's exactly what we expected. Why can't these rogue assholes at least be original? Now you two move your pitiful asses. You have two hours."

Kenoe's chuckle accompanied Collins' gruff acknowledgement as they dropped off the line.

Now, only one more call to make.

"Group mode. Connect all Seekers." The digital tweep-tweep-tweep of the state-of-the-art communications device was followed by a short, low tone. Alaan's clipped words relayed his mood—black and deadly. "Every Seeker and Iudex Judge to the library. One minute."

Alaan's long strides carried him into the packed library. A horde of black-clad, leather trench coat-wearing, weapon-toting vampires all stood at attention at the table or against the wall. Alaan tossed the now balled-up note into the middle of the conference table. The eyes of his team burned into his. Stiff to the point of tension, every nerve pulled taut until the base of his spine tingled. Damn he hadn't been this angry since Carin's kidnapping three years ago.

He snapped an, "at ease", took his seat, leaned back in the chair with his hands behind his head and waited.

His longtime friend and partner looked his way. "All right,

big guy?" Bix asked.

"Yep." Alaan motioned his head towards the scrap of paper. "Read it to them."

Bix snatched up the note delivered by the young boy. A sarcastic snort and a smirk accompanied the anticipation in his eyes before he relayed the contents to the group.

"Tonight. My brother for Sher. No questions asked. Come alone. LH-S."

A stunned hush fell over the room.

"LH-S?" Slade asked, breaking the eerie quiet.

"Lowan Hatsept-Shean, you idiot," Alex replied, gifting his teammate with a solid smack on the back of the neck.

With a frightening grin, Alaan gained his feet. "All right, they've delivered their ultimatum. No one will be attacking us today. Everyone get some sleep since nobody got any last night or early this morning. We'll get together later to complete the plans."

Everyone had their orders, yet Tameth continued to survey the room as if there was unfinished business. Unable to resist, he leaned her way and inhaled. Even after lovingly soaping every inch of her decadently curved body, he could still catch his scent lingering on her skin.

"Where's Kenoe and Collins?" she asked.

Damned woman. Too perceptive by half. Nobody but he and Bix knew what the two missing Seekers were up to. But he couldn't lie to her, she'd sense it along their bond. Resigned to telling her the truth, sort of, he opened his mouth to halfway explain.

"And what about me?" Carin challenged, stepping silently into the room. One perfectly ached brow winged its way upward in prepared defiance.

God, how Alaan loved the woman's timing. Loved her spirit even more. But her question was ridiculous and easy to answer.

"You're staying here, Carin. That's an order." Alaan crossed his arms over his chest. He'd laid down the law but knew the conversation was far from over.

"I don't think so. Kicking the skinny bitch's ass and skewering this Lowan character sounds like more fun to me."

"You're defying an order, woman?"

"Woman?" Her neck did that sideways thing only she could pull off. "First of all, I'm not a Seeker so I don't have to follow orders. Second, if the order is to stay here and cower like a girl—no disrespect intended, Tam—then hell yes, I'm defying it." Followed by an unmistakably sarcastic, "Sir."

Alaan turned to his best friend for help, but not sure why he bothered.

"Bix?"

Hands thrown up in the universal salute of surrender, Bix pushed back from the table and laughed. "Don't look at me. Carin and I are still officially on vacation. That means you, my friend, are still Head Seeker, so it's your call. Besides, she's *your* sister."

"Hell, she's *your* woman," Alaan bellowed, slamming a hand down on the solid wood table hard enough to make the nails holding it together groan.

"Like I said, it's your call, man," Bix fired back with a snarky grin

It would be so satisfying to wipe that smirk off Bix's face, best friend or not. But if he hit the man, he'd be in trouble for striking his superior officer. Not to mention Carin's foot buried up his ass for hitting her mate. Great. Just great. Now he had two women to worry about.

"No need to worry about me, handsome, nor Carin. Remember, I trained her personally," Tameth reassured.

"Yeah, but..."

"Just try telling her she can't go." Tameth's chuckle echoed around the inside of his skull.

Fine, it was settled. With a seriously hard scowl, he addressed the group at large. "Whatever part Bix and his mate play in this little drama stays in this room, understood?"

A muted, "Yes sir," was quickly followed by twenty-two knowing glances as he stalked from the room, pulling Tameth by the hand behind him.

Hell, everyone knew Bix wouldn't pass up the opportunity to have some bone-crunching, rogue-beating fun, vacation or not. Everyone also knew his mate was no punk bitch, and they wouldn't make it three feet out the front door without Carin on their heels, secret Seeker mission or not.

୧

Damn, his head hurt. Kenoe held back a groan as he struggled to lift it. His neck felt so stretched and stiff, he must have been knocked out for at least an hour. Forcing his protesting muscles to move, he raised his head, not surprised by the blindfold over his eyes, nor the ropes digging into his well-defined arms and chest. Even his legs were tied wide open, securely lashed to the legs of the wooden chair on which he sat.

A deep, but subtle, inhale—as much as the ropes would allow—revealed all he needed to know. Lowan. A scent he'd never forget in a million years.

"I should have known your misplaced sense of honor would catch up with you one day." Lowan's oily voice slid over Kenoe's skin like water mixed with spilled diesel fuel—tainted, repulsive, and full of evil stench. Pushing down the automatic revulsion roiling around in his stomach, he clenched his teeth and prepared to do his job.

He knew this man. Knew he expected Kenoe to flinch away from the coming blow. But Kenoe was not the boy who'd run from Lowan's harem all those years ago. He was a man who'd been looking forward to this day for forty long, impatient years.

A meaty, solid fist connected with Kenoe's jaw. The pain was nothing, drowned in seething rage and coldly calculated revenge. Perfectly calm and focused on the task at hand, Kenoe forced himself to shiver. Forced a tremble and a whimper into his voice. Shit, he hated acting scared. But he needed to buy himself and his teammates some time.

"Oh God, where am I?" Kenoe gasped, hoping he sounded convincing. "Alaan is supposed to comply with your wishes. Why have you brought me here?" His head snapped sideways from another blow. "Don't hurt me, please!"

"How you ever made it past Seeker training is beyond me," another voice hissed a hair's breadth away from his ear. Myles. "Sure you've filled in a bit, looks like you've even been working out. But inside, you're still a mewling little puke. Tying you up is just a waste of good rope."

Another blow landed. This time Kenoe scented his own blood as it oozed from the size of his mouth. Thankfully he'd thought to retract his fangs the second he came to.

"Hold, Myles," Lowan commanded, then turned to face Kenoe. "We know you came to London with the sole purpose of hunting me. So tell me what Alaan is planning, dear brother."

Kenoe hesitated just long enough to earn himself another smack, this one landing high on his cheekbone. Damn, that one hurt. He'd be sure to ask Dr. Carin for something to put on it after this was all over.

"I-I can't tell you. And you weren't supposed to take me. Your note said he was supposed to bring me here to trade for Sher. He can't trade me if he doesn't have me."

"Ah, so you are smart, after all," Lowan said with too much of a smile. "But you haven't answered my question, brother. What is Alaan planning?"

Another smack, this one from Lowan with an open palm. Stung like hell.

Kenoe half-screamed, half-whimpered. "I can't! I swore!"

"And don't think to sneak and contact that walking blond tree. We've taken all your neat electronic Seeker toys."

Myles' tainted breath filled his nostrils as something warm and wet snaked out to lick the blood from the cut at the side of Kenoe's mouth. The man had always been partial to young males. Bastard.

"Knowing Alaan Serati, he'll come anyway. For Sher, if nothing else. In the meantime, Myles, I'd like you to personally supervise my brother's reacquaintance with harem life."

The second the blindfold was removed, Kenoe forced stark terror into his eyes.

They hadn't changed a bit. As with most Hatsepts, neither kept their fangs sheathed. Lowan still wore his thick, white hair tied back into a mid-length ponytail, complementing his slender build and fine-boned features. With the exception of the hard lines around his mouth and the cruel light in his blue-white Hatsept eyes, he appeared as youthful as ever.

Myles, on the other hand, was still a big brute of a Hatsept, and the ugliest vampire this side of creation. Hair cut almost too short to consider a buzz, he sported a jagged scar. It stretched from the corner of one eye down to the base of his chin, compliments of a young terrified Kenoe, a silver blade, and a nasty allergic reaction to the knife used to inflict the wound. Myles had always believed only weaklings took allergy meds. Shortly after the cut became infected and refused to heal, he'd changed his mind.

Kenoe looked around. The vampires providing security might not all be on the Top Twenty Most Wanted list, but he recognized several of them as wanted in one capacity or another. Another vamp walked into the room, capturing Lowan's attention. This time Kenoe's eyes went wide for real. Not wanting to be noticed staring, he dropped his gaze to his lap and listened as Lowan and his new guest engaged in a hushed conversation.

This fucking vampire played both sides. Not a rogue, but an informant who'd passed information to the Council on more than one occasion. If this vamp had been his team's main source of information in London, no wonder they hadn't been able to find Lowan until the Knightsbridge Seekers double-crossed him. And there was no way Kenoe could get this information to Collins before he reported that Kenoe had been successfully apprehended. Hell.

Knife held between his teeth, Myles stepped forward and unzipped Kenoe's trench coat. With a familiar, spine-chilling gleam in his cold eyes, he slipped the blade underneath the bottom of Kenoe's black form-fitting T-shirt and cut the fabric from his body. The quiet hiss of the ruined cloth played louder in his ears than the informant's clunky departing footsteps on the stone tile outside the door.

Lowan stepped back into the room just as Myles reached to stroke Kenoe's groin.

"No," Lowan commanded harshly.

Myles growled, but backed off.

"You are only to supervise, Myles. Call Kimora. Give him a dose of Vigelium. It'll keep him hard for hours. Have Kimora suck him off until right before he orgasms, then hold him there over and over. He is not allowed to come until he tells us Alaan's plans. My guess is the Seekers will arrive sometime before midnight, but I want to be sure."

In spite of the tight rein on his emotions, Kenoe almost sighed with relief when Lowan stalked from the room. But then again, that left him alone with a disgruntled Myles.

Kenoe didn't know this Kimora person, but he wished she'd hurry up and get in here. The old saying, "Better the devil you know than the devil you don't" didn't apply. Kenoe would take any demon over Myles any day of the week.

Chapter Sixteen

So far, Collins' information had been dead on. Kenoe had been knocked on the back of the head just outside the British Museum after following the little human boy who'd delivered the note to Alaan. Collins had followed them back to Lowan's hold without detection, scoped out the whole place in half an hour, and got out of there.

They'd already taken out the majority of Lowan's security forces. Only two rooms remained. Bix and a team of veterans stood in front of one of them.

Easing the door open a crack, Bix spotted no one, but keen ears picked up sounds of obvious distress. Collins' intel revealed there were only two Hatsept primes in the building— Lowan and his Second, a man named Myles. Bix's years of combat experience told him one of the rogues was in this room. The other person sounded like they were trying desperately to bite their lip to keep from screaming. It had to be one of two people—a punished harem mate. Or Kenoe.

Just then, a gruff, scratchy voice said, "Tell me more, and I'll stop Kimora's torture."

"Fuck you!"

Oh, yeah. Definitely Kenoe.

Kicking the door wide, Bix tore into the room. He and his team came to a halt just inside.

"Well, it's about damned time," Kenoe screeched from a chair in the middle of the floor. "Help, damn it!"

A well-built, cocoa-skinned human female knelt between his wide-spread thighs, lips wrapped firmly around his swollen flesh. His clothes, obviously cut from his body, lay tattered and shredded around the legs of the chair. And the woman practically inhaled him with loud slurping sounds while another Hatsept stood off to the side, eyeing every inch of cock disappearing into the woman's mouth.

"Dayum!" Carin whispered in awe, eyes wide and gaze plastered firmly on the hard cock jutting out from Kenoe's body.

"Stop looking at his dick, woman!" Bix ground out between clenched teeth as the biggest, burliest, white-haired vampire he'd ever seen left Kenoe's side and stalked his way. While shorter than Bix, the vamp outweighed him by at least twenty pounds. Sword already free of the scabbard, a deadly, determined Seeker edged his way towards his teammate tied to the chair. The woman just kept right on giving the blowjob of the century.

"If somebody doesn't get this woman off me, I'm gonna lose it!" Kenoe struggled and pulled against the tight ropes, squeezing his eyes shut in what looked like prayer.

Bix circled his newest prey. Alex started off to the right towards the cock-sucking female. It was no surprise to hear the snap of Carin's voice crackling through the room.

"I've got this, Alex. Just back on up, sweetie."

Who in all of vampiredom called a deadly Seeker "sweetie" except Carin?

"Why don't you just shoot her?" Alex questioned, obviously confused.

"Because the modified rounds don't work on her. She's human."

Bix rolled his eyes in exasperation. God, they really didn't have time for this chitchat.

"Kenoe?" Bix called.

"Shit!" A particularly lusty swipe of pink tongue over the head of Kenoe's fleshy cock. "What?" he yelled impatiently.

"Which rogue is this?"

"He's Myles, now get my ass untied!"

Turning to his bondmate with a snort, Bix said, "Carin, just kick this woman's ass and get it over with so we can go, please?"

Bix's sharp blade successfully backed up a charging Myles with his first swipe. More than ready to get it on, a smile tipped up the corner of his mouth as he taunted the big Hatsept. Myles advanced again with a roar.

Meanwhile, out of the corner of his eye, Bix saw his feisty woman run over to a captive Kenoe. She dropped into a perfect horse stance and challenged the woman giving what looked like an endless round of head.

The kneeling woman ignored them all. If anything she sucked harder. Kenoe held his breath on a tense gurgle and turned from beet red to a strange shade of purple. Bix had never seen a Hatsept turn so many colors.

A second later, the harem 'ho's head snapped back on her shoulders, eyes wide with disbelief as a pissed off, hard-as-nails biogeneticist let a sidekick fly, then dropped back into her stance. Three more well-placed blows had the beautiful, but obviously misguided, harem babe knocked out.

Meanwhile, Bix delivered a quick half cut followed by a kendo block that sent Myles sprawling.

Tameth and Alaan's fireteams streamed into the wide corridor from every direction, rushing their adversaries. There were more rogues in the building than Seekers, but being better equipped had its advantages. Those who resisted arrest got a taste of Carin's biological agents, courtesy of silenced 9mm handguns and tainted blades. After watching their wounded comrades crumple into heaps of whimpering uselessness, puking their guts up on the floor until the contents were laced with blood, most of the rogues gave up without a fight.

No doubt they could take down these bad guys. But what they didn't know was how many more were on the other side of these hulking, and most likely well-secured, doors. Rather than blowing open the thick, solid wood structures, Tameth simply held a gun against the temple of the vamp closest to where they wanted to go.

Alaan winked. *"That's my girl."*

"Damned straight," she teased without taking her eyes off the vamp she was successfully intimidating.

Alaan paused outside a set of huge double doors at the end of this particular hallway and tapped his earpiece.

Bix's hushed words eased through. "All secure here. We've got Kenoe and we're on our way to you."

"Area secure outside Lowan's rooms. We're going in after the target. Leaving Betas in the hallway to watch our backs. Serati, out."

"Bixler, out."

The doors slid silently open. With a double schwing, Alaan and Tameth's swords cleared their scabbards. Cautiously, they entered the room, leaving the entrance so the rest of their team could guard their backs in case of a trap.

Alaan surveyed the huge layout of the sparsely furnished area and came to a fast conclusion—Lowan had an ego the size of Mars. There in the center of the room, number four on the V.C.O.E. Most Wanted list sat on a throne, a fucking *throne*, in the middle of a red carpet. Talk about conceited. His big head had to be the largest muscle on his pale, skinny Hatsept body.

"You're early," Lowan said absently, looking towards the wall of windows in his bedroom. Pale blue early morning sky was visible though the open drapes. The only exception was the panes closest to his bed, covered by heavy drapes to keep the sunlight from streaming directly onto his sleeping place. "Kenoe told us not to expect you until ten o'clock tonight."

"That's what happens when you trust someone who wants nothing more than to see your ass fry," Alaan replied calmly with a glance over at Tameth. She shrugged, her focus on the four vamps who'd just eased through another doorway at the very back of the oversized room. All carried wicked-looking curved long knives and positioned themselves between the Seekers and their prey.

No problem. Two Seekers against four vampires? Almost unfair...for the rogues. Then three more vampires armed with handguns slithered in and added to the growing wall of bodies between Alaan, Tameth and their target. Okay, two Seekers against seven rogues? Now the odds evened out a little bit. At least the bad guys couldn't cry foul play to the Council after they got their asses whipped.

"Do you want to know what I did to her?"

Alaan yawned. "Not particularly."

In truth, Alaan would rather skewer the rogue and have done with it, but the mission was to bring the vamp back alive, if possible. And since Lowan hadn't murdered Sher, the bastard couldn't be punished for it. Not unless Alaan could get enough of a confession for other charges.

Lowan called to someone off to the side and behind him. The former love of Alaan's life walked boldly towards her lover, stopped just short of the carpet and kneeled on the floor.

Alaan growled. The bastard knew they wouldn't attack with Sher sitting right there, especially with some of them packing guns. Lowan continued as if Alaan hadn't said a word. Alaan hated being ignored.

"I took her right out of V.C.O.E. headquarters in Vienna, right under your so-called Seeker nose. I took her into my harem, raped her, over and over again. Fucked her silly until all she wanted was more of my cock. I even gave her the chance to leave me, to return home to you and your pathetic Seeker ass." Lowan motioned wildly, baring his fangs with a murdurous hiss. "Know what she said? She'd rather stay in my harem, service me whenever I wanted, however I wanted, than return to you or anyone like you. Soft bunch, the lot of you Seratis. Allowing yourselves to be ruled by a bunch of females!" he spat. "Sher, come to me."

She scurried onto the carpet with more cuts and bruises than she'd sported while lying in the bed at their temporary headquarters recuperating. Though the old wounds appeared to be healing, there were new ones swelling up one side of her face. A split bottom lip and a deep cut high on her eyebrow joined a myriad of rainbow-colored bruises covering every patch of visible skin.

"I must admit, I had no idea what Sher was up to. Rather ambitious, I must say. Having one of the guards slap her around a little then plant her in that alley for your men to find was a stroke of genius." Lowan looked his lover over with a sneer. "You could have at least cleaned her up a little."

Alaan smirked, turned to Tameth and silently asked,

"Damn, baby, did you leave any spot on her body unbruised?"

"Not me. That's all Carin's handiwork after the woman tried to get to little Alaina this morning."

"So," Alaan asked out loud, "what about the note you had delivered to me? How the hell was I supposed to comply with your wishes if you were going to kidnap Kenoe in the first place?"

"Actually, I'd planned to simply have you ambushed and killed."

Lowan could have stopped right there. Conspiracy to murder a Seeker was all Alaan needed to lock the bastard away for the rest of his life. But the idiot just couldn't seem to stop talking. A soft beep in Alaan's ear let him know Iudex Judge Collins, a man with the power to convict Lowan on the spot, listened to every word.

"Note, you say? Not my style. Sher?" Lowan demanded. A white eyebrow arched upward as he eyed the woman at his feet.

Quietly, she replied, "I arranged to have the boy deliver the note. It was the only way I could think to get your brother here. I know how much you wanted him back."

"In the meantime..." Lowan's words trailed off with a quiet snap and a single finger pointed to his groin. Without a single glance at Alaan, Sher immediately untied the little scrap of cloth draped around the man's hips and spread it wide.

There were now sixteen armed male vampires dancing nervously on the balls of their feet in front of Lowan, protecting him. But Alaan had what he needed. The ass kicking could now commence.

Alaan snarled low in his throat. The speed at which Sher's lips wrapped Lowan's quickly stiffening cock—no shame, no care—didn't make him jealous. It pissed him off. Rankled that he'd been duped, pined for her for all those years, lost so much time that could've been spent loving a woman like Tameth. And all along, Sher, the one he'd fancied himself in love with and almost mated, brazenly aligned herself with a man like Lowan. The fury and shame of it all, held down to a low simmer while he did his duty, was now free to erupt and take out everyone and anyone close enough to get burned.

The bond with Tameth pulled taut and grew hot. His woman's sentiments echoed his own, and she was beyond ready to tear someone a new one.

Slowly, Lowan's cronies spread out and began to circle the Seekers. Back to back, Alaan and Tameth faced their enemies and relished the coming fight amidst the humming and slurping of a very enthusiastic Sher.

ᘓ

Suddenly Alaan and Tameth were surrounded as the place erupted in fierce action. Kenoe, eyes flashing white fire, streaked into the midst of the fray. Making his way to their side, each deadly stroke of his razor-sharp samurai met its target with unerring accuracy. Bix was on his heels, blade in one hand, gun in the other.

More bad guys crowded into the warehouse-sized space to aid their fallen friends and were met by a score of Seekers.

Total mayhem. Shots were fired. Blades flashed and cut. Some hurled and vomited. Others yelled, screamed...died.

One after another, Lowan's rogue colleagues fell prey to either blade-inflicted fatal wounds or the stomach-wrenching results of the Seekers' biological weapons.

A booming explosion rocked the building.

All eyes turned to the source of the deafening noise.

Carin stood framed in the doorway. A fierce frown knit her brow. Her thick coiled hair was all over her head, blown back by the force of the blast. A titanium crossbow armed with incendiary arrows gleamed dully in the bright light streaming in from the windows. Her weapon pierced clean through three loyalist males running for the farthest corner of the room. One behind the other, they fell to the ground sporting big black ragged holes in their chests. Stunned silence reigned as the fighting came to an astonished halt. It was just long enough for Alaan to unholster the gun under his arm and plant a round of nausea-inducing rounds into the rogues to his left.

Disgust threatened to overtake rage with a single glance at Lowan's throne. The bastard remained seated, bare chest gleaming with sweat as he strained for completion. With a loud, satisfied yell, his back bowed up off the chair as his twitching cock erupted into Sher's eager mouth. Pearlescent fluid dribbled from the seam of her lips as she smiled up at him. Then he petted her hair like a damned dog before settling his short kilt over his softening cock. Legs out in front of him, crossed at the ankles, he seemed completely at ease with the chaos surrounding him. But Alaan didn't miss the almost imperceptible flash of fear in his eyes as the bodies began to pile up and his line of defense grew thin.

Kenoe's voice rose over the din. "I see an opening. I'm taking it."

"No!" Alaan yelled.

"What? Screw that, Alaan. I've waited my whole life to kill this bastard." Kenoe's tainted blade sliced the ear off a tall, muscular rogue dressed in tactical gear. The male's blade dropped to the floor, followed by his body as he crumpled in a heap, heaving and gagging.

"We have our orders, damn it." Alaan cut a diagonal slice

through the chest of the closest criminal.

"Fuck you, asshole!" Kenoe spun around and planted his blade just above the kneecap of an approaching opponent.

೮

Tameth couldn't believe it. Two elite Seekers stood in the middle of a fierce battle arguing over a criminal. It was obvious they trusted her and their teammates to guard their backs. If it hadn't been so serious a situation, she would have planted the tip of her bio-treated blade into the perfectly lacquered floor and watched them fight it out. Either that or cut them both, then refuse to give them the antidote until they admitted how ridiculous they were.

A hardbodied, six-foot, athletically built Kenoe glared unflinchingly up at Alaan's six-foot-five, heavily-muscled frame. Perfect, sparkling white locs whipped around his head as he and a wicked blade motioned his intentions towards Lowan's throne. The other hand poked at the center of Alaan's right sculpted pec. And Alaan poked right back as the fighting continued around them.

Their ridiculous exchange took seconds off the opportunity to secure Lowan. And neither of the knuckleheads noticed the bad guy had pushed Sher away and headed their way with a perfectly bronzed replica of a sharpened, ancient Egyptian Temet Axe in his hand. One direct pass of that deadly weapon could sever their numb skulls from their bodies.

Tameth shook her head with a snort of disbelief. Men.

With two steps, Tameth executed a precise, controlled slice across the muscle in Lowan's shoulder and rendered his arm useless. The ax thunked to the floor as the loss of blood and the introduction of foreign bodies from her tainted blade took effect. Sher rushed to his side and wrapped her arms around the shivering, vomiting, cursing, pale-skinned rogue.

Alaan and Kenoe both shot Tameth a stormy glare as she calmly wiped the well-used, bloody weapon on a thick cleaning cloth.

Careful not to touch the blade or the soiled area on the cloth, Tameth resheathed the three-foot piece of steel beneath her trench coat. Moving towards the door to make room for the arriving mop-up crew, she glanced over her shoulder and asked, "Can we go now?"

Mopping up the crime scene was relatively easy. With very few dead vampires to dispose of, Collins, standing in his office as Iudex Judge, handed down sentences on the spot. The wounded were patched up and airlifted to the private airstrip where Stealth One waited to shuttle them to V.C.O.E. headquarters in Vienna.

This had been, by far, one of the cleanest missions in Seeker history, courtesy of the nasty coating on their blades and ammunition. As for the harem members, all were given the option to return to their previous lives or go to other more traditional Hatsept harems for some gentle retraining.

Among the dead: One. Myles, skewered on the end of Bix's katana during Kenoe's rescue from a fierce nonstop blowjob.

Sher's voice reached above the hushed efficiency of the mop up crew. Screeching wildly, she yelled and clawed at her captors.

"No! Please don't take me away from him!" she screamed, fully submerged in hysteria. "I need him. Please!"

The one male who'd been her life's anchor was now secured

and on his way to prison. And she would join him there, though it was doubtful they would ever actually see each other again.

Her desperate gaze landed on Alaan. "I hate you! I'll never forgive you. He is four times the man you are. You're nothing without the Matriarchy. Nothing!"

Her anger and loathing pierced Alaan's heart. Not because he wanted her, but because he felt so sorry for her.

His gaze followed her trembling form as she was bustled out the door. Tameth's slightly calloused hand slipped into his, followed by an even sweeter telepathic caress of love along their bond. A bond he'd never experienced with anyone else.

The most destructive and hurtful period of his life was finally dead and buried. For real, this time. And he and Tameth had ushered each other into a new life together.

Finally, it was over.

Chapter Seventeen

Hand in hand, in matching black Seeker dress uniforms, Tameth and Alaan entered the packed Council chambers of the Vampire Council of Ethics Eastern European headquarters. Black cargo pants, perfectly creased, were set off by black silk double-breasted dress shirts. For their mating, they wore no trench coats, no gloves and no weapons.

Bix and Carin stood with their two children and the rest of the elite team at the bottom of the wide carpeted stairs at the end of a long, royal blue runner. Alaana Serati, Alaan's mother and the Matriarch of their clan, waited at the top of a raised dais. Her blue eyes, so much like Alaan's, sparkled with inordinate pleasure. A hush fell over the crowd as they climbed the steps onto the platform with purposeful strides.

Bowing low in respect to the Elders, the couple waited until all ten members of the Council rose from their ornate chairs. Alaana's voice rang clear over the hushed mass.

"You may rise now. Tameth Serati-Cole, daughter of Clan Serati and Seeker of the Vampire Council of Ethics, we wish to acknowledge the finding of your mate and bondmate, Seeker Alaan Serati, son of the Elders Serati."

After a short round of applause, whistles and well wishes, "Do the Elders of Clans Serati, Vigee, Li and Sewell recognize the mating of Seeker Serati-Cole and Seeker Serati?" Alaana continued with the traditional questioning of the Council until each name was called and answered in the affirmative.

"Seeker Tameth Serati-Cole and Seeker Alaan Serati, we the Elders of the vampire clans, representatives of the Vampire Council of Ethics, recognize not only your mating but your bonding as well. We wish you goodly success. Seeker Serati-Cole, as a female of our Clan, you may now claim your bondmate."

As a sign of her acceptance of Alaan, Tameth would give him the honor of her blood. Having already experienced the fierce and addictive rush that accompanied the taste of the rich red liquid, Alaan practically shook with anticipation of the pleasure. He let his fangs drop into place as she snapped open the cuff at her wrist and pushed the sleeve past her forearm.

And that lovely arm was presented in all its smooth, golden loveliness for his taking. Stroking the skin with a tease of his fingertips, he felt a shudder work its way through Tameth's body. There was nothing like being able to give his mate goose bumps and make her tremble.

Gently, he eased his incisors into the fleshy part of her forearm near the crease at her elbow. The second the thin stream of blood flowed over his tongue the hard-on he'd exerted supreme control over snatched itself free of his will and sprang forward to push against his zipper. The clean, electrical blitz of Tameth's lifeblood, her very energy, pulsed into him with a fierceness that swept his breath away. Caressed him everywhere at once, inside and out. He looked up and watched her little pink tongue skim over the tips of her incisors. The sight was so damned erotic his suddenly double-sized cock wanted out of his pants. Desperately.

"Oooh, that feels so good," she hissed for his ears alone. Yes, it was exquisite. He wished he could make her come right here on the dais, but they weren't finished yet. Not by half.

Sucking gently while swirling his tongue over her smooth skin, Alaan's eyes closed. Immediately his mind overflowed with images of her plump, soft lips wrapped around his flesh, taking his life into herself from one of the thick veins twined around his pounding rod. He'd always fantasized of sharing something so intimate with a mate. And now that they were joined and supposed to share everything, why not let her in on it?

He knew the second she'd picked up on his thoughts when a wicked smile spread across her lips. Alaan licked the flesh to stem the sluggish flow of blood from her arm. Then he waited. As a female of his Clan, it was her choice as to where she would give him the ceremonial bite.

The slender fingers of his new wife slowly undid the buttons on the front of his shirt. One hand slowly spread the lapels, fingertips flitted over the tense, jumping pectorals and skimmed up and down the smooth, toned skin. His body tensed in anticipation of whether she'd choose the pecs or the neck. Either one, he couldn't wait to feel her mouth on him.

"Tease." He grinned.

"Damned straight."

She buried her hand in the short cropped curls of his hair and rose up on her toes. With no resistance, he allowed his head to be pulled sideways, baring the hard beat of his pulse. The nick of her incisors almost sent him to his knees.

Nothing prepared Tameth for the barely controllable lust that wracked her body the second she took Alaan's blood. Soul-stirring, intimate and wildly electric. This is what he'd experienced each time he'd bitten her as they made love. Now she understood why he wanted it. And now she was addicted, but only to him.

The thick ridge of living, swollen flesh pressed into her belly as Alaan pulled her close. Oh, the things the man could do with his cock. And if the erect shaft was any indication, he obviously wanted to do them right now. Panting into her thoughts, he spilled all his cravings into her very being.

"Oh, yes, Tam. Bite me, baby. Take me."

She pulled harder with her lips, taking more of his blood. A tremor worked its way up and through her ribs.

"Damn, baby. That's it, give me what I want," he demanded.

The answering call of her body was instantaneous. Damn, if her pussy quivered any harder, she'd look like she was break dancing across the floor. The damp trickles between her legs urged her to move a little faster and complete the ceremony. She needed him inside her, buried so deep his beautiful blue eyes reflected behind her brown ones.

With a final rasping lick, she pulled away from the rigid column of his neck and almost stumbled, dizzy with passion.

Just that quickly, the bond completed, slammed into place and shook her down to her toes. She felt Alaan in every pore of her body, every corner of her soul. Closer to him than any person she'd ever known. Shaken, oblivious to her own tears, she stood trembling as Alaan gently wiped them away.

With a strong hand, he helped her down the stairs on wobbly knees.

"Woman, I need you right now. If you can't move any faster than that I'll just have to carry you."

Whoa! A Clan Serati female didn't get carted around, tossed over her mate's shoulder like a sack of potatoes. She commanded her legs to move faster, but they didn't give a damn. And honestly, neither did she. Her life was now joined to a man who loved her with every piece of his heart. A lover who genuinely cared about her needs but was no pushover. The perfect man for her. Suddenly she felt liberated, enlightened even. And all the care about propriety, what people thought and said, flew right out the window.

Stopping just short of the dais, she lifted her arms and said simply, "Carry me, handsome."

The surprise on his face was replaced by sheer determination as she was tossed over a broad, and thankfully strong, shoulder. The collective gasp of the Council followed by a round of raucous applause said perhaps Clan Serati was in for a few changes. If not this century, then perhaps the next.

Back in their rooms, he stripped her naked, tossed her in the center of the bed and stepped back. He needed to practice undressing faster. Here she was again, bare-assed naked, and the man was fully dressed. He must have a thing for being the last one out of his clothes.

"Tameth, baby, I have a surprise for you."

The twinkle in his eye should have warned her that his gift would be the last thing she expected.

He must have left the living room door open to the suites because a quiet knock sounded at Alaan's bedroom door.

"Come in," he called.

"Alaan, we don't even know who it is." Sputtering wildly, she grabbed for the sheets, scrambled underneath them, and yanked them up to cover her bare breasts. The door slid silently open. She looked up when it closed with a snap. This had better be impor...what?

"Kenoe, what are you doing here?"

Alaan answered, "He came to give you a wedding present."

"Couldn't it have waited until morning?"

"No, baby. This is something special. Kenoe is leaving in the morning and it couldn't wait."

"Leaving? Why? We're all on leave for the next month and a half. Where are you going?"

Kenoe still hadn't said a word. And she liked to died when he began shedding his clothes as he walked towards the bed.

Oh my God! Was he crazy? The last thing she needed was Alaan flying into Seeker, me-prime-male-back-away-from-my-woman mode.

Kenoe was barechested now. Rippling, toned flesh danced a pale translucent in the candlelight. And Alaan just sat on the bed, reclined on his back, arms folded behind his head. And he was...smiling? No, he was grinning! And now just about all of Kenoe's pearly whites were showing, too.

Quieting her mind, she reached for her husband. Since neither of the boneheaded men in the room were saying anything, it was up to her to head off a potentially volatile situation before it got started. Sending a gentle probe along the bond, Tameth encountered...peace and quiet. No thoughts of shredding Kenoe or even harming him. Alaan's emotions were either under a tight rein or the bastard did a hell of a job shielding her, damn it.

But that didn't make sense either. The bond didn't work that way. Once fully in place telepathic shielding of a mate was impossible unless Alaan was unconscious, which he obviously was not. He had to be genuinely at ease about this.

She snapped her head around to look at him. That damned cheesy smirk was firmly in place as he shed his clothing, returned to the bed and yanked her into his lap. Damned man.

"Do you trust, me, Tam?" he asked seriously. Still, the bond remained quiet and content.

"Of course I trust you, but I..."

"No, sweetheart, no buts. You deserve this. It's my way of making up for the past six years of not being with you. And for being jealous of your close friendship with Kenoe when I wasn't willing to be a friend to you. He's a worthy man, Tam."

"And," Kenoe chimed in, "it's my way of saying I love you and goodbye."

Immediately her throat choked with tears. He was leaving, and this was his gift to her.

"Goodbye? But why? Are you coming back?"

"Alaan will fill you in, sweetheart. For now, congratulations on both your mating and your bonding. You deserve to be happy, Tam, and I'm very pleased things worked out."

One prime male vamp crawled towards Tameth while the other was deliciously hard behind her. Sitting between Alaan's legs, leaning back against his wonderfully wide chest, it was difficult not to relax under the firm fingers easing over her skin. Between index finger and thumb, Alaan pulled and twisted her instantly hard nipples before palming the weight of her breasts.

It felt so good. She'd always been particularly sensitive there, but as Alaan touched her, the stillness of the bond was a thing of the past. It flared and hummed with almost tangible desire. And the more he stroked her, the stronger the need grew between them.

Alaan leaned forward and reached for her thighs. A palm to the back of each knee, Tameth found herself spread wide like a banana split down the middle with her juices flowing freely down her slit like hot honey.

Then Kenoe was there. Strong, slender fingers parted her pussy to make more room for his nose. Buried in her center, he inhaled deeply then sighed with pure contentment. The face-first dive into her tender pussy had her gasping like she'd been too long underwater. Fingers dug into the meat of Alaan's thighs, looking for the smallest piece of an anchor to reality.

Her clit throbbed and ached as Kenoe lapped at her creamy folds without actually touching her where she needed pressure the most. Hanging on the edge of the precipice of pleasure made her squirm, twitch, moan and gasp.

Well, it appeared she was going to spend some time begging tonight.

"So good. Oh, please. More," she groaned, head falling back against Alaan's chest, hips writhing all on their own.

"You hear that, Kenoe?" Alaan growled in that sexy baritone of his. "She needs more."

The answering hum against her soaked flesh sent her senses reeling towards the ceiling.

Alaan's strong hand slipped beneath her ass and lifted her clean off the bed. The thick cock that had been pressed into the small of her back now nudged at her pouty labial lips, seeking entrance. God, she could feel the walls of her channel pulse and flex for release. Suddenly, he was there, pressing, inch by delicious inch into her soaked pussy from behind, grinding and flexing until he was seated to the hilt.

The second he was settled, Kenoe spread her wide, wrapped his talented lips around her clit, and sucked it completely out of its hood and into his warm, wet mouth.

Orgasm burst through her hungry cunt, spiraled up and out until her cries engulfed them. With no rest or recovery, she was immediately thrown into another bone-melting climax when Alaan's cock began shuttling in and out of her willing body as Kenoe followed the movement with his mouth, keeping hold of her clit.

She looked down between her legs and sucked in a breath at the sight of Alaan's thick cock pounding into her cunt as Kenoe gobbled up the flesh spread around her husband's hard length. Both men groaned their pleasure but she was taken aback by the untamed, lust-filled gleam in Kenoe's blue-white eyes. He'd occasionally taken up this position a few times over the years, but he'd never looked as intense as this.

He sucked harder, his face covered with her juices as Alaan increased the depth of his strokes. She flew apart again, but knew they were far from finished with her.

༽༠

Just before dawn, Alaan rolled over and gathered an exhausted Tameth in his arms. She deserved some rest. Between Kenoe and himself, the woman had rode, sucked and received more cock in one night than she ever had in her long vampire life. In the early morning darkness, Kenoe stole out of the bed with a quick kiss on the side of Tameth's slumbering face.

Alaan couldn't help but grin as he remembered Kenoe's satisfied, languorous stretch before rising. Then the vamp had climbed naked from the bed. He'd declined Alaan's offer of a hot shower, declaring Tameth's scent would remain on his body until the last possible moment. With that, he'd headed off to pack.

Before the little pissant—a term of endearment between them now—had departed, they'd agreed to keep in touch during his leave of absence. Besides, Tameth might be Alaan's mate but if anything ever happened to the Hatsept pipsqueak, she'd never let him hear the end of it. Kenoe was a good Seeker. He was also partly responsible for helping Alaan realize Tameth was the one for him. Because of that alone, Kenoe would always be welcome as more than just a teammate, but a friend.

Smoothing a few silky dark strands away from Tameth's

beautiful face, he gazed down at the peaceful loveliness sleeping perched atop his shoulder.

He'd been utterly undone, as completely as if the Indian goddess of love, Kama, had reached down into his heart, stirred it up, and spoiled him for every other woman. His life was so intertwined with Tameth's, nothing came even close to the importance of her happiness.

He'd never cared about anything as much as Seeking and bringing justice. But now he wanted to Seek and bring justice just to protect his woman.

The revelation unnerved and humbled him.

Their lives were fraught with danger, chasing one rogue after another to the ends of the earth. But if he could make her smile in her sleep every night, just like this, everything he'd ever fought for, every hell he'd ever been through, every enemy he'd ever fought and continued to fight...would all be worth it.

About the Author

Born into a musically eclectic family, TJ's first love is music. She enjoys singing, even outside of the shower. So, where does this writing stuff come in? It actually began with reading. TJ is an avid reader and you'll find her with her head buried in a book every day of the week, whether it's her own creation or something snagged at the bookstore.

And now that books have caught up to technology, TJ's eBook reader is shown no mercy, forced to entertain her at all hours of the day or night. Even in the dark!

Her favorite compositions are multicultural romances in various genres, some naughty, none nice. With several works in the wings, TJ loves to create and explore whatever world her mind decides to conjure. She currently lives out West with her two children, and enjoys working as a technical resource with a company that provides analytical solutions to lifesciences companies.

To learn more about TJ Michaels, please visit www.tjmichaels.com. Send an email to TJ@tjmichaels.com, subscribe to her newsletter, *TJ On A Tangent* to join in the fun with other readers and authors, as well as TJ.

She's his target…and his mate. Aw, hell!

Carinian's Seeker
© 2007 TJ Michaels

Beautiful genius Carinian Derrickson wants to live long enough to date a man from the future generations of spacemen, complete with ray guns and starships. She's not crazy, she's just afraid of dying young of some dreaded disease, like all the rest of her family. Her research into gene therapy has shown her the way to extend her life is by emulating traits only before seen in fiction. Vampire fiction. Only the beings that shouldn't exist are very real indeed.

Unknown to her, there's a bad boy vampire in the lab next door with a goal quite the opposite of hers. If he has his way, he'll bring the Vampire Council of Ethics (V.C.O.E.) to its knees.

Jon Bixler is a Seeker for the Council—an assassin and undercover operative in a world of humans. Bix must get close enough to this rogue to find out exactly how he plans to dismantle the Council. And Carinian is just the ticket. But when he meets her, all his vampire common sense flies out the window as his libido leaps off the charts. What's he going to do now that the woman is in danger and secretly trying to do the impossible?

Bix and Carin can't deny the combustion of love and lust between them. They accept their mating. But can they stay alive long enough to enjoy it?

Available now in ebook and print from Samhain Publishing.

Enjoy the following excerpt from Carinian's Seeker...

"Kiss me, Bix," she whispered fiercely, tilting her head up with eyes closed. She knew he'd give her what she asked for. No need to look. Just feel. Bix would take care of her. She felt his mouth move towards her, but he didn't meet her lips. Instead he tipped her chin up more and licked the side of her neck, from her pulse point up to her ear.

The intense answering ripple in her womb almost made her forget to erect a psychic shield.

"Oh damn, that was nasty. Do it again."

Bix gave her another hot swipe of his wet tongue along her sensitive skin. She shivered as her head fell back. Her skin felt much too tight and her body grew hotter by the second. She barely registered the crooning of the music in the background as she reached into his tailored jacket, grabbed two fists full of his shirt and held on under a sensual assault that almost bent her over backward. Moisture gathered at the entrance of her channel and even *she* could smell her arousal waft up from between her thighs. Finally, he captured her lips. Bix started growling again, but for a whole new set of reasons, all of which she agreed with wholeheartedly.

"I can smell you, baby. Makes me want to go down on my knees and bury my head under your dress right here in the middle of this dance floor."

Lord knows she wanted nothing more than to find a dark corner, flip up her skirt and let him have at it. A primal need rose up in her, a need for him to take her. To make her his in every way. Forever. Her kneecaps quivered and she spoke to them. *Don't you dare dump me on my ass. Stand firm, girl, stand firm.*

"Firm? I've got something firm for you, baby," Bix whispered

into her head and pressed his long, swollen ridge of flesh firmly against her belly.

Her shield dropped like a stone. Bix, along with a horde of other horny vamps, heard her telepathic scream. *"Oh, Bix, I'm yours, baby. Please... Oh God, bite me."*

He looked directly into her eyes, fangs clearly visible. "Are you sure, Carin? There's no going back if we do this."

She rubbed feverishly against him, trying to do her best to look like she was still dancing rather than humping against his leg. "Yes, I'm sure, Bix. I'm yours, and you're mine. I can't imagine being with anyone else or sharing you with anyone else. Ever."

"The mating is to bind you to me, not the other way around," Bix said firmly, all smug Seeker confidence.

Alpha to the bone, arrogant and self-assured. And right now, she didn't give a rat's ass. "So you say, damn it. You're mine."

She knew she could be a stubborn bitch on wheels, but this man was going to be wholly and completely hers and love it. Even if she had to kill him. Her breathing hitched with anticipation as he lowered his head to the sweet pulse on her neck. She could feel his fangs aching fiercely, his need to bite so strong, *her* gums tingled. So powerful it burned from where his mouth touched her down to the little hairs on her toes. He rubbed his incisors against her tender skin.

A sharp voice cut through the fog of lust and need.

"Bix and Carin, please join me on the dais." Alaana Serati stood there, calling to them. "And no necking on the dance floor for you two. We will do this according to tradition." Then she smiled at Bix's grimace at having his love play interrupted.

"Damn, her timing sucks," Carin growled into his chest.

*Trapped in the dark, can two lost souls find their way
back to the light?*

Tempting Darkness
© 2007 Rene Lyons

Book Three of the Templar Vampire series

Once a proud Templar Knight, Lucian of Penwick lost his
faith when God damned him as a vampire. Tormented by guilt,
he is dragged back to his ancestral home and forced to confront
the sins of his past. As he struggles to uphold his oath, Lucian
knows if he falters, it's not just his own soul on the line...

Ripped from life as she knew it, Jessica Vargo is held
prisoner in a world of darkness and torment. Deep in the
bowels of a medieval castle, the line between myth and reality
blurs and the only one she can trust is the seven-hundred-year-
old vampire.

But as darkness tempts, can Lucian and Jessica find their
light?

Available now in ebook and print from Samhain Publishing.

GET IT NOW

MyBookStoreAndMore.com

GREAT EBOOKS, GREAT DEALS . . . AND MORE!

Don't wait to run to the bookstore down the street, or
waste time shopping online at one of the "big boys." Now,
all your favorite Samhain authors are all in one place—at
MyBookStoreAndMore.com. Stop by today and discover
great deals on Samhain—and a whole lot more!

Samhain
Publishing, ltd

WWW.SAMHAINPUBLISHING.COM

GREAT
cheap
fun

Discover eBooks!